THE WONDERFUL
WIZARD OF OZ
&
GLINDA OF OZ

The Wonderful Wizard of Oz

AND

Glinda of Oz

L. FRANK BAUM

WORDSWORTH CLASSICS

For my husband
ANTHONY JOHN RANSON
with love from your wife, the publisher.
Eternally grateful for your unconditional love.

Readers who are interested in other titles from
Wordsworth Editions are invited to visit our website at
www.wordsworth-editions.com

For our latest list and a full mail-order service, contact
Bibliophile Books, 5 Datapoint, South Crescent, London E16 4TL
TEL: +44 (0)20 7474 2474 FAX: +44 (0)20 7474 8589
ORDERS: orders@bibliophilebooks.com
WEBSITE: www.bibliophilebooks.com

First published in 1993 by Wordsworth Editions Limited
8B East Street, Ware, Hertfordshire SG12 9HJ
The *Glinda of Oz* story added in 2012

ISBN 978 1 84022 694 2

Text © Wordsworth Editions Limited 1993 and 2012

Wordsworth® is a registered trade mark of
Wordsworth Editions Limited

Wordsworth Editions
is the company founded in 1987 by
MICHAEL TRAYLER

Typeset in Great Britain by Antony Gray
Printed and bound by Clays Ltd, St Ives plc

CONTENTS

The Wonderful Wizard of Oz

This book is dedicated to
my good friend and comrade
MY WIFE

CONTENTS

INTRODUCTION

Folklore, legends, myths and fairy tales have followed childhood through the ages, for every healthy youngster has a wholesome and instinctive love of stories fantastic, marvellous and manifestly unreal. The winged fairies of Grimm and Andersen have brought more happiness to childish hearts than all other human creations.

Yet the old-time fairy tale, having served for generations, may now be classed as 'historical' in the children's library; for the time has come for a series of newer 'wonder tales' in which the stereotyped genie, dwarf and fairy are eliminated, together with all the horrible and blood-curdling incidents devised by their authors to point a fearsome moral to each tale. Modern education includes morality; therefore the modern child seeks only entertainment in its wonder-tales and gladly dispenses with all disagreeable incident.

Having this thought in mind, the story of the wonderful Wizard of Oz was written solely to pleasure children of today. It aspires to being a modernised fairy tale, in which the wonderment and joy are retained and the heartaches and nightmares are left out.

L. Frank Baum
Chicago, April 1900

CHAPTER ONE

The Cyclone

Dorothy lived in the midst of the great Kansas prairies, with Uncle Henry, who was a farmer, and Aunt Em, who was the farmer's wife. Their house was small, for the lumber to build it had to be carried by wagon many miles. There were four walls, a floor and a roof, which made one room; and this room contained a rusty looking cooking stove, a cupboard for the dishes, a table, three or four chairs, and the beds. Uncle Henry and Aunt Em had a big bed in one corner and Dorothy a little bed in another corner. There was no garret at all, and no cellar – except a small hole, dug in the ground, called a cyclone cellar, where the family could go in case one of those great whirlwinds arose, mighty enough to crush any building in its path. It was reached by a trap-door in the middle of the floor, from which a ladder led down into the small, dark hole.

When Dorothy stood in the doorway and looked around, she could see nothing but the great grey prairie on every side. Not a tree nor a house broke the broad sweep of flat country that reached the edge of the sky in all directions. The sun had baked the ploughed land into a grey mass, with little cracks running through it. Even the grass was not green, for the sun had burned the tops of the long blades until they were the same grey colour to be seen everywhere. Once the house had been painted, but the sun blistered the paint and the rains washed it away, and now the house was as dull and grey as everything else.

When Aunt Em came there to live she was a young, pretty wife. The sun and wind had changed her, too. They had taken the sparkle from her eyes and left them a sober grey; they had taken the red from her cheeks and lips, and they were grey also. She was thin and gaunt, and never smiled, now. When Dorothy, who was an orphan, first came to her, Aunt Em had been so startled by the child's laughter that she would scream and press her hand upon her heart whenever Dorothy's merry voice reached her ears; and she still looked at the little girl with wonder that she could find anything to laugh at.

Uncle Henry never laughed. He worked hard from morning till night and did not know what joy was. He was grey also, from his long beard to his rough boots, and he looked stern and solemn, and rarely spoke.

It was Toto that made Dorothy laugh, and saved her from growing as grey as her other surroundings. Toto was not grey; he was a little black dog, with long silky hair and small black eyes that twinkled merrily on either side of his funny, wee nose. Toto played all day long, and Dorothy played with him, and loved him dearly.

Today, however, they were not playing. Uncle Henry sat upon the doorstep and looked anxiously at the sky, which was even greyer than usual. Dorothy stood in the door with Toto in her arms, and looked at the sky too. Aunt Em was washing the dishes.

From the far north they heard a low wail of the wind, and Uncle Henry and Dorothy could see where the long grass bowed in waves before the coming storm. There now came a sharp whistling in the air from the south, and as they turned their eyes that way they saw ripples in the grass coming from that direction also.

Suddenly Uncle Henry stood up.

'There's a cyclone coming, Em,' he called to his wife; 'I'll go look after the stock.' Then he ran towards the sheds where the cows and horses were kept.

Aunt Em dropped her work and came to the door. One glance told her of the danger close at hand.

'Quick, Dorothy!' she screamed; 'run for the cellar!'

Toto jumped out of Dorothy's arms and hid under the bed, and the girl started to get him. Aunt Em, badly frightened, threw open the trap-door in the floor and climbed down the ladder into the small, dark hole. Dorothy caught Toto at last, and started to follow her aunt. When she was halfway across the room there came a great shriek from the wind, and the house shook so hard that she lost her footing and sat down suddenly upon the floor.

A strange thing then happened.

The house whirled around two or three times and rose slowly through the air. Dorothy felt as if she were going up in a balloon.

The north and south winds met where the house stood, and made it the exact centre of the cyclone. In the middle of a cyclone the air is generally still, but the great pressure of the wind on every side of the house raised it up higher and higher, until it was at the very top of the cyclone; and there it remained and was carried miles and miles away as easily as you could carry a feather.

It was very dark, and the wind howled horribly around her, but Dorothy found she was riding quite easily. After the first few whirls around, and one other time when the house tipped badly, she felt as if she were being rocked gently, like a baby in a cradle.

Toto did not like it. He ran about the room, now here, now there, barking loudly; but Dorothy sat quite still on the floor and waited to see what would happen.

Once Toto got too near the open trap-door, and fell in; and at first the little girl thought she had lost him. But soon she saw one of his ears sticking up through the hole, for the strong pressure of the air was keeping him up so that he could not fall. She crept to the hole, caught Toto by the ear, and dragged him into the room again; afterwards closing the trap-door so that no more accidents could happen.

Hour after hour passed away, and slowly Dorothy got over her fright; but she felt quite lonely, and the wind shrieked so loudly all about her that she nearly became deaf. At first she had wondered if she would be dashed to pieces when the house fell again; but as the hours passed and nothing terrible happened, she stopped worrying and resolved to wait calmly and see what the future would bring. At last she crawled over the swaying floor to her bed, and lay down upon it; and Toto followed and lay down beside her.

In spite of the swaying of the house and the wailing of the wind, Dorothy soon closed her eyes and fell fast asleep.

CHAPTER TWO

The Council with the Munchkins

She was awakened by a shock, so sudden and severe that if Dorothy had not been lying on the soft bed she might have been hurt. As it was, the jar made her catch her breath and wonder what had happened; and Toto put his cold little nose into her face and whined dismally. Dorothy sat up and noticed that the house was not moving; nor was it dark, for the bright sunshine came in at the window, flooding the little room. She sprang from her bed and with Toto at her heels ran and opened the door.

The little girl gave a cry of amazement and looked about her, her eyes growing bigger and bigger at the wonderful sights she saw.

The cyclone had set the house down, very gently – for a cyclone – in the midst of a country of marvellous beauty. There were lovely patches of green sward all about, with stately trees bearing rich and luscious fruits. Banks of gorgeous flowers were on every hand, and birds with rare and brilliant plumage sang and fluttered in the trees and bushes. A little way off was a small brook, rushing and sparkling along between green banks, and murmuring in a voice very grateful to a little girl who had lived so long on the dry, grey prairies.

While she stood looking eagerly at the strange and beautiful sights, she noticed coming towards her a group of the queerest people she had ever seen. They were not as big as the grown folk she had always been used to; but neither were they very small. In fact, they seemed about as tall as Dorothy, who was a well-grown child for her age, although they were, so far as looks go, many years older.

Three were men and one a woman, and all were oddly dressed. They wore round hats that rose to a small point a foot above their heads, with little bells around the brims that tinkled sweetly as they moved. The hats of the men were blue; the little woman's hat was white, and she wore a white gown that hung in pleats from her shoulders; over it were sprinkled little stars that glistened in the sun like diamonds. The men were dressed in blue, of the same shade as their hats, and wore well-polished boots with a deep roll of blue at the tops. The men, Dorothy thought, were about as old as Uncle Henry, for two of them had beards. But the little woman was doubtless much older: her face was covered with wrinkles, her hair was nearly white, and she walked rather stiffly.

When these people drew near the house where Dorothy was standing in the doorway, they paused and whispered among themselves, as if afraid to come farther. But the little old woman walked up to Dorothy, made a low bow and said, in a sweet voice: 'You are welcome, most noble Sorceress, to the land of the Munchkins. We are so grateful to you for having killed the Wicked Witch of the East, and for setting our people free from bondage.'

Dorothy listened to this speech with wonder. What could

the little woman possibly mean by calling her a sorceress, and saying she had killed the Wicked Witch of the East? Dorothy was an innocent, harmless little girl, who had been carried by a cyclone many miles from home; and she had never killed anything in all her life.

But the little woman evidently expected her to answer; so Dorothy said, with hesitation.

'You are very kind; but there must be some mistake. I have not killed anything.'

'Your house did, anyway,' replied the little old woman, with a laugh; 'and that is the same thing. See!' she continued, pointing to the corner of the house; 'there are her two toes, still sticking out from under a block of wood.'

Dorothy looked, and gave a little cry of fright. There, indeed, just under the corner of the great beam the house rested on, two feet were sticking out, shod in silver shoes with pointed toes. 'Oh dear! oh dear!' cried Dorothy, clasping her hands together in dismay; 'the house must have fallen on her. What ever shall we do?'

'There is nothing to be done,' said the little woman, calmly.

'But who was she?' asked Dorothy.

'She was the Wicked Witch of the East, as I said,' answered the little woman. 'She has held all the Munchkins in bondage for many years, making them slave for her night and day. Now they are all set free and are grateful to you for the favour.'

'Who are the Munchkins?' enquired Dorothy.

'They are the people who live in this land of the East, where the Wicked Witch ruled.'

'Are you a Munchkin?' asked Dorothy.

'No; but I am their friend, although I live in the land of the North. When they saw the Witch of the East was dead the Munchkins sent a swift messenger to me, and I came at once. I am the Witch of the North.'

'Oh, gracious!' cried Dorothy; 'are you a real witch?'

'Yes, indeed,' answered the little woman. 'But I am a good witch, and the people love me. I am not as powerful as the Wicked Witch was who ruled here, or I should have set the people free myself.'

'But I thought all witches were wicked,' said the girl, who was half frightened at facing a real witch.

'Oh, no; that is a great mistake. There were only four witches in all the Land of Oz, and two of them, those who live in the North and the South, are good witches. I know this is true, for I am one of them myself, and cannot be mistaken. Those who dwelt in the East and the West were, indeed, wicked witches; but now that you have killed one of them, there is but one wicked Witch in all the Land of Oz – the one who lives in the West.'

'But,' said Dorothy, after a moment's thought, 'Aunt Em has told me that the witches were all dead – years and years ago.'

'Who is Aunt Em?' enquired the little old woman.

'She is my aunt who lives in Kansas, where I came from.'

The Witch of the North seemed to think for a time, with her head bowed and her eyes upon the ground. Then she looked up and said, 'I do not know where Kansas is, for I have never heard that country mentioned before. But tell me, is it a civilised country?'

'Oh, yes,' replied Dorothy.

'Then that accounts for it. In the civilised countries I believe there are no witches left; nor wizards, nor sorceresses, nor magicians. But, you see, the Land of Oz has never been civilised, for we are cut off from all the rest of the world. Therefore we still have witches and wizards amongst us.'

'Who are the wizards?' asked Dorothy.

'Oz himself is the Great Wizard,' answered the Witch, sinking her voice to a whisper. 'He is more powerful than all the rest of us together. He lives in the City of Emeralds.'

Dorothy was going to ask another question, but just then the Munchkins, who had been standing silently by, gave a loud shout and pointed to the corner of the house where the Wicked Witch had been lying.

'What is it?' asked the little old woman; and looked, and began to laugh. The feet of the dead witch had disappeared entirely and nothing was left but the silver shoes.

'She was so old,' explained the Witch of the North, 'that she dried up quickly in the sun That is the end of her. But the silver shoes are yours, and you shall have them to wear.' She reached down and picked up the shoes, and after shaking the dust out of them handed them to Dorothy.

'The Witch of the East was proud of those silver shoes,' said one of the Munchkins; 'and there is some charm connected with them; but what is it we never knew.'

Dorothy carried the shoes into the house and placed them on the table. Then she came out again to the Munchkins and said, 'I am anxious to get back to my Aunt and Uncle, for I am sure they will worry about me. Can you help me find my way?'

The Munchkins and the Witch first looked at one another, and then at Dorothy, and then shook their heads.

'At the East, not far from here,' said one, 'there is a great desert, and none could live to cross it.'

'It is the same at the South,' said another, 'for I have been there and seen it. The South is the country of the Quadlings.'

'I am told,' said the third man, 'that it is the same at the West. And that country, where the Winkies live, is ruled by the Wicked Witch of the West, who would make you her slave if you passed her way.'

'The North is my home,' said the old lady, 'and at its edge is the same great desert that surrounds this land of Oz. I'm afraid, my dear, you will have to live with us.'

Dorothy began to sob, at this, for she felt lonely among all these strange people. Her tears seemed to grieve the kind-hearted Munchkins, for they immediately took out their handkerchiefs and began to weep also. As for the little old woman, she took off her cap and balanced the point on the end of her nose, while she counted 'one, two, three' in a solemn voice. At once the cap changed to a slate, on which was written in big, white chalk marks: Let Dorothy Go to the City of Emeralds

The little old woman took the slate from her nose, and having read the words on it, asked, 'Is your name Dorothy, my dear?'

'Yes,' answered the child, looking up and drying her tears.

'Then you must go to the City of Emeralds. Perhaps Oz will help you.'

'Where is this city?' asked Dorothy.

'It is exactly in the centre of the country, and is ruled by Oz, the Great Wizard I told you of.'

'Is he a good man?' enquired the girl, anxiously.

'He is a good wizard. Whether he is a man or not I cannot tell, for I have never seen him.'

'How can I get there?' asked Dorothy.

'You must walk. It is a long journey, through a country that is sometimes pleasant and sometimes dark and terrible. However, I will use all the magic arts I know of to keep you from harm.'

'Won't you go with me?' pleaded the girl, who had begun to look upon the little old woman as her only friend.

'No, I cannot do that,' she replied; 'but I will give you my kiss, and no one will dare injure a person who has been kissed by the Witch of the North.'

She came close to Dorothy and kissed her gently on the forehead. Where her lips touched the girl they left a round, shining mark, as Dorothy found out soon after.

'The road to the City of Emeralds is paved with yellow

brick,' said the Witch; 'so you cannot miss it. When you get to Oz do not be afraid of him, but tell your story and ask him to help you. Goodbye, my dear.'

The three Munchkins bowed low to her and wished her a pleasant journey, after which they walked away through the trees. The witch gave Dorothy a friendly little nod, whirled around on her left heel three times, and straightway disappeared, much to the surprise of little Toto, who barked after her loudly enough when she had gone, because he had been afraid even to growl while she stood by.

But Dorothy, knowing her to be a witch, had expected her to disappear in just that way, and was not surprised in the least.

CHAPTER THREE

*How Dorothy Saved
the Scarecrow*

When Dorothy was left alone she began to feel hungry. So she went to the cupboard and cut herself some bread, which she spread with butter. She gave some to Toto, and taking a pail from the shelf she carried it down to the little brook and filled it with clear, sparkling water. Toto ran over to the trees and began to bark at the birds sitting there. Dorothy went to get him, and saw such delicious fruit hanging from the branches that she gathered some of it, finding it just what she wanted to help out her breakfast.

Then she went back to the house, and having helped herself and Toto to a good drink of the cool, clear water, she set about making ready for the journey to the City of Emeralds.

Dorothy had only one other dress, but that happened to be clean and was hanging on a peg beside her bed. It was gingham, with checks of white and blue; and although the blue was somewhat faded with many washings, it was still a pretty frock. The girl washed herself carefully, dressed herself in the clean gingham, and tied her pink sunbonnet on her head. She took a little basket and filled it with bread from the cupboard, laying a white cloth over the top. Then she looked down at her feet and noticed how old and worn her shoes were.

'They surely will never do for a long journey, Toto,' she said. And Toto looked up into her face with his little black eyes and wagging his tail to show he knew what she meant.

At that moment Dorothy saw lying on the table the silver shoes that had belonged to the Witch of the East.

'I wonder if they will fit me,' she said to Toto. 'They would be just the thing to take a long walk in, for they could not wear out.'

She took off her old leather shoes and tried on the silver ones, which fitted her as well as if they had been made for her.

Finally she picked up her basket.

'Come along, Toto,' she said, 'we will go to the Emerald City and ask the great Oz how to get back to Kansas again.'

She closed the door, locked it, and put the key carefully in the pocket of her dress. And so, with Toto trotting along soberly behind her, she started on her journey.

There were several roads near by, but it did not take her long to find the one paved with yellow brick. Within a short time she was walking briskly towards the Emerald City, her silver shoes tinkling merrily on the hard yellow roadbed. The sun shone bright and the birds sang sweetly and Dorothy did not feel nearly so bad as you might think a little girl would who had been suddenly whisked away from her own country and set down in the midst of a strange land.

She was surprised, as she walked along, to see how pretty the country was about her. There were neat fences at the sides of the road, painted a dainty blue colour, and beyond them were fields of grain and vegetables in abundance. Evidently the Munchkins were good farmers and able to raise large crops. Once in a while she would pass a house, and the people came out to look at her and bow low as she went by; for everyone knew she had been the means of destroying the Wicked Witch and setting them free from bondage. The houses of the Munchkins were odd looking dwellings, for each was round, with a big dome for a roof. All were painted blue, for in this country of the East blue was the favourite colour.

Towards evening, when Dorothy was tired with her long wait and began to wonder where she should pass the night, she came to a house rather larger than the rest. On the green lawn before it many men and women were dancing. Five little fiddlers played as loudly as possible and the people were laughing and singing, while a big table near by was loaded with delicious fruits and nuts, pies and cakes, and many other good things to eat.

The people greeted Dorothy kindly, and invited her to supper and to pass the night with them; for this was the home of one of the richest Munchkins in the land, and his friends were gathered with him to celebrate their freedom from the bondage of the Wicked Witch.

Dorothy ate a hearty supper and was waited upon by the rich Munchkin himself, whose name was Boq. Then she sat down upon a settee and watched the people dance.

When Boq saw her silver shoes, he said, 'You must be a great sorceress.'

'Why?' asked the girl.

'Because you wear silver shoes and have killed the Wicked Witch. Besides, you have white in your frock, and only witches and sorceresses wear white.'

'My dress is blue and white checked,' said Dorothy, smoothing out the wrinkles in it.

'It is kind of you to wear that,' said Boq. 'Blue is the

You must be a great sorceress.

colour of the Munchkins, and white is the witch colour; so we know you are a friendly witch.'

Dorothy did not know what to say to this, for all the people seemed to think her a witch, and she knew very well she was only an ordinary little girl who had come by the chance of a cyclone into a strange land.

When she had tired watching the dancing, Boq led her into the house, where he gave her a room with a pretty bed in it. The sheets were made of blue cloth, and Dorothy slept soundly in them till morning, with Toto curled up on the blue rug beside her.

She ate a hearty breakfast, and watched a wee Munchkin baby, who played with Toto and pulled his tail and crowed and laughed in a way that greatly amused Dorothy. Toto was a fine curiosity to all the people, for they had never seen a dog before.

'How far is it to the Emerald City?' the girl asked.

'I do not know,' answered Boq, gravely, 'for I have never been there. It is better for people to keep away from Oz, unless they have business with him. But it is a long way to the Emerald City, and it will take you many days. The country here is rich and pleasant, but you must pass through rough and dangerous places before you reach the end of your journey.'

This worried Dorothy a little, but she knew that only the great Oz could help her get to Kansas again, so she bravely resolved not to turn back.

She bade her friends goodbye, and again started along the road of yellow brick. When she had gone several miles she thought she would stop to rest, and so climbed to the top of the fence beside the road and sat down. There was a great cornfield beyond the fence, and not far away she saw a Scarecrow, placed high on a pole to keep the birds from the ripe corn.

Dorothy leaned her chin upon her hand and gazed

thoughtfully at the Scarecrow. Its head was a small sack stuffed with straw, with eyes, nose and mouth painted on it to represent a face. An old, pointed blue hat, that had belonged to some Munchkin, was perched on this head, and the rest of the figure was a blue suit of clothes, worn and faded, which had also been stuffed with straw. On the feet were some old boots with blue tops, such as every man wore in this country, and the figure was raised above the stalks of corn by means of the pole stuck up its back.

While Dorothy was looking earnestly into the queer, painted face of the Scarecrow, she was surprised to see one of the eyes slowly wink at her. She thought she must have been mistaken, at first, for none of the scarecrows in Kansas ever wink; but presently the figure nodded its head to her in a friendly way. Then she climbed down from the fence and walked up to it, while Toto ran around the pole and barked.

'Good-day,' said the Scarecrow, in a rather husky voice.

'Did you speak?' asked the girl, in wonder.

'Certainly,' answered the Scarecrow; 'how do you do?'

'I'm pretty well, thank you,' replied Dorothy, politely; 'how do you do?'

'I'm not feeling well,' said the Scarecrow, with a smile, 'for it is very tedious being perched up here night and day to scare away crows.'

'Can't you get down?' asked Dorothy.

'No, for this pole is stuck up my back. If you will please take away the pole I shall be greatly obliged to you.'

Dorothy reached up both arms and lifted the figure off the pole; for, being stuffed with straw, it was quite light.

'Thank you very much,' said the Scarecrow, when he had been set down on the ground. 'I feel like a new man.'

Dorothy was puzzled at this, for it sounded queer to hear a stuffed man speak, and to see him bow and walk along beside her.

'Who are you?' asked the Scarecrow when he had stretched himself and yawned, 'and where are you going?'

'My name is Dorothy,' said the girl, 'and I am going to the Emerald City, to ask the great Oz to send me back to Kansas.'

'Where is the Emerald City?' he enquired; 'and who is Oz?'

'Why, don't you know?' she returned, in surprise.

'No, indeed; I don't know anything. You see, I am stuffed, so I have no brains at all,' he answered, sadly.

'Oh,' said Dorothy, 'I'm awfully sorry for you.'

'Do you think,' he asked, 'if I go to the Emerald City with you, that Oz would give me some brains?'

'I cannot tell,' she returned; 'but you may come with me, if you like. If Oz will not give you any brains you will be no worse off than you are now.'

'That is true,' said the Scarecrow. 'You see,' he continued, confidentially, 'I don't mind my legs and arms and body being stuffed, because I cannot get hurt. If anyone treads on my toes or sticks a pin into me, it doesn't matter, for I can't feel it. But I do not want people to call me a fool, and if my head stays stuffed with straw instead of with brains, as yours is, how am I ever to know anything?'

'I understand how you feel,' said the little girl, who was truly sorry for him. 'If you will come with me I'll ask Oz to do all he can for you.'

'Thank you,' he answered, gratefully.

They walked back to the road, Dorothy helped him over the fence, and they started along the path of yellow brick for the Emerald City.

Toto did not like this addition to the party, at first. He smelled around the stuffed man as if he suspected there might be a nest of rats in the straw, and he often growled in an unfriendly way at the Scarecrow.

'Don't mind Toto,' said Dorothy, to her new friend; 'he never bites.'

'Oh, I'm not afraid,' replied the Scarecrow, 'he can't hurt the straw. Do let me carry that basket for you. I shall not mind it, for I can't get tired. I'll tell you a secret,' he continued, as he walked along; 'there is only one thing in the world I am afraid of.'

'What is that?' asked Dorothy; 'the Munchkin farmer who made you?'

'No,' answered the Scarecrow; 'it's a lighted match.'

CHAPTER FOUR

The Road through the Forest

After a few hours the road began to be rough, and the walking grew so difficult that the Scarecrow often stumbled over the yellow bricks, which were here very uneven. Sometimes, indeed, they were broken or missing altogether, leaving holes that Toto jumped across and Dorothy walked around. As for the Scarecrow, having no brains, he walked straight ahead, and so stepped into the holes and fell at full length on the hard bricks. It never hurt him, however, and Dorothy would pick him up and set him upon his feet again, while he joined her in laughing merrily at his own mishap.

The farms were not nearly so well cared for here as they were farther back. There were fewer houses and fewer fruit trees, and the farther they went the more dismal and lonesome the country became.

At noon they sat down by the roadside, near a little brook,

and Dorothy opened her basket and got out some bread. She offered a piece to the Scarecrow, but he refused.

'I am never hungry,' he said; 'and it is a lucky thing I am not. For my mouth is only painted, and if I should cut a hole in it so I could eat, the straw I am stuffed with would come out, and that would spoil the shape of my head.'

Dorothy saw at once that this was true, so she only nodded and went on eating her bread.

'Tell me something about yourself, and the country you came from,' said the Scarecrow, when she had finished her dinner. So she told him all about Kansas, and how grey everything was there, and how the cyclone had carried her to this queer land of Oz. The Scarecrow listened carefully, and said, 'I cannot understand why you should wish to leave this beautiful country and go back to the dry, grey place you call Kansas.'

'That is because you have no brains,' answered the girl. 'No matter how dreary and grey our homes are, we people of flesh and blood would rather live there than in any other country, be it ever so beautiful. There is no place like home.'

The Scarecrow sighed.

'Of course I cannot understand it,' he said. 'If your heads were stuffed with straw, like mine, you would probably all live in the beautiful places, and then Kansas would have no people at all. It is fortunate for Kansas that you have brains.'

'Won't you tell me a story, while we are resting?' asked the child.

The Scarecrow looked at her reproachfully, and answered, 'My life has been so short that I really know nothing whatever. I was only made day before yesterday. What happened in the world before that time is all unknown to me. Luckily, when the farmer made my head, one of the first things he did was to paint my ears, so that I heard what was going on. There was another Munchkin with him, and the first thing

I heard was the farmer saying, "How do you like those ears?"

' "They aren't straight," answered the other.

' "Never mind," said the farmer; "they are ears just the same," which was true enough.

' "Now I'll make the eyes," said the farmer. So he painted my right eye, and as soon as it was finished I found myself looking at him and at everything around me with a great deal of curiosity, for this was my first glimpse of the world.

' "That's a rather pretty eye," remarked the Munchkin who was watching the farmer; "blue paint is just the colour for eyes."

' "I think I'll make the other a little bigger," said the farmer; and when the second eye was done I could see much better than before. Then he made my nose and my mouth; but I did not speak, because at that time I didn't know what a mouth was for. I had the fun of watching them make my body and my arms and legs; and when they fastened on my head, at last, I felt very proud, for I thought I was just as good a man as anyone.

' "This fellow will scare the crows fast enough," said the farmer; "he looks just like a man."

' "Why, he is a man," said the other, and I quite agreed with him. The farmer carried me under his arm to the cornfield, and set me up on a tall stick, where you found me. He and his friend soon after walked away and left me alone.

'I did not like to be deserted this way; so I tried to walk after them, but my feet would not touch the ground, and I was forced to stay on that pole. It was a lonely life to lead, for I had nothing to think of, having been made such a little while before. Many crows and other birds flew into the cornfield, but as soon as they saw me they flew away again, thinking I was a Munchkin; and this pleased me and made me feel that I was quite an important person. By and by an old crow flew near me, and after looking at me carefully he perched upon my shoulder and said, "I wonder if that farmer thought to fool me in this clumsy manner. Any crow of sense could see that you are only stuffed with straw." Then he hopped down at my feet and ate all the corn he wanted. The other birds, seeing he was not harmed by me, came to eat the corn too, so in a short time there was a great flock of them about me.

'I felt sad at this, for it showed I was not such a good Scarecrow after all; but the old crow comforted me, saying: "If you only had brains in your head you would be as good a man as any of them, and a better man than some of them. Brains are the only things worth having in this world, no matter whether one is a crow or a man."

'After the crows had gone I thought this over, and decided I would try hard to get some brains. By good luck, you came along and pulled me off the stake, and from what you say I am sure the great Oz will give me brains as soon as we get to the Emerald City.'

'I hope so,' said Dorothy, earnestly, 'since you seem anxious to have them.'

'Oh, yes; I am anxious,' returned the Scarecrow. 'It is such an uncomfortable feeling to know one is a fool.'

'Well,' said the girl, 'let us go.' And she handed the basket to the Scarecrow.

There were no fences at all by the roadside now, and the land was rough and untilled. Towards evening they came to a great forest, where the trees grew so big and close together that their branches met over the road of yellow brick. It was almost dark under the trees, for the branches shut out the daylight; but the travellers did not stop, and went on into the forest.

'If this road goes in, it must come out,' said the Scarecrow, 'and as the Emerald City is at the other end of the road, we must go wherever it leads us.'

'Anyone would know that,' said Dorothy.

'Certainly; that is why I know it,' returned the Scarecrow. 'If it required brains to figure it out, I never should have said it.'

After an hour or so the light faded away, and they found themselves stumbling along in the darkness. Dorothy could not see at all, but Toto could, for some dogs see very well in the dark; and the Scarecrow declared he could see as well as by day. So she took hold of his arm, and managed to get along fairly well.

'If you see any house, or any place where we can pass the night,' she said, 'you must tell me; for it is very uncomfortable walking in the dark.'

Soon after the Scarecrow stopped.

'I see a little cottage at the right of us,' he said, 'built of logs and branches. Shall we go there?'

'Yes, indeed,' answered the child. 'I am all tired out.'

So the Scarecrow led her through the trees until they reached the cottage, and Dorothy entered and found a bed of dried leaves in one corner. She lay down at once, and with Toto beside her soon fell into a sound sleep. The Scarecrow, who was never tired, stood up in another corner and waited patiently until morning came.

CHAPTER FIVE

The Rescue of the Tin Woodman

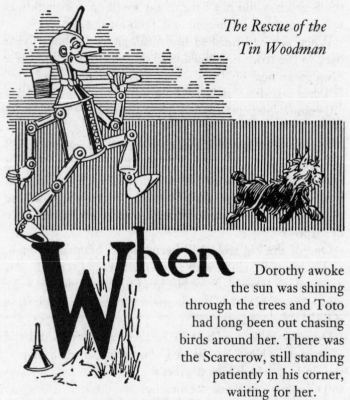

When Dorothy awoke the sun was shining through the trees and Toto had long been out chasing birds around her. There was the Scarecrow, still standing patiently in his corner, waiting for her.

'We must go and search for water,' she said to him.

'Why do you want water?' he asked.

'To wash my face clean after the dust of the road, and to drink, so the dry bread will not stick in my throat.'

'It must be inconvenient to be made of flesh,' said the Scarecrow, thoughtfully; 'for you must sleep, and eat and drink. However, you have brains, and it is worth a lot of bother to be able to think properly.'

They left the cottage and walked through the trees until they found a little spring of clear water, where Dorothy drank and bathed and ate her breakfast. She saw there was not much bread left in the basket, and the girl was thankful the Scarecrow did not have to eat anything, for there was scarcely enough for herself and Toto for the day.

When she had finished her meal, and was about to go back to the road of yellow brick, she was startled to hear a deep groan near by.

'What was that?' she asked, timidly.

'I cannot imagine,' replied the Scarecrow; 'but we can go and see.'

Just then another groan reached their ears, and the sound seemed to come from behind them. They turned and walked through the forest a few steps, when Dorothy discovered something shining in a ray of sunshine, that fell between the trees. She ran to the place and then stopped short, with a cry of surprise.

One of the big trees had been partly chopped through, and standing beside it, with an uplifted axe in his hands, was a man made entirely of tin. His head and arms and legs were jointed upon his body, but he stood perfectly motionless, as if he could not stir at all.

Dorothy looked at him in amazement, and so did the Scarecrow, while Toto barked sharply and made a snap at the tin legs, which hurt his teeth.

'Did you groan?' asked Dorothy.

'Yes,' answered the tin man; 'I did. I've been groaning for more than a year, and no one has ever heard me before or come to help me.'

'What can I do for you?' she enquired, softly, for she was moved by the sad voice in which the man spoke.

'Get an oilcan and oil my joints,' he answered. 'They are rusted so badly that I cannot move them at all; if I am well oiled I shall soon be all right again. You will find an oilcan on a shelf in my cottage.'

Dorothy at once ran back to the cottage and found the

oilcan, and then she returned and asked, anxiously, 'Where are your joints?'

'Oil my neck, first,' replied the Tin Woodman. So she oiled it, and as it was quite badly rusted the Scarecrow took hold of the tin head and moved it gently from side to side until it worked freely, and then the man could turn it himself.

'Now oil the joints in my arms,' he said. And Dorothy oiled them and the Scarecrow bent them carefully until they were quite free from rust and as good as new.

The Tin Woodman gave a sigh of satisfaction and lowered his axe, which he leaned against the tree.

'This is a great comfort,' he said. 'I have been holding that axe in the air ever since I rusted, and I'm glad to be able to put it down at last. Now, if you will oil the joints of my legs, I shall be all right once more.'

So they oiled his legs until he could move them freely; and he thanked them again and again for his release, for he seemed a very polite creature, and very grateful.

'I might have stood there always if you had not come along,' he said; 'so you have certainly saved my life. How did you happen to be here?'

'We are on our way to the Emerald City, to see the great Oz,' she answered, 'and we stopped at your cottage to pass the night.'

'Why do you wish to see Oz?' he asked.

'I want him to send me back to Kansas; and the Scarecrow wants him to put a few brains into his head,' she replied.

The Tin Woodman appeared to think deeply for a moment. Then he said: 'Do you suppose Oz could give me a heart?'

'Why, I guess so,' Dorothy answered; 'it would be as easy as to give the Scarecrow brains.'

'True,' the Tin Woodman returned. 'So, if you will allow me to join your party, I will also go to the Emerald City and ask Oz to help me.'

'Come along,' said the Scarecrow, heartily; and Dorothy added that she would be pleased to have his company. So the Tin Woodman shouldered his axe and they all passed through the forest until they came to the road that was paved with yellow brick.

The Tin Woodman had asked Dorothy to put the oilcan in her basket. 'For,' he said, 'if I should get caught in the rain, and rust again, I would need the oilcan badly.'

It was a bit of good luck in have their new comrade join the party, for soon after they had begun their journey again they came to a place where the trees and branches grew so thick over the road that the travellers could not pass. But the Tin Woodman set to work with his axe and chopped so well that soon he cleared a passage for the entire party.

Dorothy was thinking so earnestly as they walked along that she did not notice when the Scarecrow stumbled into a hole and rolled over to the side of the road. Indeed he was obliged to call to her to help him up again.

'Why didn't you walk around the hole?' asked the Tin Woodman.

'I don't know enough,' replied the Scarecrow, cheerfully. 'My head is stuffed with straw, you know, and that is why I am going to Oz to ask him for some brains.'

'Oh, I see,' said the Tin Woodman. 'But, after all, brains are not the best things in the world.'

'Have you any?' enquired the Scarecrow.

'No, my head is quite empty,' answered the Woodman; 'but once I had brains, and a heart also; so, having tried them both, I should much rather have a heart.'

'And why is that?' asked the Scarecrow.

'I will tell you my story, and then you will know.'

So, while they were walking through the forest, the Tin Woodman told the following story: 'I was born the son of a woodman who chopped down trees in the forest and sold the wood for a living. When I grew up I too became a wood-chopper, and after my father died I took care of my old mother as long as she lived. Then I made up my mind that instead of living alone I would marry, so that I might not become lonely.

'There was one of the Munchkin girls who was so beautiful that I soon grew to love her with all my heart. She, on her part, promised to marry me as soon as I could earn enough money to build a better house for her; so I set to work harder than ever. But the girl lived with an old woman who did not want her to marry anyone, for she was so lazy she wished the girl to remain with her and do the cooking and the housework. So the old woman went to the Wicked Witch of the East, and promised her two sheep and a cow if she would prevent the marriage. Thereupon the Wicked Witch enchanted my axe, and when I was chopping away at my best one day, for I was anxious to get the new house and my wife as soon as possible, the axe slipped all at once and cut off my left leg.

'This at first seemed a great misfortune, for I knew a one-legged man could not do very well as a wood-chopper. So I went to a tin-smith and had him make me a new leg out of tin. The leg worked very well, once I was used to it; but my action angered the Wicked Witch of the East, for she had promised the old woman I should not marry the pretty Munchkin girl. When I began chopping again my axe slipped and cut off my right leg. Again I went to the tinner, and again he made me a leg out of tin. After this the enchanted axe cut off my arms, one after the other; but, nothing daunted, I had them replaced with tin ones. The Wicked Witch then made the axe slip and cut off my head, and at first I thought that was the end of me. But the tinner happened to come along, and he made me a new head out of tin.

'I thought I had beaten the Wicked Witch then, and I worked harder than ever; but I little knew how cruel my enemy could be. She thought of a new way to kill my love for the beautiful Munchkin maiden, and made my axe slip again, so that it cut right through my body, splitting me into two halves. Once more the tinner came to my help and made me a body of tin, fastening my tin arms and legs and head to it, by means of joints, so that I could move around as well as ever. But, alas! I had now no heart, so that I lost all my love for the Munchkin girl, and did not care whether I married her or not. I suppose she is still living with the old woman, waiting for me to come after her.

'My body shone so brightly in the sun that I felt very proud of it and it did not matter now if my axe slipped, for it could not cut me. There was only one danger – that my joints would rust; but I kept an oilcan in my cottage and took care to oil myself whenever I needed it. However, there came a day when I forgot to do this, and, being caught in a rainstorm, before I thought of the danger my joints had rusted, and I was left to stand in the woods until you came to help me. It was a terrible thing to undergo, but during the year I stood there I had time to think that the greatest loss I had known was the loss of my heart. While I was in love I was the happiest man on earth; but no one can love who has not a heart, and so I am resolved to ask Oz to give me one. If he does, I will go back to the Munchkin maiden and marry her.'

Both Dorothy and the Scarecrow had been greatly interested in the story of the Tin Woodman, and now they knew why he was so anxious to get a new heart.

'All the same,' said the Scarecrow, 'I shall ask for brains instead of a heart; for a fool would not know what to do with a heart if he had one.'

'I shall take the heart,' returned the Tin Woodman; 'for brains do not make one happy, and happiness is the best thing in the world.'

Dorothy did not say anything, for she was puzzled to

*The Tin Woodman gave a sigh of satisfaction and
lowered his axe, which he leaned against the tree.*

know which of her two friends was right, and she decided if she could only get back to Kansas and Aunt Em it did not matter so much whether the Woodman had no brains and the Scarecrow no heart, or each got what he wanted.

What worried her most was that the bread was nearly gone, and another meal for herself and Toto would empty the basket. To be sure neither the Woodman nor the Scarecrow ever ate anything, but she was not made of tin nor straw, and could not live unless she was fed.

CHAPTER SIX

The Cowardly Lion

All this time Dorothy and her companions had been walking through the thick woods. The road was still paved with yellow bricks, but these were much covered by dried branches and dead leaves from the trees, and the walking was not at all good.

There were few birds in this part of the forest, for birds love the open country where there is plenty of sunshine; but now and then there came a deep growl from some wild animal hidden among the trees. These sounds made the little girl's heart beat fast, for she did not know what made them; but Toto knew, and he walked close to Dorothy's side, and did not even bark in return.

'How long will it be,' the child asked of the Tin Woodman, 'before we are out of the forest?'

'I cannot tell,' was the answer, 'for I have never been to the Emerald City. But my father went there once, when I was a boy, and he said it was a long journey through a dangerous country, although nearer to the city where Oz dwells the country is beautiful. But I am not afraid so long as I have my oilcan, and nothing can hurt the Scarecrow, while you bear upon your forehead the mark of the good Witch's kiss, and that will protect you from harm.'

'But Toto!' said the girl anxiously; 'what will protect him?'

'We must protect him ourselves, if he is in danger,' replied the Tin Woodman.

Just as he spoke there came from the forest a terrible roar, and the next moment a great Lion bounded into the road. With one blow of his paw he sent the Scarecrow spinning over and over to the edge of the road, and then he struck at the Tin Woodman with his sharp claws. But, to the Lion's surprise, he could make no impression on the tin, although the Woodman fell over in the road and lay still.

Little Toto, now that he had an enemy to face, ran barking towards the Lion, and the great beast had opened his mouth to bite the dog, when Dorothy, fearing Toto would be killed, and heedless of danger, rushed forward and slapped the Lion upon his nose as hard as she could, while she cried out: 'Don't you dare to bite Toto! You ought to be ashamed of yourself, a big beast like you, to bite a poor little dog!'

'I didn't bite him,' said the Lion, as he rubbed his nose with his paw where Dorothy had hit it.

'No, but you tried to,' she retorted. 'You are nothing but a big coward.'

'I know it,' said the Lion, hanging his head in shame; 'I've always known it. But how can I help it?'

'I don't know, I'm sure. To think of you striking a stuffed man, like the poor Scarecrow!'

'Is he stuffed?' asked the Lion, in surprise, as he watched her pick up the Scarecrow and set him upon his feet, while she patted him into shape again.

'Of course he's stuffed,' replied Dorothy, who was still angry.

'That's why he went over so easily,' remarked the Lion. 'It astonished me to see him whirl around so. Is the other one stuffed, also?'

'No,' said Dorothy, 'he's made of tin. And she helped the Woodman up again.

'That's why he nearly blunted my claws,' said the Lion. 'When they scratched against the tin it made a cold shiver run down my back. What is that little animal you are so tender of?'

'He is my dog, Toto,' answered Dorothy.

'Is he made of tin, or stuffed?' asked the Lion.

'Neither. He's a–a–a meat dog,' said the girl.

'Oh! He's a curious animal, and seems remarkably small, now that I look at him. No one would think of biting such a little thing except a coward like me,' continued the Lion, sadly.

'What makes you a coward?' asked Dorothy, looking at the great beast in wonder, for he was as big as a small horse.

'It's a mystery,' replied the Lion. 'I suppose I was born that way. All the other animals in the forest naturally expect me to be brave, for the Lion is everywhere thought to be the King of Beasts. I learned that if I roared very loudly every living thing was frightened and got out of my way. Whenever I've met a man I've been awfully scared; but I just roared at him, and he has always run away as fast as he could go. If the elephants and the tigers and the bears had ever tried to fight me, I should have run myself – I'm such a coward; but just as soon as they hear me roar they all try to get away from me, and of course I let them go.'

'But that isn't right. The King of Beasts shouldn't be a coward,' said the Scarecrow.

'I know it,' returned the Lion, wiping a tear from his eye with the tip of his tail; 'it is my great sorrow, and makes my life very unhappy. But whenever there is danger my heart begins to beat fast.'

'Perhaps you have heart disease,' said the Tin Woodman.

'It may be,' said the Lion.

'If you have,' continued the Tin Woodman, 'you ought to be glad, for it proves you have a heart. For my part, I have no heart; so I cannot have heart disease.'

'Perhaps,' said the Lion, thoughtfully, 'if I had no heart I should not be a coward.'

'Have you brains?' asked the Scarecrow.

'I suppose so. I've never looked to see,' replied the Lion.

'I am going to the great Oz to ask him to give me some,' remarked the Scarecrow, 'for my head is stuffed with straw.'

'And I am going to ask him to give me a heart,' said the Woodman.

'And I am going to ask him to send Toto and me back to Kansas,' added Dorothy.

'Do you think Oz could give me courage?' asked the cowardly Lion.

'Just as easily as he could give me brains,' said the Scarecrow.

'Or give me a heart,' said the Tin Woodman.

'Or send me back to Kansas,' said Dorothy.

'Then, if you don't mind, I'll go with you,' said the Lion, 'for my life is simply unbearable without a bit of courage.'

'You will be very welcome,' answered Dorothy, 'for you will help to keep away the other wild beasts. It seems to me they must be more cowardly than you are if they allow you to scare them so easily.'

'They really are,' said the Lion; 'but that doesn't make me any braver, and as long as I know myself to be a coward I shall be unhappy.'

So once more the little company set off upon the journey, the Lion walking with stately strides at Dorothy's side. Toto did not approve this new comrade at first, for he could not forget how nearly he had been crushed between the Lion's great jaws; but after a time he became more at ease, and presently Toto and the Cowardly Lion had grown to be good friends.

During the rest of that day there was no other adventure to mar the peace of their journey. Once, indeed, the Tin Woodman stepped upon a beetle that was crawling along the road, and killed the poor little thing. This made the Tin Woodman very unhappy, for he was always careful not to hurt any living creature; and as he walked along he wept several tears of sorrow and regret. These tears ran slowly down his face and over the hinges of his jaw, and there they rusted. When Dorothy presently asked him a question the Tin Woodman could not open his mouth, for his jaws were tightly rusted together. He became greatly frightened at this and made many motions to Dorothy to relieve him, but she could not understand. The Lion was also puzzled to know what was wrong. But the Scarecrow seized the oilcan from Dorothy's basket and oiled the Woodman's jaws, so that after a few moments he could talk as well as before.

'This will serve me a lesson,' said he, 'to look where I step. For if I should kill another bug or beetle I should surely cry again, and crying rusts my jaws so that I cannot speak.'

Thereafter he walked very carefully, with his eyes on the road, and when he saw a tiny ant toiling by he would step over it, so as not to harm it. The Tin Wood-man knew very well he had no heart, and therefore he took great care never to be cruel or unkind to anything.

'You people with hearts,' he said, 'have something to guide you, and need never do wrong; but I have no heart, and so I must be very careful. When Oz gives me a heart of course I needn't mind so much.'

CHAPTER SEVEN

The Journey to the Great Oz

They were obliged to camp out that night under a large tree in the forest, for there were no houses near. The tree made a good, thick covering to protect them from the dew, and the Tin Woodman chopped a great pile of wood with his axe and Dorothy built a splendid fire that warmed her and made her feel less lonely. She and Toto ate the last of their bread, and now she didn't know what they would do for breakfast.

'If you wish,' said the Lion, 'I will go into the forest and kill a deer for you. You can roast it by the fire, since your tastes so are so peculiar that you prefer cooked food, and then you will have a very good breakfast.'

'Don't! please don't,' begged the Tin Woodman. 'I should

certainly weep if you killed a poor deer, and then my jaws would rust again.'

But the Lion went away into the forest and found his own supper, and no one ever knew what it was, for he didn't mention it. And the Scarecrow found a tree full of nuts and filled Dorothy's basket with them, so that she would not be hungry for a long time. She thought this was very kind and thoughtful of the Scarecrow, but she laughed heartily at the awkward way in which the poor creature picked up the nuts. His padded hands were so clumsy and the nuts were so small that he dropped almost as many as he put in the basket. But the Scarecrow did not mind how long it took him to fill the basket, for it enabled him to keep away from the fire, as he feared a spark might get into his straw and burn him up. So he kept a good distance away from the flames, and only came near to cover Dorothy with dry leaves when she lay down to sleep. These kept her very snug and warm and she slept soundly until morning.

When it was daylight the girl bathed her face in a little rippling brook and soon after they all started towards the Emerald City.

This was to be an eventful day for the travellers. They had hardly been walking an hour when they saw before them a great ditch that crossed the road and divided the forest as far as they could see on either side. It was a very wide ditch, and when they crept up to the edge and looked into it they could see it was also very deep, and there were many big, jagged rocks at the bottom. The sides were so steep that none of them could climb down, and for a moment it seemed that their journey must end.

'What shall we do?' asked Dorothy, despairingly.

'I haven't the faintest idea,' said the Tin Woodman; and the Lion shook his shaggy mane and looked thoughtful.

But the Scarecrow said: 'We cannot fly, that is certain;

neither can we climb down into this great ditch. Therefore, if we cannot jump over it, we must stop where we are.'

'I think I could jump over it,' said the Cowardly Lion, after measuring the distance carefully in his mind.

'Then we are all right,' answered the Scarecrow, 'for you can carry us all over on your back, one at a time.'

'Well, I'll try it,' said the Lion. 'Who will go first?'

'I will,' declared the Scarecrow; 'for, if you found that you could not jump over the gulf, Dorothy would be killed, or the Tin Woodman badly dented on the rocks below. But if I am on your back it will not matter so much, for the fall would not hurt me at all.'

'I am terribly afraid of falling, myself,' said the Cowardly Lion, 'but I suppose there is nothing to do but try it. So get on my back and we will make the attempt.'

The Scarecrow sat upon the Lion's back, and the big beast walked to the edge of the gulf and crouched down.

'Why don't you run and jump?' asked the Scarecrow.

'Because that isn't the way we Lions do these things,' he replied. Then giving a great spring, he shot through the air and landed safely on the other side. They were all greatly pleased to see how easily he did it, and after the Scarecrow had got down from his back the Lion sprang across the ditch again.

Dorothy thought she would go next; so she took Toto in her arms and climbed on the Lion's back, holding tightly to his mane with one hand. The next moment it seemed as if she was flying through the air; and then, before she had time to think about it, she was safe on the other side. The Lion went back a third time and got the Tin Woodman, and then they all sat down for a few moments to give the beast a chance to rest, for his great leaps had made his breath short, and he panted like a big dog that has been running too long.

They found the forest very thick on this side, and it

looked dark and gloomy. After the Lion had rested they started along the road of yellow brick, silently wondering, each in his own mind, if ever they would come to the end of the woods and reach the bright sunshine again. To add to their discomfort, they soon heard strange noises in the depths of the forest, and the Lion whispered to them that it was in this part of the country that the Kalidahs lived.

'What are the Kalidahs?' asked the girl.

'They are monstrous beasts with bodies like bears and heads like tigers,' replied the Lion; 'and with claws so long and sharp that they could tear me in two as easily as I could kill Toto. I'm terribly afraid of the Kalidahs.'

'I'm not surprised that you are,' returned Dorothy. 'They must be dreadful beasts.'

The Lion was about to reply when suddenly they came to another gulf across the road; but this one was so broad and deep that the Lion knew at once he could not leap across it.

So they sat down to consider what they should do, and after serious thought the Scarecrow said, 'Here is a great tree, standing close to the ditch. If the Tin Woodman can chop it down, so that it will fall to the other side, we can walk across it easily.'

'That is a first-rate idea,' said the Lion. 'One would almost suspect you had brains in your head, instead of straw.'

The Woodman set to work at once, and so sharp was his axe that the tree was soon chopped nearly through. Then the Lion put his strong front legs against the tree and pushed with all his might, and slowly the big tree tipped and fell with a crash across the ditch, with its top branches on the other side.

They had just started to cross this queer bridge when a sharp growl made them all look up, and to their horror they saw running towards them two great beasts with bodies like bears and heads like tigers.

'They are the Kalidahs!' said the Cowardly Lion, beginning to tremble.

'Quick!' cried the Scarecrow, 'let us cross over.'

So Dorothy went first, holding Toto in her arms; the Tin Woodman followed, and the Scarecrow came next. The Lion, although he was certainly afraid, turned to face the Kalidahs, and then he gave so loud and terrible a roar that Dorothy screamed and the Scarecrow fell over backward, while even the fierce beasts stopped short and looked at him in surprise.

But, seeing they were bigger than the Lion, and remembering that there were two of them and only one of him, the Kalidahs again rushed forward, and the Lion crossed over the tree and turned to see what they would do next. Without stopping an instant the fierce beasts also began to cross the tree, and the Lion said to Dorothy, 'We are lost, for they will surely tear us to pieces with their sharp claws. But stand close behind me, and I will fight them as long as I am alive.'

'Wait a minute!' called the Scarecrow. He had been thinking what was best to be done, and now he asked the Woodman to chop away the end of the tree that rested on their side of the ditch. The Tin Woodman began to use his axe at once, and, just as the two Kalidahs were nearly across, the tree fell with a crash into the gulf, carrying the ugly, snarling brutes with it, and both were dashed to pieces on the sharp rocks at the bottom.

'Well,' said the Cowardly Lion, drawing a long breath of relief, 'I see we are going to live a little while longer, and I am glad of it, for it must be a very uncomfortable thing not to be alive. Those creatures frightened me so badly that my heart is beating yet.'

'Ah,' said the Tin Woodman, sadly, 'I wish I had a heart to beat.'

This adventure made the travellers more anxious than

ever to get out of the forest, and they walked so fast that Dorothy became tired, and had to ride on the Lion's back. To their great joy the trees became thinner the farther they advanced, and in the afternoon they suddenly came upon a broad river, flowing swiftly just before them. On the other side of the water they could see the road of yellow brick running through a beautiful country, with green meadows dotted with bright flowers and all the road bordered with trees hanging full of delicious fruits. They were greatly pleased to see this delightful country before them.

'How shall we cross the river?' asked Dorothy.

'That is easily done,' replied the Scarecrow. 'The Tin Woodman must build us a raft, so we can float to the other side.'

So the Woodman took his axe and began to chop down small trees to make a raft, and while he was busy at this the Scarecrow found on the river bank a tree full of fine fruit. This pleased Dorothy, who had eaten nothing but nuts all day, and she made a hearty meal of the ripe fruit.

But it takes time to make a raft, even when one is as industrious and untiring as the Tin Woodman, and when night came the work was not done. So they found a cosy place under the trees where they slept well until the morning; and Dorothy dreamed of the Emerald City, and of the good Wizard Oz, who would soon send her back to her own home again.

CHAPTER EIGHT

The Deadly Poppy Field

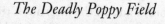

Our little party of travellers wakened the next morning refreshed and full of hope, and Dorothy breakfasted like a princess off peaches and plums from the trees beside the river. Behind them was the dark forest they had passed safely through, although they had suffered many discouragements; but before them was a lovely, sunny country that seemed to beckon them on to the Emerald City. To be sure, the broad river now cut them off from this beautiful land; but the raft was nearly done, and after the Tin Woodman had cut a few more logs and fastened them together with wooden pins, they were ready to start. Dorothy sat down in the middle of the raft and held Toto in her arms. When the Cowardly Lion stepped upon the raft it tipped badly, for he was big and heavy; but the Scarecrow and the Tin Woodman stood upon the other end to steady it, and they had long poles in their hands to push the raft through the water.

They got along quite well at first, but when they reached the middle of the river the swift current swept the raft down stream, farther and farther away from the road of yellow brick; and the water grew so deep that the long poles would not touch the bottom.

'This is bad,' said the Tin Woodman, 'for if we cannot get to the land we shall be carried into the country of the Wicked Witch of the West, and she will enchant us and make us her slaves.'

'And then I should get no brains,' said the Scarecrow.

'And I should get no courage,' said the Cowardly Lion.

'And I should get no heart,' said the Tin Woodman.

'And I should never get back to Kansas,' said Dorothy.

'We must certainly get to the Emerald City if we can,' the Scarecrow continued, and he pushed so hard on his long pole that it stuck fast in the mud at the bottom of the river, and before he could pull it out again, or let go, the raft was swept away and the poor Scarecrow left clinging to the pole in the middle of the river.

'Goodbye!' he called after them, and they were very sorry to leave him; indeed, the Tin Woodman began to cry, but fortunately remembered that he might rust, and so dried his tears on Dorothy's apron.

Of course this was a bad thing for the Scarecrow.

'I am now worse off than when I first met Dorothy,' he thought. 'Then, I was stuck on a pole in a cornfield, where I could make believe scare the crows, at any rate; but surely there is no use for a Scarecrow stuck on a pole in the middle of a river. I am afraid I shall never have any brains, after all!'

Down the stream the raft floated, and the poor Scarecrow was left far behind.

Then the Lion said: 'Something must be done to save us. I

think I can swim to the shore and pull the raft after me, if you will only hold fast to the tip of my tail.'

So he sprang into the water and the Tin Woodman caught fast hold of his tail, when the Lion began to swim with all his might towards the shore. It was hard work, although he was so big; but by and by they were drawn out of the current, and then Dorothy took the Tin Woodman's long pole and helped push the raft to the land.

They were all tired out when they reached the shore at last and stepped off upon the pretty green grass, and they also knew that the stream had carried them a long way past the road of yellow brick that led to the Emerald City.

'What shall we do now?' asked the Tin Woodman, as the Lion lay down on the grass to let the sun dry him.

'We must get back to the road, in some way,' said Dorothy.

'The best plan will be to walk along the river bank until we come to the road again,' remarked the Lion.

So, when they were rested, Dorothy picked up her basket and they started along the grassy bank, back to the road from which the river had carried them. It was a lovely country, with plenty of flowers and fruit trees and sunshine to cheer them, and had they not felt so sorry for the poor Scarecrow they could have been very happy.

They walked along as fast as they could, Dorothy only stopping once to pick a beautiful flower; and after a time the Tin Woodman cried out, 'Look!'

Then they all looked at the river and saw the Scarecrow perched upon his pole in the middle of the water, looking very lonely and sad.

'What can we do to save him?' asked Dorothy.

The Lion and the Woodman both shook their heads, for they did not know. So they sat down upon the bank and gazed wistfully at the Scarecrow until a Stork flew by, which, seeing them, stopped to rest at the water's edge.

'Who are you and where are you going?' asked the Stork.

'I am Dorothy,' answered the girl; 'and these are my friends, the Tin Woodman and the Cowardly Lion; and we are going to the Emerald City.'

'This isn't the road,' said the Stork, as she twisted her long neck and looked sharply at the queer party.

'I know it,' returned Dorothy, 'but we have lost the Scarecrow, and are wondering how we shall get him again.'

'Where is he?' asked the Stork.

'Over there in the river,' answered the girl.

'If he wasn't so big and heavy I would get him for you,' remarked the Stork.

'He isn't heavy a bit,' said Dorothy, eagerly, 'for he is stuffed with straw; and if you will bring him back to us we shall thank you ever and ever so much.'

'Well, I'll try,' said the stork; 'but if I find he is too heavy to carry I shall have to drop him in the river again.'

So the big bird flew into the air and over the water till she came to where the Scarecrow was perched upon his pole. Then the Stork with her great claws grabbed the Scarecrow by the arm and carried him up into the air and back to the bank, where Dorothy and the Lion and the Tin Woodman and Toto were sitting.

When the Scarecrow found himself among his friends again he was so happy that he hugged them all, even the Lion and Toto; and as they walked along he sang 'Tol-de-ri-de-oh!' at every step, he felt so gay.

'I was afraid I should have to stay in the river for ever,' he said, 'but the kind Stork saved me, and if I ever get any brains I shall find the Stork again and do it some kindness in return.'

'That's all right,' said the Stork, who was flying along beside them. 'I always like to help anyone in trouble. But I must go now, for my babies are waiting in the nest for me. I hope you will find the Emerald City and that Oz will help you.'

'Thank you,' replied Dorothy, and then the kind Stork flew into the air and was soon out of sight.

They walked along listening to the singing of the bright-coloured birds and looking at the lovely flowers which now became so thick that the ground was carpeted with them. There were big yellow and white and blue and purple blossoms, besides great clusters of scarlet poppies, which were so brilliant in colour they almost dazzled Dorothy's eyes.

'Aren't they beautiful?' the girl asked, as she breathed in the spicy scent of the flowers.

'I suppose so,' answered the Scarecrow. 'When I have brains I shall probably like them better.'

'If I only had a heart I should love them,' added the Tin Woodman.

'I always did like flowers,' said the Lion; 'they seem so helpless and frail. But there are none in the forest so bright as these.'

They now came upon more and more of the big scarlet poppies, and fewer and fewer of the other flowers; and soon they found themselves in the midst of a great meadow of poppies. Now it is well known that when there are many of these flowers together their odour is so powerful that any-one who breathes it falls asleep, and if the sleeper is not carried away from the scent of the flowers he sleeps on and on for ever. But Dorothy did not know this, nor could she get away from the bright red flowers that were everywhere about; so presently her eyes grew heavy and she felt she must sit down to rest and to sleep.

But the Tin Woodman would not let her do this.

'We must hurry and get back to the road of yellow brick before dark,' he said; and the Scarecrow agreed with him. So they kept walking until Dorothy could stand no longer. Her eyes closed in spite of herself and she forgot where she was and fell among the poppies, fast asleep.

*Then the Stork grabbed the Scarecrow by the arm and carried
him up into the air and back to the bank*

'What shall we do?' asked the Tin Woodman.

'If we leave her here she will die,' said the Lion. 'The smell of the flowers is killing us all. I myself can scarcely keep my eyes open and the dog is asleep already.'

It was true; Toto had fallen down beside his little mistress. But the Scarecrow and the Tin Woodman, not being made of flesh, were not troubled by the scent of the flowers.

'Run fast,' said the Scarecrow to the Lion, 'and get out of this deadly flower-bed as soon as you can. We will bring the little girl with us, but if you should fall asleep you are too big to be carried.'

So the Lion aroused himself and bounded forward as fast as he could go. In a moment he was out of sight.

'Let us make a chair with our hands, and carry her,' said the Scarecrow. So they picked up Toto and put the dog in Dorothy's lap, and then they made a chair with their hands for the seat and their arms for the arms and carried the sleeping girl between them through the flowers.

On and on they walked, and it seemed that the great carpet of deadly flowers that surrounded them would never end. They followed the bend of the river, and at last came upon their friend the Lion, lying fast asleep among the poppies. The flowers had been too strong for the huge beast and he had given up, at last, and fallen only a short distance from the end of the poppy-bed, where the sweet grass spread in beautiful green fields before them.

'We can do nothing for him,' said the Tin Woodman, sadly; 'for he is much too heavy to lift. We must leave him here to sleep on for ever, and perhaps he will dream that he has found courage at last.'

'I'm sorry,' said the Scarecrow; 'the Lion was a very good comrade for one so cowardly. But let us go on.'

They carried the sleeping girl to a pretty spot beside the river, far enough from the poppy field to prevent her breathing any more of the poison of the flowers, and here they laid her gently on the soft grass and waited for the fresh breeze to waken her.

CHAPTER NINE

The Queen of the Field-Mice

"**W**e cannot be far from the road of yellow brick now,' remarked the Scarecrow, as he stood beside the girl, 'for we have come nearly as far as the river carried us away.'

The Tin Woodman was about to reply when he heard a low growl, and turning his head (which worked beautifully on hinges) he saw a strange beast come bounding over the grass towards them. It was, indeed, a great, yellow wildcat, and the Woodman thought it must be chasing something, for its ears were lying close to its head and its mouth was wide open, showing two rows of ugly teeth, while its red eyes glowed like balls of fire. As it came nearer the Tin Woodman saw that running before the beast was a little grey field-mouse, and although he had no heart he knew it was wrong for the wildcat to try to kill such a pretty, harmless creature.

So the Woodman raised his axe, and as the wildcat ran by he gave it a quick blow that cut the beast's head clean off from its body, and it rolled over at his feet in two pieces.

The field-mouse, now that it was freed from its enemy, stopped short; and coming slowly up to the Woodman it said, in a squeaky little voice, 'Oh, thank you! Thank you ever so much for saving my life.'

'Don't speak of it, I beg of you,' replied the Woodman. 'I have no heart, you know, so I am careful to help all those who may need a friend, even if it happens to be only a mouse.'

'Only a mouse!' cried the little animal, indignantly; 'why, I am a Queen – the Queen of all the Field-Mice!'

'Oh, indeed,' said the Woodman, making a bow.

'Therefore you have done a great deed, as well as a brave one, in saving my life,' added the Queen.

At that moment several mice were seen running up as fast as their little legs could carry them, and when they saw their Queen they exclaimed, 'Oh, your Majesty, we thought you would be killed! How did you manage to escape the great Wildcat?' and they all bowed so low to the little Queen that they almost stood upon their heads.

'This funny tin man,' she answered, 'killed the Wildcat and saved my life. So hereafter you must all serve him, and obey his slightest wish.'

'We will!' cried all the mice, in a shrill chorus. And then they scampered in all directions, for Toto had awakened from his sleep, and seeing all these mice around him he gave one bark of delight and jumped right into the middle of the group. Toto had always loved to chase mice when he lived in Kansas, and he saw no harm in it.

But the Tin Woodman caught the dog in his arms and held him tight, while he called to the mice: 'Come back! come back! Toto shall not hurt you.'

At this the Queen of the Mice stuck her head out from

underneath a clump of grass and asked, in a timid voice, 'Are you sure he will not bite us?'

'I will not let him,' said the Woodman; 'so do not be afraid.'

One by one the mice came creeping back, and Toto did not bark again, although he tried to get out of the Woodman's arms, and would have bitten him had he not known very well he was made of tin. Finally one of the biggest mice spoke.

'Is there anything we can do,' it asked, 'to repay you for saving the life of our Queen?'

'Nothing that I know of,' answered the Woodman; but the Scarecrow, who had been trying to think, but could not because his head was stuffed with straw, said, quickly, 'Oh, yes; you can save our friend, the Cowardly Lion, who is asleep in the poppy bed.'

'A lion!' cried the little Queen; 'why, he would eat us all up.'

'Oh, no,' declared the Scarecrow; 'this lion is a coward.'

'Really?' asked the mouse.

'He says so himself,' answered the Scarecrow, 'and he would never hurt anyone who is our friend. If you will help us to save him I promise that he shall treat you all with kindness.'

'Very well,' said the Queen, 'we will trust you. But what shall we do?'

'Are there many of these mice which call you Queen and are willing to obey you?'

'Oh, yes; there are thousands,' she replied.

'Then send for them all to come here as soon as possible, and let each one bring a long piece of string.'

The Queen turned to the mice that attended her and told them to go at once and get all her people. As soon as they heard her orders they ran away in every direction as fast as possible.

'Now,' said the Scarecrow to the Tin Woodman, 'you must go to those trees by the riverside and make a truck that will carry the Lion.'

So the Woodman went at once to the trees and began to work; and he soon made a truck out of the limbs of trees, from which he chopped away all the leaves and branches. He fastened it together with wooden pegs and made the four wheels out of short pieces of a big tree-trunk. So fast and so well did he work that by the time the mice began to arrive the truck was all ready for them.

They came from all directions, and there were thousands of them: big mice and little mice and middle-sized mice; and each one brought a piece of string in his mouth. It was about this time that Dorothy woke from her long sleep and opened her eyes. She was greatly astonished to find herself lying upon the grass, with thousands of mice standing around and looking at her timidly.

But the Scarecrow told her about everything, and turning to the dignified little Mouse, he said, 'Permit me to introduce to you her Majesty, the Queen.'

Dorothy nodded gravely and the Queen made a curtsey, after which she became quite friendly with the little girl.

The Scarecrow and the Woodman now began to fasten the mice to the truck, using the strings they had brought. One end of a string was tied around the neck of each mouse and the other end to the truck. Of course the truck was a thousand times bigger than any of the mice who were to draw it; but when all the mice had been harnessed they were able to pull it quite easily. Even the Scarecrow and the Tin Woodman could sit on it, and were drawn swiftly by their queer little horses to the place where the Lion lay asleep.

After a great deal of hard work, for the Lion was heavy, they managed to get him up on the truck. Then the Queen hurriedly gave her people the order to start, for she feared if the mice stayed among the poppies too long they also would fall asleep.

At first the little creatures, many though they were, could hardly stir the heavily loaded truck; but the Woodman and the Scarecrow both pushed from behind, and they got along better. Soon they rolled the Lion out of the poppy bed to the green fields, where he could breathe the sweet, fresh air again, instead of the poisonous scent of the flowers.

Dorothy came to meet them and thanked the little mice warmly for saving her companion from death. She had grown so fond of the big Lion she was glad he had been rescued.

Then the mice were unharnessed from the truck and scampered away through the grass to their homes. The Queen of the Mice was the last to leave.

'If ever you need us again,' she said, 'come out into the field and call, and we shall hear you and come to your assistance. Goodbye!'

'Goodbye!' they all answered, and away the Queen ran, while Dorothy held Toto tightly lest he should run after her and frighten her.

After this they sat down beside the Lion until he should awaken; and the Scarecrow brought Dorothy some fruit from a tree nearby, which she ate for her dinner.

CHAPTER TEN

The Guardian of the Gates

It was some time before the Cowardly Lion awakened, for he had lain among the poppies a long while, breathing in their deadly fragrance; but when he did open his eyes and roll off the truck he was very glad to find himself still alive.

'I ran as fast as I could,' he said, sitting down and yawning; 'but the flowers were too strong for me. How did you get me out?'

Then they told him of the field-mice, and how they had generously saved him from death; and the Cowardly Lion laughed, and said, 'I have always thought myself very big and terrible; yet such little things as flowers came near to killing me, and such small animals as mice have saved my life. How strange it all is! But, comrades, what shall we do now?'

'We must journey on until we find the road of yellow brick again,' said Dorothy; 'and then we can keep on to the Emerald City.'

So, the Lion being fully refreshed, and feeling quite himself again, they all started upon the journey, greatly enjoying the walk through the soft, fresh grass; and it was not long before they reached the road of yellow brick and turned again towards the Emerald City where the great Oz dwelt.

The road was smooth and well paved, now, and the country about was beautiful; so that the travellers rejoiced in leaving the forest far behind, and with it the many dangers they had met in its gloomy shades. Once more they could see fences built beside the road; but these were painted green, and when they came to a small house, in which a farmer evidently lived, that also was painted green. They passed by several of these houses during the afternoon, and sometimes people came to the doors and looked at them as if they would like to ask questions; but no one came near them nor spoke to them because of the great Lion, of which they were much afraid. The people were all dressed in clothing of a lovely emerald green colour and wore peaked hats like those of the Munchkins.

'This must be the Land of Oz,' said Dorothy, 'and we are surely getting near the Emerald City.'

'Yes,' answered the Scarecrow; 'everything is green here, while in the country of the Munchkins blue was the favourite colour. But the people do not seem to be as friendly as the Munchkins and I'm afraid we shall be unable to find a place to pass the night.'

'I should like something to eat besides fruit,' said the girl, 'and I'm sure Toto is nearly starved. Let us stop at the next house and talk to the people.'

So, when they came to a good-sized farmhouse, Dorothy walked boldly up to the door and knocked. A woman opened it just far enough to look out, and said, 'What do you want, child, and why is that great lion with you?'

'We wish to pass the night with you, if you will allow us,' answered Dorothy; 'and the Lion is my friend and comrade, and would not hurt you for the world.'

'Is he tame?' asked the woman, opening the door a little wider.

'Oh, yes,' said the girl, 'and he is a great coward, too; so that he will be more afraid of you than you are of him.'

'Well,' said the woman, after thinking it over and taking another peep at the Lion, 'if that is the case you may come in, and I will give you some supper and a place to sleep.'

So they all entered the house, where there were, besides the woman, two children and a man. The man had hurt his leg, and was lying on the couch in a corner. They seemed greatly surprised to see so strange a company, and while the woman was busy laying the table the man asked, 'Where are you all going?'

'To the Emerald City,' said Dorothy, 'to see the Great Oz.'

'Oh, indeed!' exclaimed the man. 'Are you sure that Oz will see you?'

'Why not?' she replied.

'Why, it is said that he never lets anyone come into his presence. I have been to the Emerald City many times, and it is a beautiful and wonderful place; but I have never been permitted to see the Great Oz, nor do I know of any living person who has seen him.'

'Does he never go out?' asked the Scarecrow.

'Never. He sits day after day in the great Throne Room of his palace, and even those who wait upon him do not see him face to face.'

'What is he like?' asked the girl.

'That is hard to tell,' said the man, thoughtfully. 'You see, Oz is a great Wizard, and can take on any form he wishes.

So that some say he looks like a bird; and some say he looks like an elephant; and some say he looks like a cat. To others he appears as a beautiful fairy, or a brownie, or in any other form that pleases him. But who the real Oz is, when he is in his own form, no living person can tell.'

'That is very strange,' said Dorothy; 'but we must try, in some way, to see him, or we shall have made our journey for nothing.'

'Why do you wish to see the terrible Oz?' asked the man.

'I want him to give me some brains,' said the Scarecrow, eagerly.

'Oh, Oz could do that easily enough,' declared the man. 'He has more brains than he needs.'

'And I want him to give me a heart,' said the Tin Woodman.

'That will not trouble him,' continued the man, 'for Oz has a large collection of hearts, of all sizes and shapes.'

'And I want him to give me courage,' said the Cowardly Lion.

'Oz keeps a great pot of courage in his Throne Room,' said the man, 'which he has covered with a golden plate, to keep it from running over. He will be glad to give you some.'

'And I want him to send me back to Kansas,' said Dorothy.

'Where is Kansas?' asked the man, with surprise.

'I don't know,' replied Dorothy, sorrowfully; 'but it is my home, and I'm sure it's somewhere.'

'Very likely. Well, Oz can do anything; so I suppose he will find Kansas for you. But first you must get to see him, and that will be a hard task; for the great Wizard does not like to see anyone, and he usually has his own way. But what do you want?' he continued, speaking to Toto. Toto only wagged his tail; for, strange to say, he could not speak.

The woman now called to them that supper was ready, so they gathered around the table and Dorothy ate some delicious porridge and a dish of scrambled eggs and a plate of nice white bread, and enjoyed her meal. The Lion ate some of the porridge, but did not care for it, saying it was made from oats and oats was food for horses, not for lions. The Scarecrow and the Tin Woodman ate nothing at all. Toto ate a little of everything, and was glad to get a good supper again.

The woman now gave Dorothy a bed to sleep in, and Toto lay down beside her, while the Lion guarded the door of her room so she might not be disturbed. The Scarecrow and the Tin Woodman stood up in a corner and kept quiet all night, although of course they could not sleep.

The next morning, as soon as the sun was up, they started on their way, and soon saw a beautiful green glow in the sky just before them.

'That must be the Emerald City,' said Dorothy.

As they walked on, the green glow became brighter and brighter, and it seemed that at last they were nearing the end of their travels. Yet it was afternoon before they came to the great wall that surrounded the City. It was high, and thick, and of a bright green colour.

In front of them, and at the end of the road of yellow brick, was a big gate, all studded with emeralds that glittered so in the sun that even the painted eyes of the Scarecrow were dazzled by their brilliancy.

There was a bell beside the gate, and Dorothy pushed the button and heard a silvery tinkle sound within. Then the big gate swung slowly open, and they all passed through and found themselves in a high arched room, the walls of which glistened with countless emeralds.

Before them stood a little man about the same size as the Munchkins. He was clothed all in green, from his head to his feet, and even his skin was of a greenish tint. At his side was a large green box.

When he saw Dorothy and her companions the man asked, 'What do you wish in the Emerald City?'

'We came here to see the Great Oz,' said Dorothy.

The man was so surprised at this answer that he sat down to think it over.

'It has been many years since anyone asked me to see Oz,' he said, shaking his head in perplexity. 'He is powerful and terrible, and if you come on an idle or foolish errand to bother the wise reflections of the Great Wizard, he might be angry and destroy you all in an instant.'

'But it is not a foolish errand, nor an idle one,' replied the Scarecrow; 'it is important. And we have been told that Oz is a good Wizard.'

'So he is,' said the green man; 'and he rules the Emerald City wisely and well. But to those who are not honest, or who approach him from curiosity, he is most terrible, and few have ever dared ask to see his face. I am the Guardian of the Gates, and since you demand to see the Great Oz I must take you to his palace. But first you must put on the spectacles.'

'Why?' asked Dorothy.

'Because if you did not wear spectacles the brightness and glory of the Emerald City would blind you. Even those who live in the City must wear spectacles night and day. They are all locked on, for Oz so ordered it when the City was first built, and I have the only key that will unlock them.'

He opened the big box, and Dorothy saw that it was filled with spectacles of every size and shape. All of them had green glasses in them. The Guardian of the Gates found a pair that would just fit Dorothy and put them over her eyes. There were two golden bands fastened to them that passed around the back of her head, where they were looked together by a little key that was at the end of a chain the Guardian of the Gates wore around his neck. When they were on Dorothy could not take them off had she wished, but of course she did not wish to be blinded by the glare of the Emerald City so she said nothing.

Then the green man fitted spectacles for the Scarecrow and the Tin Woodman and the Lion, and even on little Toto; and all were locked fast with the key.

Then the Guardian of the Gates put on his own glasses and told them he was ready to show them to the palace. Taking a big golden key from a peg on the wall he opened another gate, and they all followed him through the portal into the streets of the Emerald City.

CHAPTER ELEVEN

The Wonderful Emerald City of Oz

Even with eyes
protected by the
green spectacles Dorothy and her friends
were at first dazzled by the brilliancy
of the wonderful City. The streets
were lined with beautiful houses all
built of green marble and studded
everywhere with sparkling emeralds. They walked over a
pavement of the same green marble, and where the blocks
were joined together were rows of emeralds, set closely,
and glittering in the brightness of the sun. The window
panes were of green glass; even the sky above the City had a
green tint, and the rays of the sun were green.

There were many people, men, women and children,
walking about, and these were all dressed in green clothes
and had greenish skins. They looked at Dorothy and her
strangely assorted company with wondering eyes, and the
children all ran away and hid behind their mothers when

they saw the Lion; but no one spoke to them. Many shops stood in the street, and Dorothy saw that everything in them was green. Green candy and green popcorn were offered for sale, as well as green shoes, green hats and green clothes of all sorts. At one place a man was selling green lemonade, and when the children bought it Dorothy could see that they paid for it with green pennies.

There seemed to be no horses nor animals of any kind; the men carried things around in little green carts, which they pushed before them. Everyone seemed happy and contented and prosperous.

The Guardian of the Gates led them through the streets until they came to a big building, exactly in the middle of the City, which was the Palace of Oz, the Great Wizard. There was a soldier before the door, dressed in a green uniform and wearing a long green beard.

'Here are strangers,' said the Guardian of the Gates to him, 'and they demand to see the Great Oz.'

'Step inside,' answered the soldier, 'and I will carry your message to him.'

So they passed through the palace gates and were led into a big room with a green carpet and lovely green furniture set with emeralds. The soldier made them all wipe their feet upon a green mat before entering this room, and when they were seated he said, politely, 'Please make yourselves comfortable while I go to the door of the Throne Room and tell Oz you are here.'

They had to wait a long time before the soldier returned.

When, at last, he came back, Dorothy asked, 'Have you seen Oz?'

'Oh, no,' returned the soldier; 'I have never seen him. But I spoke to him as he sat behind his screen, and gave him your message. He said he will grant you an audience, if you so desire; but each one of you must enter his presence alone, and he will admit but one each day. Therefore, as you must remain in the Palace for several days, I will have you shown to rooms where you may rest in comfort after your journey.'

'Thank you,' replied the girl; 'that is very kind of Oz.'

The soldier now blew upon a green whistle, and at once a young girl, dressed in a pretty green silk gown, entered the room. She had lovely green hair and green eyes, and she bowed low before Dorothy as she said, 'Follow me and I will show you your room.'

So Dorothy said goodbye to all her friends except Toto, and taking the dog in her arms followed the green girl through seven passages and up three flights of stairs until they came to a room at the front of the Palace. It was the sweetest little room in the world, with a soft comfortable bed that had sheets of green silk and a green velvet counterpane. There was a tiny fountain in the middle of the room, that shot a spray of green perfume into the air, to fall back into a beautifully carved green marble basin. Beautiful green flowers stood in the windows, and there was a shelf with a row of little green books. When Dorothy had time to open these books she found them full of queer green pictures that made her laugh, they were so funny.

In a wardrobe were many green dresses, made of silk and satin and velvet; and all of them fitted Dorothy exactly.

'Make yourself perfectly at home,' said the green girl, 'and if you wish for anything ring the bell. Oz will send for you tomorrow morning.'

She left Dorothy alone and went back to the others.

These she also led to rooms, and each one of them found himself lodged in a very pleasant part of the Palace. Of course this politeness was wasted on the Scarecrow; for when he found himself alone in his room he stood stupidly in one spot, just within the doorway, to wait till morning. It would not rest him to lie down, and he could not close his eyes; so he remained all night staring at a little spider which was weaving its web in a corner of the room, just as if it were not one of the most wonderful rooms in the world. The Tin Woodman lay down on his bed from force of habit, for he remembered when he was made of flesh; but not being able to sleep he passed the night moving his joints up and down to make sure they kept in good working order. The Lion would have preferred a bed of dried leaves in the forest, and did not like being shut up in a room; but he had too much sense to let this worry him, so he sprang upon the bed and rolled himself up like a cat and purred himself asleep in a minute.

The next morning, after breakfast, the green maiden came to fetch Dorothy, and she dressed her in one of the prettiest gowns – made of green brocaded satin. Dorothy put on a green silk apron and tied a green ribbon around Toto's neck, and they started for the Throne Room of the Great Oz.

First they came to a great hall in which were many ladies and gentlemen of the court, all dressed in rich costumes. These people had nothing to do but talk to each other, but they always came to wait outside the Throne Room every morning, although they were never permitted to see Oz. As Dorothy entered they looked at her curiously, and one of them whispered, 'Are you really going to look upon the face of Oz the Terrible?'

'Of course,' answered the girl, 'if he will see me.'

'Oh, he will see you,' said the soldier who had taken her message to the Wizard, 'although he does not like to have people ask to see him. Indeed, at first he was angry, and said I should send you back where you came from. Then he asked me what you looked like, and when I mentioned your silver shoes he was very much interested. At last I told him about the mark upon your forehead, and he decided he would admit you to his presence.'

Just then a bell rang, and the green girl said to Dorothy,

'That is the signal. You must go into the Throne Room alone.'

She opened a little door and Dorothy walked boldly through and found herself in a wonderful place. It was a big, round room with a high arched roof, and the walls and ceiling and floor were covered with large emeralds set closely together. In the centre of the roof was a great light, as bright as the sun, which made the emeralds sparkle in a wonderful manner.

But what interested Dorothy most was the big throne of green marble that stood in the middle of the room. It was shaped like a chair and sparkled with gems, as did everything else. In the centre of the chair was an enormous Head, without a body to support it or any arms or legs whatever. There was no hair upon this head, but it had eyes and nose and mouth, and was much bigger than the head of the biggest giant.

As Dorothy gazed upon this in wonder and fear, the eyes turned slowly and looked at her sharply and steadily. Then the mouth moved, and Dorothy heard a voice say, 'I am Oz, the Great and Terrible. Who are you, and why do you seek me?'

It was not such an awful voice as she had expected to come from the big Head; so she took courage and answered, 'I am Dorothy, the Small and Meek. I have come to you for help.'

The eyes looked at her thoughtfully for a full minute. Then said the voice: 'Where did you get the silver shoes?'

'I got them from the Wicked Witch of the East, when my house fell on her and killed her,' she replied.

'Where did you get the mark upon your forehead?' continued the voice.

'That is where the good Witch of the North kissed me when she bade me goodbye and sent me to you,' said the girl.

Again the eyes looked at her sharply, and they saw she was telling the truth. Then Oz asked, 'What do you wish me to do?'

'Send me back to Kansas, where my Aunt Em and Uncle Henry are,' she answered earnestly. 'I don't like your country, although it is so beautiful. And I am sure Aunt Em will be dreadfully worried over my being away so long.'

The eyes winked three times, and then they turned up to the ceiling and down to the floor and rolled around so queerly that they seemed to see every part of the room. And at last they looked at Dorothy again.

'Why should I do this for you?' asked Oz.

'Because you are strong and I am weak; because you are a Great Wizard and I am only a helpless little girl.'

'But you were strong enough to kill the Wicked Witch of the East,' said Oz.

'That just happened,' returned Dorothy, simply; 'I could not help it.'

'Well,' said the Head, 'I will give you my answer. You have no right to expect me to send you back to Kansas unless you do something for me in return. In this country everyone must pay for everything he gets. If you wish me to use my magic power to send you home again you must do something for me first. Help me and I will help you.'

'What must I do?' asked the girl.

'Kill the Wicked Witch of the West,' answered Oz.

'But I cannot!' exclaimed Dorothy, greatly surprised.

'You killed the Witch of the East and you wear the silver shoes, which bear a powerful charm. There is now but one Wicked Witch left in all this land, and when you can tell me she is dead I will send you back to Kansas – but not before.'

The little girl began to weep, she was so much disappointed and the eyes winked again and looked upon her anxiously, as if the Great Oz felt that she could help him if she would.

'I never killed anything, willingly,' she sobbed; 'and even if I wanted to, how could I kill the Wicked Witch? If you, who are Great and Terrible, cannot kill her yourself, how do you expect me to do it?'

'I do not know,' said the Head; 'but that is my answer, and until the Wicked Witch dies you will not see your uncle and aunt again. Remember that the Witch is wicked – tremendously wicked – and ought to be killed. Now go, and do not ask to see me again until you have done your task.'

Sorrowfully Dorothy left the Throne Room and went back where the Lion and the Scarecrow and the Tin Woodman were waiting to hear what Oz had said to her.

'There is no hope for me,' she said sadly, 'for Oz will not send me home until I have killed the Wicked Witch of the West; and that I can never do.'

Her friends were sorry, but could do nothing to help her; so she went to her own room and lay down on the bed and cried herself to sleep.

The next morning the soldier with the green whiskers came to the Scarecrow and said, 'Come with me, for Oz has sent for you.'

So the Scarecrow followed him and was admitted into the great Throne Room, where he saw, sitting in the emerald throne, a most lovely lady. She was dressed in green silk gauze and wore upon her flowing green locks a crown of jewels. Growing from her shoulders were wings, gorgeous in colour and so light that they fluttered if the slightest breath of air reached them.

When the Scarecrow had bowed, as prettily as his straw stuffing would let him, before this beautiful creature, she looked upon him sweetly, and said, 'I am Oz, the Great and Terrible. Who are you, and why do you seek me?'

Now the Scarecrow, who had expected to see the great

Head Dorothy had told him of, was much astonished; but he answered her bravely, 'I am only a Scarecrow, stuffed with straw. Therefore I have no brains, and I come to you praying that you will put brains in my head instead of straw, so that I may become as much a man as any other in your dominions.'

'Why should I do this for you?' asked the lady.

'Because you are wise and powerful, and no one else can help me,' answered the Scarecrow.

'I never grant favours without some return,' said Oz; 'but this much I will promise. If you will kill for me the Wicked Witch of the West I will bestow upon you a great many brains, and such good brains that you will be the wisest man in the Land of Oz.'

'I thought you asked Dorothy to kill the Witch,' said the Scarecrow, in surprise.

'So I did. I don't care who kills her. But until she is dead I will not grant your wish. Now go, and do not seek me again until you have earned the brains you so greatly desire.'

The Scarecrow went sorrowfully back to his friends and told them what Oz had said; and Dorothy was surprised to find that the great Wizard was not a Head, as she had seen him, but a lovely lady.

'All the same,' said the Scarecrow, 'she needs a heart as much as the Tin Woodman.'

On the next morning the soldier with the green whiskers came to the Tin Woodman and said, 'Oz has sent for you. Follow me.'

So the Tin Woodman followed him and came to the great Throne Room. He did not know whether he would find Oz a lovely lady or a Head, but he hoped it would be a lovely lady. 'For,' he said to himself, 'if it is the Head, I am sure I shall not be given a heart, since a head has no heart of its own and therefore cannot feel for me. But if it is the lovely lady I shall beg hard for a heart, for all ladies are themselves said to be kindly hearted.'

But when the Woodman entered the great Throne Room he saw neither the Head nor the Lady, for Oz had taken the shape of a most terrible Beast. It was nearly as big as an elephant, and the green throne seemed hardly strong enough to hold its weight. The Beast had a head like that of a rhinoceros, only there were five eyes in its face. There were five long arms growing out of its body and it also had five long, slim legs. Thick, woolly hair covered every part of it, and a more dreadful looking monster could not be imagined. It was fortunate the Tin Woodman had no heart at that moment, for it would have beat loud and fast from terror. But being only tin, the Woodman was not at all afraid, although he was much disappointed.

'I am Oz, the Great and Terrible,' spake the Beast, in a voice that was one great roar. 'Who are you, and why do you seek me?'

'I am a Woodman, and made of tin. Therefore I have no heart, and cannot love. I pray you to give me a heart that I may be as other men are.'

'Why should I do this?' demanded the Beast.

'Because I ask it, and you alone can grant my request,' answered the Woodman.

Oz gave a low growl at this, but said, gruffly, 'If you indeed desire a heart, you must earn it.'

'How?' asked the Woodman.

'Help Dorothy to kill the Wicked Witch of the West,' replied the Beast. 'When the Witch is dead, come to me, and I will then give you the biggest and kindest and most loving heart in all the Land of Oz.'

So the Tin Woodman was forced to return sorrowfully to his friends and tell them of the terrible Beast he had seen. They all wondered greatly at the many forms the great Wizard could take upon himself, and the Lion said, 'If he is a beast when I go to see him, I shall roar my loudest and so frighten him that he will grant all I ask. And if he is the lovely lady, I shall pretend to spring upon her, and so compel her to do my bidding. And if he is the great Head, he will be at my mercy; for I will roll this head all about the room until he promises to give us what we desire. So be of good cheer, my friends, for all will yet be well.'

The next morning the soldier with the green whiskers led the Lion to the great Throne Room and bade him enter the presence of Oz.

The Lion at once passed through the door, and glancing around saw, to his surprise, that before the throne was a Ball of Fire, so fierce and glowing he could scarcely bear to gaze upon it. His first thought was that Oz had by accident caught on fire and was burning up; but, when he tried to go nearer, the heat was so intense that it singed his whiskers, and he crept back tremblingly to a spot nearer the door.

Then a low, quiet voice came from the Ball of Fire, and these were the words it spoke: 'I am Oz, the Great and Terrible. Who are you, and why do you seek me?'

And the Lion answered, 'I am a Cowardly Lion, afraid of everything. I come to you to beg that you give me courage, so that in reality I may become the King of Beasts, as men call me.'

'Why should I give you courage?' demanded Oz.

'Because of all Wizards you are the greatest, and alone have power to grant my request,' answered the Lion.

The Ball of Fire burned fiercely for a time, and the voice said, 'Bring me proof that the Wicked Witch is dead, and that moment I will give you courage. But as long as the Witch lives you must remain a coward.'

The Lion was angry at this speech, but could say nothing in reply, and while he stood silently gazing at the Ball of Fire it became so furiously hot that he turned tail and rushed from the room. He was glad to find his friends waiting for him, and told them of his terrible interview with the Wizard.

'What shall we do now?' asked Dorothy, sadly.

'There is only one thing we can do,' returned the Lion, and that is to go to the land of the Winkies, seek out the Wicked Witch, and destroy her.'

'But suppose we cannot?' said the girl.

'Then I shall never have courage,' declared the Lion.

'And I shall never have brains,' added the Scarecrow.

'And I shall never have a heart,' spoke the Tin Woodman.

'And I shall never see Aunt Em and Uncle Henry,' said Dorothy, beginning to cry.

'Be careful!' cried the green girl, 'the tears will fall on your green silk gown, and spot it.'

So Dorothy dried her eyes and said, 'I suppose we must try it; but I am sure I do not want to kill anybody, even to see Aunt Em again.'

'I will go with you; but I'm too much of a coward to kill the Witch,' said the Lion.

'I will go too,' declared the Scarecrow; 'but I shall not be of much help to you, I am such a fool.'

'I haven't the heart to harm even a Witch,' remarked the Tin Woodman; 'but if you go I certainly shall go with you.'

Therefore it was decided to start upon their journey the next morning, and the Woodman sharpened his axe on a green grindstone and had all his joints properly oiled. The Scarecrow stuffed himself with fresh straw and Dorothy put new paint on his eyes that he might see better. The green girl, who was very kind to them, filled Dorothy's basket with good things to eat, and fastened a little bell around Toto's neck with a green ribbon.

They went to bed quite early and slept soundly until daylight, when they were awakened by the crowing of a green cock that lived in the back yard of the palace, and the cackling of a hen that had laid a green egg.

CHAPTER TWELVE

The Search for the Wicked Witch

The soldier with the green whiskers led them through the streets of the Emerald City until they reached the room where the Guardian of the Gates lived. This officer unlocked their spectacles to put them back in his great box, and then he politely opened the gate for our friends.

'Which road leads to the Wicked Witch of the West?' asked Dorothy.

'There is no road,' answered the Guardian of the Gates; 'no one ever wishes to go that way.'

'How, then, are we to find her?' enquired the girl.

'That will be easy,' replied the man; 'for when she knows you are in the country of the Winkies she will find you, and make you all her slaves.'

'Perhaps not,' said the Scarecrow, 'for we mean to destroy her.'

'Oh, that is different,' said the Guardian of the Gates. 'No one has ever destroyed her before, so I naturally thought she would make slaves of you, as she has of the rest. But take care; for she is wicked and fierce, and may not allow you to destroy her. Keep to the West, where the sun sets, and you cannot fail to find her.'

They thanked him and bade him goodbye, and turned towards the West, walking over fields of soft grass dotted here and there with daisies and buttercups. Dorothy still wore the pretty silk dress she had put on in the palace, but now, to her surprise, she found it was no longer green, but pure white. The ribbon around Toto's neck had also lost its green colour and was white as Dorothy's dress.

The Emerald City was soon left far behind. As they advanced the ground became rougher and hillier, for there were no farms nor houses in this country of the West, and the ground was untilled.

In the afternoon the sun shone hot in their faces, for there were no trees to offer them shade; so that before night Dorothy and Toto and the Lion were tired, and lay down upon the grass and fell asleep, with the Woodman and the Scarecrow keeping watch.

Now the Wicked Witch of the West had but one eye, yet that was as powerful as a telescope, and could see every-where. So, as she sat in the door of her castle, she happened to look around and saw Dorothy lying asleep, with her friends all about her. They were a long distance off, but the Wicked Witch was angry to find them in her country; so she blew upon a silver whistle that hung around her neck.

At once there came running to her from all directions a pack of great wolves. They had long legs and fierce eyes and sharp teeth.

'Go to those people,' said the Witch, 'and tear them to pieces.'

'Are you not going to make them your slaves?' asked the leader of the wolves.

'No,' she answered, 'one is of tin, and one of straw; one is a girl and another a Lion. None of them is fit to work, so you may tear them into small pieces.'

'Very well,' said the wolf, and he dashed away at full speed, followed by the others.

It was lucky the Scarecrow and the Woodman were wide awake and heard the wolves coming.

'This is my fight,' said the Woodman; 'so get behind me and I will meet them as they come.'

He seized his axe, which he had made very sharp, and as the leader of the wolves came on the Tin Woodman swung his arm and chopped the wolf's head from its body, so that it immediately died. As soon as he could raise his axe another wolf came up, and he also fell under the sharp edge of the Tin Woodman's weapon. There were forty wolves, and forty times a wolf was killed; so that at last they all lay dead in a heap before the Woodman.

Then he put down his axe and sat beside the Scarecrow, who said, 'It was a good fight, friend.'

They waited until Dorothy awoke the next morning. The little girl was quite frightened when she saw the great pile of shaggy wolves, but the Tin Woodman told her all. She thanked him for saving them and sat down to breakfast, after which they started again upon their journey.

Now this same morning the Wicked Witch came to the door of her castle and looked out with her one eye that could see afar off. She saw all her wolves lying dead, and the strangers still travelling through her country. This made her angrier than before, and she blew her silver whistle twice.

Straightway a great flock of wild crows came flying towards her, enough to darken the sky. And the Wicked Witch said to the King Crow, 'Fly at once to the strangers; peck out their eyes and tear them to pieces.'

The wild crows flew in one great flock towards Dorothy

and her companions. When the little girl saw them coming she was afraid. But the Scarecrow said, 'This is my battle; so lie down beside me and you will not be harmed.'

So they all lay upon the ground except the Scarecrow, and he stood up and stretched out his arms. And when the crows saw him they were frightened, as these birds always are by scarecrows, and did not dare to come any nearer. But the King Crow said, 'It is only a stuffed man. I will peck his eyes out.'

The King Crow flew at the Scarecrow, who caught it by the head and twisted its neck until it died. And then another crow flew at him, and the Scarecrow twisted its neck also. There were forty crows, and forty times the Scarecrow twisted a neck, until at last all were lying dead beside him. Then he called to his companions to rise, and again they went upon their journey.

When the Wicked Witch looked out again and saw all her crows lying in a heap, she got into a terrible rage, and blew three times upon her silver whistle.

Forthwith there was heard a great buzzing in the air, and a swarm of black bees came flying towards her.

'Go to the strangers and sting them to death!' commanded the Witch, and the bees turned and flew rapidly until they came to where Dorothy and her friends were walking. But the Woodman had seen them coming and the Scarecrow had decided what to do.

'Take out my straw and scatter it over the little girl and the dog and the lion,' he said to the Woodman, 'and the bees cannot sting them.' This the Woodman did, and as Dorothy lay close beside the Lion and held Toto in her arms, the straw covered them entirely.

The bees came and found no one but the Woodman to sting, so they flew at him and broke off all their stings against the tin, without hurting the Woodman at all. And as bees cannot live when their stings are broken that was the end of the black bees, and they lay scattered thick about the Woodman, like little heaps of fine coal.

Then Dorothy and the Lion got up, and the girl helped the Tin Woodman put the straw back into the Scarecrow again, until he was as good as ever. So they started upon their journey once more.

The Wicked Witch was so angry when she saw her black bees in little heaps like fine coal that she stamped her foot and tore her hair and gnashed her teeth. And then she called a dozen of her slaves, who were the Winkies, and gave them sharp spears, telling them to go to the strangers and destroy them.

The Winkies were not a brave people, but they had to do as they were told; so they marched away until they came near to Dorothy. Then the Lion gave a great roar and sprang towards them, and the poor Winkies were so frightened that they ran back as fast as they could.

When they returned to the castle the Wicked Witch beat them well with a strap, and sent them back to their work, after which she sat down to think what she should do next. She could not understand how all her plans to destroy these strangers had failed; but she was a powerful Witch, as well as a wicked one, and she soon made up her mind how to act.

There was, in her cupboard, a Golden Cap, with a circle of diamonds and rubies running round it. This Golden cap had a charm. Whoever owned it could call three times upon the Winged Monkeys, who would obey any order they were given. But no person could command these strange creatures more than three times. Twice already the Wicked Witch had used the charm of the Cap. Once was when she had made the Winkies her slaves, and set herself to rule over their country. The Winged Monkeys had helped her do this. The second time was when she had fought against the Great Oz himself, and driven him out of the land of the

West. The Winged Monkeys had also helped her in doing this. Only once more could she use this Golden Cap, for which reason she did not like to do so until all her other powers were exhausted. But now that her fierce wolves and her wild crows and her stinging bees were gone, and her slaves had been scared away by the Cowardly Lion, she saw there was only one way left to destroy Dorothy and her friends.

So the Wicked Witch took the Golden Cap from her cupboard and placed it upon her head. Then she stood upon her left foot and said, slowly, 'Ep-pe, pep-pe, kak-ke!'

Next she stood upon her right foot and said, 'Hil-lo, hol-lo, hel-lo!'

After this she stood upon both feet and cried in a loud voice, 'Ziz-zy, zuz-zy, zik!'

Now the charm began to work. The sky was darkened, and a low rumbling sound was heard in the air. There was a rushing of many wings; a great chattering and laughing; and the sun came out of the dark sky to show the Wicked Witch surrounded by a crowd of monkeys, each with a pair of immense and powerful wings on his shoulders.

One, much bigger than the others, seemed to be their leader. He flew close to the Witch and said, 'You have called us for the third and last time. What do you command?'

'Go to the strangers who are within my land and destroy them all except the Lion,' said the Wicked Witch. 'Bring that beast to me, for I have a mind to harness him like a horse, and make him work.'

'Your commands shall be obeyed,' said the leader; and then, with a great deal of chattering and noise, the Winged Monkeys flew away to the place where Dorothy and her friends were walking.

Some of the Monkeys seized the Tin Woodman and carried him through the air until they were over a country thickly covered with sharp rocks. Here they dropped the poor Woodman, who fell a great distance to the rocks, where he lay so battered and dented that he could neither move nor groan.

Others of the Monkeys caught the Scarecrow, and with their long fingers pulled all of the straw out of his clothes and head. They made his hat and boots and clothes into a small bundle and threw it into the top branches of a tall tree.

The remaining Monkeys threw pieces of stout rope around the Lion and wound many coils about his body and head and legs, until he was unable to bite or scratch or struggle in any way. Then they lifted him up and flew away with him to the Witch's castle, where he was placed in a small yard with a high iron fence around it, so that he could not escape.

But Dorothy they did not harm at all. She stood, with Toto in her arms, watching the sad fate of her comrades and thinking it would soon be her turn. The leader of the Winged Monkeys flew up to her, his long, hairy arms stretched out and his ugly face grinning terribly; but he saw the mark of the Good Witch's kiss upon her forehead and stopped short, motioning the others not to touch her.

'We dare not harm this little girl,' he said to them, 'for she is protected by the Power of Good, and that is greater than the Power of Evil. All we can do is to carry her to the castle of the Wicked Witch and leave her there.'

So, carefully and gently, they lifted Dorothy in their arms and carried her swiftly through the air until they came to the castle, where they set her down upon the front doorstep.

Then the leader said to the Witch, 'We have obeyed you as far as we were able. The Tin Woodman and the Scarecrow are destroyed, and the Lion is tied up in your yard. The little girl we dare not harm, nor the dog she carries in her arms. Your power over our band is now ended, and you will never see us again.'

Then all the Winged Monkeys, with much laughing and chattering and noise, flew into the air and were soon out of sight.

The Wicked Witch was both surprised and worried when she saw the mark on Dorothy's forehead, for she knew well that neither the winged monkeys nor she, herself, dare hurt the girl in any way. She looked down at Dorothy's feet, and seeing the silver shoes, began to tremble with fear, for she knew what a powerful charm belonged to them. At first the Witch was tempted to run away from Dorothy; but she happened to look into the child's eyes and saw how simple the soul behind them was, and that the little girl did not know of the wonderful power the Silver Shoes gave her. So the Wicked Witch laughed to herself, and thought, 'I can still make her my slave, for she does not know how to use her power.'

Then she said to Dorothy, harshly and severely, 'Come with me; and see that you mind everything I tell you, for if you do not I will make an end of you, as I did of the Tin Woodman and the Scarecrow.'

Dorothy followed her through many of the beautiful rooms in her castle until they came to the kitchen, where the Witch bade her clean the pots and kettles and sweep the floor and keep the fire fed with wood.

Dorothy went to work meekly, with her mind made up to work as hard as she could; for she was glad the Wicked Witch had decided not to kill her.

With Dorothy hard at work, the Witch thought she would go into the courtyard and harness the Cowardly Lion like a horse; it would amuse her, she was sure, to make him draw her chariot whenever she wished to go to drive. But as she opened the gate the Lion gave a loud roar and bounded at her so fiercely that the Witch was afraid, and ran out and shut the gate again.

'If I cannot harness you,' said the Witch to the Lion,

speaking through the bars of the gate, 'I can starve you. You shall have nothing to eat until you do as I wish.'

So after that she took no food to the imprisoned Lion; but every day she came to the gate at noon and asked, 'Are you ready to be harnessed like a horse?'

And the Lion would answer, 'No. If you come in this yard I will bite you.'

The reason the Lion did not have to do as the Witch wished was that every night, when the woman was asleep, Dorothy carried him food from the cupboard. After he had eaten he would lie down on his bed of straw, and Dorothy would lie beside him and put her head on his soft, shaggy mane, while they talked of their troubles and tried to plan some way to escape. But they could find no way to get out of the castle, for it was constantly guarded by the yellow Winkies, who were the slaves of the Wicked Witch and too afraid of her not to do as she told them.

The girl had to work hard during the day, and often the Witch threatened to beat her with the same old umbrella she always carried in her hand. But, in truth, she did not dare to strike Dorothy, because of the mark upon her forehead. The child did not know this, and was full of fear for herself and Toto. Once the Witch struck Toto a blow with her umbrella and the brave little dog flew at her and bit her leg, in return. The Witch did not bleed where she was bitten, for she was so wicked that the blood in her had dried up many years before.

Dorothy's life became very sad as she grew to understand that it would be harder than ever to get back to Kansas and Aunt Em again. Sometimes she would cry bitterly for hours, with Toto sitting at her feet and looking into her face, whining dismally to show how sorry he was for his little mistress. Toto did not really care whether he was in Kansas or the Land of Oz so long as Dorothy was with him; but he knew the little girl was unhappy, and that made him unhappy too.

Now the Wicked Witch had a great longing to have for her own the Silver Shoes which the girl always wore. Her Bees and her Crows and her Wolves were lying in heaps and drying up, and she had used up all the power of the Golden Cap; but if she could only get hold of the Silver Shoes they would give her more power than all the other things she had lost. She watched Dorothy carefully, to see if she ever took off her shoes, thinking she might steal them. But the child was so proud of her pretty shoes that she never took them off except at night and when she took her bath. The Witch was too much afraid of the dark to dare go in Dorothy's room at night to take the shoes, and her dread of water was greater than her fear of the dark, so she never came near when Dorothy was bathing. Indeed, the old Witch never touched water, nor ever let water touch her in any way.

But the wicked creature was very cunning, and she finally thought of a trick that would give her what she wanted. She placed a bar of iron in the middle of the kitchen floor, and then by her magic arts made the Lion invisible to human eyes. So that when Dorothy walked across the floor she stumbled over the bar, not being able to see it, and fell at full length. She was not much hurt, but in her fall one of the Silver Shoes came off, and before she could reach it the Witch had snatched it away and put it on her own skinny foot.

The wicked woman was greatly pleased with the success of her trick, for as long as she had one of the shoes she owned half the power of their charm, and Dorothy could not use it against her, even had she known how to do so.

The little girl, seeing she had lost one of her pretty shoes, grew angry, and said to the witch, 'Give me back my shoe!'

'I will not,' retorted the Witch, 'for it is now my shoe, and not yours.'

'You are a wicked creature!' cried Dorothy. 'You have no right to take my shoe from me.'

'I shall keep it, just the same,' said the Witch, laughing at her, 'and someday I shall get the other one from you, too.'

This made Dorothy so very angry that she picked up the bucket of water that stood near and dashed it over the Witch, wetting her from head to foot.

Instantly the wicked woman gave a loud cry of fear, and then, as Dorothy looked at her in wonder, the Witch began to shrink and fall away.

'See what you have done!' she screamed. 'In a minute I shall melt away.'

'I'm very sorry, indeed,' said Dorothy, who was truly frightened to see the Witch actually melting away like brown sugar before her very eyes.

'Didn't you know water would be the end of me?' asked the Witch, in a wailing, despairing voice.

'Of course not,' answered Dorothy; 'how should I?'

'Well, in a few minutes I shall be all melted, and you will have the castle to yourself. I have been wicked in my day, but I never thought a little girl like you would ever be able to melt me and end my wicked deeds. Look out – here I go!'

With these words the Witch fell down in a brown, melted, shapeless mass and began to spread over the clean boards of the kitchen floor. Seeing that she had really melted away to nothing, Dorothy drew another bucket of water and threw it over the mess. She then swept it all out the door. After picking out the silver shoe, which was all that was left of the old woman, she cleaned and dried it with a cloth, and put it on her foot again. Then, being at last free to do as she chose, she ran out to the courtyard to tell the Lion that the Wicked Witch of the West had come to an end, and that they were no longer prisoners in a strange land.

CHAPTER THIRTEEN

The Rescue

cowardly Lion was very pleased to hear that the Wicked Witch had been melted by a bucket of water, and Dorothy at once unlocked the gate of his prison and set him free.

They went in together to the castle, where Dorothy's first act was to call all the Winkies together and tell them that they were no longer slaves.

There was great rejoicing among the yellow Winkies, for they had been made to work hard during many years for the Wicked Witch, who had always treated them with great cruelty. They kept this day as a holiday, then and ever after, and spent the time in feasting and dancing.

'If our friends, the Scarecrow and the Tin Woodman, were only with us,' said the Lion, 'I should be quite happy.'

'Don't you suppose we could rescue them?' asked the girl anxiously.

'We can try,' answered the Lion.

So they called the yellow Winkies and asked them if they would help to rescue their friends, and the Winkies said that they would be delighted to do all in their power for Dorothy, who had set them free from bondage. So she chose a number of the Winkies who looked as if they knew the most, and they all started away. They travelled that day and part of the next until they came to the rocky plain where the Tin Woodman lay, all battered and bent. His axe was near him, but the blade was rusted and the handle was broken off short.

The Winkies lifted him tenderly in their arms, and carried him back to the yellow castle again, Dorothy shedding a few tears by the way at the sad plight of her old friend, and the Lion looking sober and sorry.

When they reached the castle Dorothy said to the Winkies, 'Are any of your people tinsmiths?'

'Oh, yes; some of them are very good tinsmiths,' they told her.

'Then bring them to me,' she said. And when the tinsmiths came, bringing with them all their tools in baskets, she enquired, 'Can you straighten out those dents in the Tin Woodman, and bend him back into shape again, and solder him together where he is broken?'

The tinsmiths looked the Woodman over carefully and then answered that they thought they could mend him so he would be as good as ever. So they set to work in one of the big yellow rooms of the castle and worked for three days and four nights, hammering and twisting and bending and soldering and polishing and pounding at the legs and body and head of the Tin Woodman, until at last he was straightened out into his old form, and his joints worked as well as ever. To be sure, there were several patches on him, but the tinsmiths did a good job, and as the Woodman was not a vain man he did not mind the patches at all.

When, at last, he walked into Dorothy's room and thanked

her for rescuing him, he was so pleased that he wept tears of joy, and Dorothy had to wipe every tear carefully from his face with her apron, so his joints would not be rusted. At the same time her own tears fell thick and fast at the joy of meeting her old friend again, and these tears did not need to be wiped away. As for the Lion, he wiped his eyes so often with the tip of his tail that it became quite wet, and he was obliged to go out into the courtyard and hold it in the sun till it dried.

'If we only had the Scarecrow with us again,' said the Tin Woodman, when Dorothy had finished telling him everything that had happened, 'I should be quite happy.'

'We must try to find him,' said the girl.

So she called the Winkies to help her, and they walked all that day and part of the next until they came to the tall tree in the branches of which the Winged Monkeys had tossed the Scarecrow's clothes.

It was a very tall tree, and the trunk was so smooth that no one could climb it; but the Woodman said at once, 'I'll chop it down, and then we can get the Scarecrow's clothes.'

Now while the tinsmiths had been at work mending the Woodman himself, another of the Winkies, who was a goldsmith, had made an axe-handle of solid gold and fitted it to the Woodman's axe, instead of the old broken handle. Others polished the blade until all the rust was removed and it glistened like burnished silver.

As soon as he had spoken, the Tin Woodman began to chop, and in a short time the tree fell over with a crash, when the Scarecrow's clothes fell out of the branches and rolled off on the ground.

Dorothy picked them up and had the Winkies carry them back to the castle, where they were stuffed with nice clean straw; and, behold! here was the Scarecrow, as good as ever, thanking them over and over again for saving him.

Now they were reunited, Dorothy and her friends spent a

The tinsmiths worked for three days and four nights

few happy days at the Yellow Castle, where they found everything they needed to make them comfortable. But one day the girl thought of Aunt Em, and said, 'We must go back to Oz, and claim his promise.'

'Yes,' said the Woodman, 'at last I shall get my heart.'

'And I shall get my brains,' added the Scarecrow, joyfully.

'And I shall get my courage,' said the Lion, thoughtfully.

'And I shall get back to Kansas,' cried Dorothy, clapping her hands. 'Oh, let us start for the Emerald City tomorrow!'

This they decided to do. The next day they called the Winkies together and bade them goodbye. The Winkies were sorry to have them go, and they had grown so fond of the Tin Woodman that they begged him to stay and rule over them and the Yellow Land of the West. Finding they were determined to go, the Winkies gave Toto and the Lion each a golden collar; and to Dorothy they presented a beautiful bracelet, studded with diamonds; and to the Scarecrow they gave a gold-headed walking stick, to keep him from stumbling; and to the Tin Woodman they offered a silver oilcan, inlaid with gold and set with precious jewels.

Every one of the travellers made the Winkies a pretty speech in return, and all shook hands with them until their arms ached.

Dorothy went to the Witch's cupboard to fill her basket with food for the journey, and there she saw the Golden Cap. She tried it on her own head and found that it fitted her exactly. She did not know anything about the charm of the Golden Cap, but she saw that it was pretty, so she made up her mind to wear it and carry her sun-bonnet in the basket.

Then, being prepared for the journey, they all started for the Emerald City; and the Winkies gave them three cheers and many good wishes to carry with them.

CHAPTER FOURTEEN

The Winged Monkeys

YOU will remember there was no road – not even a pathway – between the castle of the Wicked Witch and the Emerald City. When the four travellers went in search of the Witch she had seen them coming, and so sent the Winged Monkeys to bring them to her.

It was much harder to find their way back through the big fields of buttercups and bright daisies than it was being carried. They knew, of course, they must go straight east, towards the rising sun and they started off in the right way. But at noon, when the sun was over their heads, they did not know which was east and which was west, and that was the reason they were lost in the great fields. They kept on walking, however, and at night the moon came out and shone brightly. So they lay down among the sweet-smelling scarlet flowers and slept soundly until morning – all but the Scarecrow and the Tin Woodman.

The next morning the sun was behind a cloud, but they started on, as if they were quite sure which way they were going.

'If we walk far enough,' said Dorothy, 'we shall sometime come to some place, I am sure.'

But day by day passed away, and they still saw nothing before them but the scarlet fields. The Scarecrow began to grumble a bit.

'We have surely lost our way,' he said, 'and unless we find it again in time to reach the Emerald City I shall never get my brains.'

'Nor I my heart,' declared the Tin Woodman. 'It seems to me I can scarcely wait till I get to Oz, and you must admit this is a very long journey.'

'You see,' said the Cowardly Lion, with a whimper, 'I haven't the courage to keep tramping for ever, without getting anywhere at all.'

Then Dorothy lost heart. She sat down on the grass and looked at her companions, and they sat down and looked at her, and Toto found that for the first time in his life he was too tired to chase a butterfly that flew past his head; so he put out his tongue and panted and looked at Dorothy as if to ask what they should do next.

'Suppose we call the Field-Mice,' she suggested. 'They could probably tell us the way to the Emerald City.'

'To be sure they could,' cried the Scarecrow; 'why didn't we think of that before?'

Dorothy blew the little whistle she had always carried about her neck since the Queen of the Mice had given it to her. In a few minutes they heard the pattering of tiny feet, and many of the small grey mice came running up to her. Among them was the Queen herself, who asked, in her squeaky little voice, 'What can I do for my friends?'

'We have lost our way,' said Dorothy. 'Can you tell us where the Emerald City is?'

'Certainly,' answered the Queen; 'but it is a great way off, for you have had it at your backs all this time.' Then she noticed Dorothy's Golden Cap, and said, 'Why don't you use the charm of the Cap, and call the Winged Monkeys to you? They will carry you to the City of Oz in less than an hour.'

'I didn't know there was a charm,' answered Dorothy, in surprise. 'What is it?'

'It is written inside the Golden Cap,' replied the Queen of the Mice; 'but if you are going to call the Winged Monkeys we must run away, for they are full of mischief and think it great fun to plague us.'

'Won't they hurt me?' asked the girl, anxiously.

'Oh, no; they must obey the wearer of the Cap. Goodbye!' And she scampered out of sight, with all the mice hurrying after her.

Dorothy looked inside the Golden Cap and saw some words written upon the lining. These, she thought, must be the charm, so she read the directions carefully and put the Cap upon her head.

'Ep-pe, pep-pe, kak-ke!' she said, standing on her left foot.

'What did you say?' asked the Scarecrow, who did not know what she was doing.

'Hil-lo, hol-lo, hel-lo!' Dorothy went on, standing this time on her right foot.

'Hello!' replied the Tin Woodman, calmly.

'Ziz-zy, zuz-zy, zik!' said Dorothy, who was now standing on both feet. This ended the saying of the charm, and they heard a great chattering and flapping of wings, as the band of Winged Monkeys flew up to them.

The King bowed low before Dorothy, and asked, 'What is your command?'

'We wish to go to the Emerald City,' said the child, 'and we have lost our way.'

'We will carry you,' replied the King, and no sooner had he spoken than two of the Monkeys caught Dorothy in their arms and flew away with her. Others took the Scarecrow and the Woodman and the Lion, and one little Monkey seized Toto and flew after them, although the dog tried hard to bite him.

The Scarecrow and the Tin Woodman were rather frightened at first, for they remembered how badly the Winged Monkeys had treated them before; but they saw that no harm was intended, so they rode through the air quite cheerfully, and had a fine time looking at the pretty gardens and woods far below them.

Dorothy found herself riding easily between two of the biggest Monkeys, one of them the King himself. They had made a chair of their hands and were careful not to hurt her.

'Why do you have to obey the charm of the Golden Cap?' she asked.

'That is a long story,' answered the King, with a laugh; 'but as we have a long journey before us I will pass the time by telling you about it, if you wish.'

'I shall be glad to hear it,' she replied.

'Once,' began the leader, 'we were a free people, living happily in the great forest, flying from tree to tree, eating nuts and fruit, and doing just as we pleased without calling anybody master. Perhaps some of us were rather too full of mischief at times, flying down to pull the tails of the animals that had no wings, chasing birds, and throwing nuts at the people who walked in the forest. But we were careless and happy and full of fun, and enjoyed every minute of the day. This was many years ago, long before Oz came out of the clouds to rule over this land.

'There lived here then, away at the North, a beautiful

princess, who was also a powerful sorceress. All her magic was used to help the people, and she was never known to hurt anyone who was good. Her name was Gayelette, and she lived in a handsome palace built from great blocks of ruby. Everyone loved her, but her greatest sorrow was that she could find no one to love in return, since all the men were much too stupid and ugly to mate with one so beautiful and wise. At last, however, she found a boy who was handsome and manly and wise beyond his years. Gayelette made up her mind that when he grew to be a man she would make him her husband, so she took him to her ruby palace and used all her magic powers to make him as strong and good and lovely as any woman could wish. When he grew to manhood, Quelala, as he was called, was said to be the best and wisest man in all the land, while his manly beauty was so great that Gayelette loved him dearly, and hastened to make everything ready for the wedding.

'My grandfather was at that time the King of the Winged Monkeys which lived in the forest near Gayelette's palace, and the old fellow loved a joke better than a good dinner. One day, just before the wedding, my grandfather was flying out with his band when he saw Quelala walking beside the river. He was dressed in a rich costume of pink silk and purple velvet, and my grandfather thought he would see what he could do. At his word the band flew down and seized Quelala, carried him in their arms until they were over the middle of the river, and then dropped him into the water.

' "Swim out, my fine fellow," cried my grandfather, "and see if the water has spotted your clothes." Quelala was much too wise not to swim, and he was not in the least spoiled by all his good fortune. He laughed, when he came to the top of the water, and swam in to shore. But when Gayelette came running out to him she found his silks and velvet all ruined by the river.

'The princess was very angry, and she knew, of course, who did it. She had all the Winged Monkeys brought before her, and she said at first that their wings should be tied and they should be treated as they had treated Quelala, and dropped in the river. But my grandfather pleaded hard, for he knew the Monkeys would drown in the river with their wings tied, and Quelala said a kind word for them also; so that Gayelette finally spared them, on condition that the Winged Monkeys should ever after do three times the bidding of the owner of the Golden Cap. This Cap had been made for a wedding present to Quelala, and it is said to have cost the princess half her Kingdom. Of course my grandfather and all the other Monkeys at once agreed to the condition, and that is how it happens that we are three times the slaves of the owner of the Golden Cap, whosoever he may be.'

'And what became of them?' asked Dorothy, who had been greatly interested in the story.

'Quelala being the first owner of the Golden Cap,' replied the Monkey, 'he was the first to lay his wishes upon us. As his bride could not bear the sight of us, he called us all to him in the forest after he had married her and ordered us always to keep where she could never again set eyes on a Winged Monkey, which we were glad to do, for we were all afraid of her.

'This was all we ever had to do until the Golden Cap fell into the hands of the Wicked Witch of the West, who made us enslave the Winkies, and afterward drive Oz himself out of the Land of the West. Now the Golden Cap is yours, and three times you have the right to lay your wishes upon us.'

As the Monkey King finished his story Dorothy looked down and saw the green, shining walls of the Emerald City before them. She wondered at the rapid flight of the Monkeys, but was glad the journey was over. The strange creatures set the travellers down carefully before the gate of the City, the King bowed low to Dorothy, and then flew swiftly away, followed by all his band.

'That was a good ride,' said the little girl.

'Yes, and a quick way out of our troubles,' replied the Lion. 'How lucky it was you brought away that wonderful Cap!'

CHAPTER FIFTEEN

The Discovery of Oz the Terrible

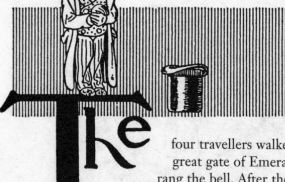

The four travellers walked up to the great gate of Emerald City and rang the bell. After they had rung several times it was opened by the same Guardian of the Gates they had met before.

'What! are you back again?' he asked, in surprise.

'Do you not see us?' answered the Scarecrow.

'But I thought you had gone to visit the Wicked Witch of the West.'

'We did visit her,' said the Scarecrow.

'And she let you go again?' asked the man, in wonder.

'She could not help it, for she is melted,' explained the Scarecrow.

'Melted! Well, that is good news, indeed,' said the man. 'Who melted her?'

'It was Dorothy,' said the Lion, gravely.

'Good gracious!' exclaimed the man, and he bowed very low indeed before her.

Then he led them into his little room and locked the spectacles from the great box on all their eyes, just as he had done before. Afterward they passed on through the gate into the Emerald City, and when the people heard from the Guardian of the Gates that they had melted the Wicked Witch of the West they all gathered around the travellers, and followed them in a great crowd to the Palace of Oz.

The soldier with the green whiskers was still on guard before the door, but he let them in at once, and they were again met by the beautiful green girl, who showed each of them to their old rooms at once, so they might rest until the Great Oz was ready to receive them.

The soldier had the news carried straight to Oz that Dorothy and the other travellers had come back again, after destroying the Wicked Witch; but Oz made no reply. They thought the Great Wizard would send for them at once, but he did not. They had no word from him the next day, nor the next, nor the next. The waiting was tiresome and wearing, and at last they grew vexed that Oz should treat them in so poor a fashion, after sending them to undergo hardships and slavery. So the Scarecrow at last asked the green girl to take another message to Oz, saying if he did not let them in to see him at once they would call the Winged Monkeys to help them, and find out whether he kept his promises or not. When the Wizard was given this message he was so frightened that he sent word for them to come to the Throne Room at four minutes after nine o'clock the next morning. He had once met the Winged Monkeys in the Land of the West, and he did not wish to meet them again.

The four travellers passed a sleepless night, each thinking

of the gift Oz had promised to bestow on him. Dorothy fell asleep only once, and then she dreamed she was in Kansas, where Aunt Em was telling her how glad she was to have her little girl at home again.

Promptly at nine o'clock he next morning the green whiskered soldier came to them, and four minutes later they all went into the Throne Room of the Great Oz.

Of course each one of them expected to see the Wizard in the shape he had taken before, and all were greatly surprised when they looked about and saw no one at all in the room. They kept close to the door and closer to one another, for the stillness of the empty room was more dreadful than any of the forms they had seen Oz take.

Presently they heard a voice, seeming to come from somewhere near the top of the great dome, and it said, solemnly, 'I am Oz, the Great and Terrible. Why do you seek me?'

They looked again in every part of the room, and then, seeing no one, Dorothy asked, 'Where are you?'

'I am everywhere,' answered the Voice, 'but to the eyes of common mortals I am invisible. I will now seat myself upon my throne, that you may converse with me.'

Indeed, the Voice seemed just then to come straight from the throne itself; so they walked towards it and stood in a row while Dorothy said: 'We have come to claim our promise, O Oz.'

'What promise?' asked Oz.

'You promised to send me back to Kansas when the Wicked Witch was destroyed,' said the girl.

'And you promised to give me brains,' said the Scarecrow.

'And you promised to give me a heart,' said the Tin Woodman.

'And you promised to give me courage,' said the Cowardly Lion.

'Is the Wicked Witch really destroyed?' asked the Voice, and Dorothy thought it trembled a little.

'Yes,' she answered, 'I melted her with a bucket of water.'

'Dear me,' said the Voice; 'how sudden! Well, come to me tomorrow, for I must have time to think it over.'

'You've had plenty of time already,' said the Tin Woodman, angrily.

'We shan't wait a day longer,' said the Scarecrow.

'You must keep your promises to us!' exclaimed Dorothy.

The Lion thought it might be as well to frighten the Wizard. So he gave a large, loud roar, which was so fierce and dreadful that Toto jumped away from him in alarm and tipped over the screen that stood in a corner. As it fell with a crash they looked that way, and the next moment all of them were filled with wonder. For they saw, standing in just the spot the screen had hidden, a little, old man, with a bald head and a wrinkled face, who seemed to be as much surprised as they were.

The Tin Woodman, raising his axe, rushed towards the little man and cried out, 'Who are you?'

'I am Oz, the Great and Terrible,' said the little man, in a trembling voice, 'but don't strike me – please don't – and I'll do anything you want me to.'

Our friends looked at him in surprise and dismay.

'I thought Oz was a great Head,' said Dorothy.

'And I thought Oz was a lovely Lady,' said the Scarecrow.

'And I thought Oz was a terrible Beast,' said the Tin Woodman.

'And I thought Oz was a Ball of Fire,' exclaimed the Lion.

'No; you are all wrong,' said the little man, meekly. 'I have been making believe.'

'Making believe!' cried Dorothy. 'Are you not a great Wizard?'

'Hush, my dear,' he said; 'don't speak so loud, or you will be overheard – and I should be ruined. I'm supposed to be a Great Wizard.'

'And aren't you?' she asked.

'Not a bit of it, my dear; I'm just a common man.'

'You're more than that,' said the Scarecrow, in a grieved tone; 'you're a humbug.'

'Exactly so!' declared the little man, rubbing his hands together as if it pleased him, 'I am a humbug.'

'But this is terrible,' said the Tin Woodman; 'how shall I ever get my heart?'

'Or I my courage?' asked the Lion.

'Or I my brains?' wailed the Scarecrow, wiping the tears from his eyes with his coat-sleeve.

'My dear friends,' said Oz, 'I pray you not to speak of these little things. Think of me, and the terrible trouble I'm in at being found out.'

'Doesn't anyone else know you're a humbug?' asked Dorothy.

'No one knows it but you four – and myself,' replied Oz. 'I have fooled everyone so long that I thought I should never be found out. It was a great mistake my ever letting you into the Throne Room. Usually I will not see even my subjects, and so they believe I am something terrible.'

'But, I don't understand,' said Dorothy, in bewilderment. 'How was it you appeared to me as a great Head?'

'That was one of my tricks,' answered Oz. 'Step this way, please, and I will tell you all about it.'

He led the way to a small chamber in the rear of the Throne Room, and they all followed him. He pointed to one corner, in which lay the Great Head, made out of many thicknesses of paper, and with a carefully painted face.

'This I hung from the ceiling by a wire,' said Oz; 'I stood behind the screen and pulled a thread, to make the eyes move and the mouth open.'

'But how about the voice?' she enquired.

'Oh, I am a ventriloquist,' said the little man, 'and I can throw the sound of my voice whenever I wish; so that you thought it was coming out of the Head. Here are the other

'Exactly so!' declared the little man, 'I am a humbug.'

things I used to deceive you.' He showed the Scarecrow the dress and the mask he had worn when he seemed to be the lovely Lady; and the Tin Woodman saw that his terrible Beast was nothing but a lot of skins, sewn together, with slats to keep their sides out. As for the Ball of Fire, the false Wizard had hung that also from the ceiling. It was really a ball of cotton, but when oil was poured upon it the ball burned fiercely.

'Really,' said the Scarecrow, 'you ought to be ashamed of yourself for being such a humbug.'

'I am – I certainly am,' answered the little man, sorrowfully; 'but it was the only thing I could do. Sit down, please, there are plenty of chairs; and I will tell you my story.'

So they sat down and listened while he told the following tale: 'I was born in Omaha – '

'Why, that isn't very far from Kansas!' cried Dorothy.

'No; but it's farther from here,' he said, shaking his head at her, sadly. 'When I grew up I became a ventriloquist, and at that I was very well trained by a great master. I can imitate any kind of a bird or beast.' Here he mewed so like a kitten that Toto pricked up his ears and looked everywhere to see where she was. 'After a time,' continued Oz, 'I tired of that, and became a balloonist.'

'What is that?' asked Dorothy.

'A man who goes up in a balloon on circus day, so as to draw a crowd of people together and get them to pay to see the circus,' he explained.

'Oh,' she said; 'I know.'

'Well, one day I went up in a balloon and the ropes got twisted, so that I couldn't come down again. It went way up above the clouds, so far that a current of air struck it and carried it many, many miles away. For a day and a night I travelled through the air, and on the morning of the second day I awoke and found the balloon floating over a strange and beautiful country.

'It came down gradually, and I was not hurt a bit. But I found myself in the midst of a strange people, who, seeing me come from the clouds, thought I was a great Wizard. Of course I let them think so, because they were afraid of me, and promised to do anything I wished them to.

'Just to amuse myself, and keep the good people busy, I ordered them to build this City, and my palace; and they did it all willingly and well. Then I thought, as the country was so green and beautiful, I would call it the Emerald City, and to make the name fit better I put green spectacles on all the people, so that everything they saw was green.'

'But isn't everything here green?' asked Dorothy.

'No more than in any other city,' replied Oz; 'but when you wear green spectacles, why of course everything you see looks green to you. The Emerald City was built a great many years ago, for I was a young man when the balloon brought me here, and I am a very old man now. But my people have worn green glasses on their eyes so long that most of them think it really is an Emerald City, and it certainly is a beautiful place, abounding in jewels and precious metals, and every good thing that is needed to make one happy. I have been good to the people, and they like me; but ever since this Palace was built I have shut myself up and would not see any of them.

'One of my greatest fears was the Witches, for while I had no magical powers at all I soon found out that the Witches were really able to do wonderful things. There were four of them in this country, and they ruled the people who live in the North and South and East and West. Fortunately, the Witches of the North and South were good, and I knew they would do me no harm; but the Witches of the East and West were terribly wicked, and had they not thought I was more powerful than they themselves, they would surely have destroyed me. As it was, I lived in deadly fear of them for many years; so you can imagine how pleased I was when I heard your house had fallen on the Wicked Witch of the East. When you came to me I was willing to promise anything if you would only do away with the other Witch; but, now that you have melted her, I am ashamed to say that I cannot keep my promises.'

'I think you are a very bad man.' said Dorothy.

'Oh, no, my dear; I'm really a very good man; but I'm a very bad Wizard, I must admit.'

'Can't you give me brains?' asked the Scarecrow.

'You don't need them. You are learning something every day. A baby has brains, but it doesn't know much. Experience is the only thing that brings knowledge, and the longer you are on earth the more experience you are sure to get.'

'That may all be true,' said the Scarecrow, 'but I shall be very unhappy unless you give me brains.'

The false Wizard looked at him carefully.

'Well,' he said with a sigh, 'I'm not much of a magician, as I said; but if you will come to me tomorrow morning, I will stuff your head with brains. I cannot tell you how to use them, however; you must find that out for yourself.'

'Oh, thank you – thank you!' cried the Scarecrow. 'I'll find a way to use them, never fear!'

'But how about my courage?' asked the Lion, anxiously.

'You have plenty of courage, I am sure,' answered Oz. 'All you need is confidence in yourself. There is no living thing that is not afraid when it faces danger. True courage is in facing danger when you are afraid, and that kind of courage you have in plenty.'

'Perhaps I have, but I'm scared just the same,' said the Lion. 'I shall really be very unhappy unless you give me the sort of courage that makes one forget he is afraid.'

'Very well; I will give you that sort of courage tomorrow,' replied Oz.

'How about my heart?' asked the Tin Woodman.

'Why, as for that,' answered Oz, 'I think you are wrong to want a heart. It makes most people unhappy. If you only knew it, you are in luck not to have a heart.'

'That must be a matter of opinion,' said the Tin Woodman. 'For my part, I will bear all the unhappiness without a murmur, if you will give me the heart.'

'Very well,' answered Oz, meekly. 'Come to me tomorrow and you shall have a heart. I have played Wizard for so many years that I may as well continue the part a little longer.'

'And now,' said Dorothy, 'how am I to get back to Kansas?'

'We shall have to think about that,' replied the little man. 'Give me two or three days to consider the matter and I'll try to find a way to carry you over the desert. In the meantime you shall all be treated as my guests, and while you live in the Palace my people will wait upon you and obey your slightest wish. There is only one thing I ask in return for my help – such as it is. You must keep my secret and tell no one I am a humbug.'

They agreed to say nothing of what they had learned, and went back to their rooms in high spirits. Even Dorothy had hope that 'The Great and Terrible Humbug', as she called him, would find a way to send her back to Kansas, and if he did she was willing to forgive him everything.

CHAPTER SIXTEEN

The Magic Art of the Great Humbug

Next morning the Scarecrow said to his friends: 'Congratulate me. I am going to Oz to get my brains at last. When I return I shall be as other men are.'

'I have always liked you as you were,' said Dorothy simply.

'It is kind of you to like a Scarecrow,' he replied. 'But surely you will think more of me when you hear the splendid thoughts my new brain is going to turn out.'

Then he said goodbye to them all in a cheerful voice and went to the Throne Room, where he rapped upon the door.

'Come in,' said Oz.

The Scarecrow went in and found the little man sitting down by the window, engaged in deep thought.

'I have come for my brains,' remarked the Scarecrow, a little uneasily.

'Oh, yes; sit down in that chair, please,' replied Oz. 'You must excuse me for taking your head off, but I shall have to do it in order to put your brains in their proper place.'

'That's all right,' said the Scarecrow. 'You are quite welcome to take my head off, as long as it will be a better one when you put it on again.'

So the Wizard unfastened his head and emptied out the straw. Then he entered the back room and took up a measure of bran, which he mixed with a great many pins and needles. Having shaken them together thoroughly, he filled the top of the Scarecrow's head with the mixture and stuffed the rest of the space with straw, to hold it in place. When he had fastened the Scarecrow's head on his body again he said to him, 'Hereafter you will be a great man, for I have given you a lot of bran-new brains.'

The Scarecrow was both pleased and proud at the fulfilment of his greatest wish, and having thanked Oz warmly he went back to his friends.

Dorothy looked at him curiously. His head was quite bulged out at the top with brains.

'How do you feel?' she asked.

'I feel wise indeed,' he answered earnestly. 'When I get used to my brains I shall know everything.'

'Why are those needles and pins sticking out of your head?' asked the Tin Woodman.

'That is proof that he is sharp,' remarked the Lion.

'Well, I must go to Oz and get my heart,' said the Woodman. So he walked to the Throne Room and knocked at the door.

'Come in,' called Oz, and the Woodman entered and said, 'I have come for my heart.'

'Very well,' answered the little man. 'But I shall have to cut a hole in your breast, so I can put your heart in the right place. I hope it won't hurt you.'

'Oh, no,' answered the Woodman. 'I shall not feel it at all.'

So Oz brought a pair of tinner's shears and cut a small, square hole in the left side of the Tin Woodman's breast. Then, going to a chest of drawers, he took out a pretty heart, made entirely of silk and stuffed with sawdust.

'Isn't it a beauty?' he asked.

'It is, indeed!' replied the Woodman, who was greatly pleased. 'But is it a kind heart?'

'Oh, very!' answered Oz. He put the heart in the Woodman's breast and then replaced the square of tin, soldering it neatly together where it had been cut.

'There,' said he; 'now you have a heart that any man might be proud of; I'm sorry I had to put a patch on your breast, but it really couldn't be helped.'

'Never mind the patch,' exclaimed the happy Woodman. 'I am very grateful to you, and shall never forget your kindness.'

'Don't speak of it,' replied Oz.

Then the Tin Woodman went back to his friends, who wished him every joy on account of his good fortune.

The Lion now walked to the Throne Room and knocked at the door.

'Come in,' said Oz.

'I have come for my courage,' announced the Lion, entering the room.

'Very well,' answered the little man; 'I will get it for you.'

He went to a cupboard and reaching up to a high shelf took down a square green bottle, the contents of which he poured into a green-gold dish, beautifully carved. Placing this before the Cowardly Lion, who sniffed at it as if he did not like it, the Wizard said, 'Drink.'

'What is it?' asked the Lion.

'Well,' answered Oz, 'if it were inside of you, it would be courage. You know, of course, that courage is always inside one; so that this really cannot be called courage until you have swallowed it. Therefore I advise you to drink it as soon as possible.'

The Lion hesitated no longer but drank till the dish was empty.

'How do you feel now?' asked Oz.

'Full of courage,' replied the Lion, who went joyfully back to his friends to tell them of his good fortune.

Oz, left to himself, smiled to think of his success in giving the Scarecrow and the Tin Woodman and the Lion exactly what they thought they wanted. 'How can I help being a humbug,' he said, 'when all these people make me do things that everybody knows can't be done? It was easy to make the Scarecrow and the Lion and the Woodman happy, because they imagined I could do anything. But it will take more imagination to carry Dorothy back to Kansas, and I'm sure I don't know how it can be done.'

CHAPTER SEVENTEEN

How the Balloon was Launched

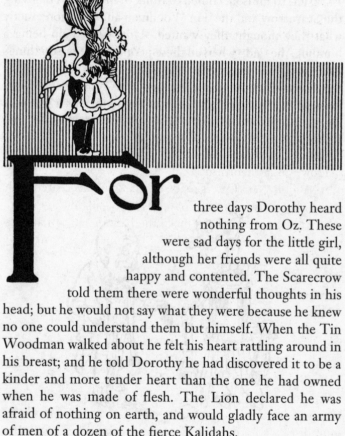

three days Dorothy heard nothing from Oz. These were sad days for the little girl, although her friends were all quite happy and contented. The Scarecrow told them there were wonderful thoughts in his head; but he would not say what they were because he knew no one could understand them but himself. When the Tin Woodman walked about he felt his heart rattling around in his breast; and he told Dorothy he had discovered it to be a kinder and more tender heart than the one he had owned when he was made of flesh. The Lion declared he was afraid of nothing on earth, and would gladly face an army of men of a dozen of the fierce Kalidahs.

Thus each of the little party was satisfied except Dorothy, who longed more than ever to get back to Kansas.

On the fourth day, to her great joy, Oz sent for her, and when she entered the Throne Room he said, pleasantly: 'Sit down, my dear; I think I have found the way to get you out of this country.'

'And back to Kansas?' she asked eagerly.

'Well, I'm not sure about Kansas,' said Oz; 'for I haven't the faintest notion which way it lies. But the first thing to do is to cross the desert, and then it should be easy to find your way home.'

'How can I cross the desert?' she enquired.

'Well, I'll tell you what I think,' said the little man. 'You see, when I came to this country it was in a balloon. You also came through the air, being carried by a cyclone. So I believe the best way to get across the desert will be through the air. Now, it is quite beyond my powers to make a cyclone; but I've been thinking the matter over, and I believe I can make a balloon.'

'How?' asked Dorothy.

'A balloon,' said Oz, 'is made of silk, which is coated with glue to keep the gas in it. I have plenty of silk in the Palace, so it will be no trouble to make the balloon. But in all this country there is no gas to fill the balloon with, to make it float.'

'If it won't float,' remarked Dorothy, 'it will be of no use to us.'

'True,' answered Oz. 'But there is another way to make it float, which is to fill it with hot air. Hot air isn't as good as gas, for if the air should get cold the balloon would come down in the desert, and we should be lost.'

'We!' exclaimed the girl; 'are you going with me?'

'Yes, of course,' replied Oz. 'I am tired of being such a humbug. If I should go out of this Palace my people would soon discover I am not a Wizard, and then they would be vexed with me for having deceived them. So I have to stay shut up in these rooms all day, and it gets tiresome. I'd much rather go back to Kansas with you and be in a circus again.'

'I shall be glad to have your company,' said Dorothy.

'Thank you,' he answered. 'Now, if you will help me sew the silk together, we will begin to work on our balloon.'

So Dorothy took a needle and thread, and as fast as Oz cut the strips of silk into proper shape the girl sewed them neatly together. First there was a strip of light green silk, then a strip of dark green and then a strip of emerald green; for Oz had a fancy to make the balloon in different shades of the colour about them. It took three days to sew all the strips together, but when it was finished they had a big bag of green silk more than twenty feet long.

Then Oz painted it on the inside with a coat of thin glue, to make it airtight, after which he announced that the balloon was ready.

'But we must have a basket to ride in,' he said. So he sent the soldier with the green whiskers for a big clothes basket, which he fastened with many ropes in the bottom of the balloon.

When it was all ready, Oz sent word to his people that he was going to make a visit to a great brother Wizard who lived in the clouds. The news spread rapidly throughout the city and everyone came to see the wonderful sight.

Oz ordered the balloon carried out in front of the Palace, and the people gazed upon it with much curiosity. The Tin Woodman had chopped a big pile of wood, and now he made a fire of it, and Oz held the bottom of the balloon over the fire so that the hot air that arose from it would be caught in the silken bag. Gradually the balloon swelled out and rose into the air, until finally the basket just touched the ground.

Then Oz got into the basket and said to all the people in a loud voice: 'I am now going away to make a visit. While I am gone the Scarecrow will rule over you. I command you to obey him as you would me.'

The balloon was by this time tugging hard at the rope

that held it to the ground, for the air within it was hot, and this made it so much lighter in weight than the air without that it pulled hard to rise in the sky.

'Come, Dorothy!' cried the Wizard; 'hurry up, or the balloon will fly away.'

'I can't find Toto anywhere,' replied Dorothy, who did not wish to leave her little dog behind. Toto had run into the crowd to bark at a kitten, and Dorothy at last found him. She picked him up and ran towards the balloon.

She was within a few steps of it, and Oz was holding out his hands to help her into the basket, when, crack! went the ropes, and the balloon rose into the air without her.

'Come back!' she screamed; 'I want to go, too!'

'I can't come back, my dear,' called Oz from the basket. 'Goodbye!'

'Goodbye!' shouted everyone, and all eyes were turned upward to where the Wizard was riding in the basket, rising every moment farther and farther into the sky.

And that was the last any of them ever saw of Oz, the Wonderful Wizard, though he may have reached Omaha safely, and be there now, for all we know.

But the people remembered him lovingly, and said to one another, 'Oz was always our friend. When he was here he built for us this beautiful Emerald City, and now he is gone he has left the Wise Scarecrow to rule over us.'

Still, for many days they grieved over the loss of the Wonderful Wizard, and would not be comforted.

CHAPTER EIGHTEEN

Away to the South

Dorothy wept bitterly at the passing of her hope to get home to Kansas again; but when she thought it all over she was glad she had not gone up in the balloon. And she also felt sorry at losing Oz, and so did her companions.

The Tin Woodman came to her and said, 'Truly I should be ungrateful if I failed to mourn for the man who gave me my lovely heart. I should like to cry a little because Oz is gone, if you will kindly wipe away my tears, so that I shall not rust.'

'With pleasure,' she answered, and brought a towel at once. Then the Tin Woodman wept for several minutes, and she watched the tears carefully and wiped them away with the towel. When he had finished he thanked her kindly and oiled himself thoroughly with his jewelled oil can, to guard against mishap.

The Scarecrow was now the ruler of the Emerald City, and although he was not a Wizard the people were proud of him. 'For,' they said, 'there is not another city in all the world that is ruled by a stuffed man.' And, so far as they knew, they were quite right.

The morning after the balloon had gone up with Oz the four travellers met in the Throne Room and talked matters over. The Scarecrow sat in the big throne and the others stood respectfully before him.

'We are not so unlucky,' said the new ruler; 'for this Palace and the Emerald City belong to us, and we can do just as we please. When I remember that a short time ago I was up on a pole in a farmer's cornfield, and that now I am the ruler of this beautiful City, I am quite satisfied with my lot.'

'I also,' said the Tin Woodman, 'am well pleased with my new heart; and, really, that was the only thing I wished in all the world.'

'For my part, I am content in knowing I am as brave as any beast that ever lived, if not braver,' said the Lion, modestly.

'If Dorothy would only be contented to live in the Emerald City,' continued the Scarecrow, 'we might all be happy together.'

'But I don't want to live here,' cried Dorothy. 'I want to go to Kansas, and live with Aunt Em and Uncle Henry.'

'Well, then, what can be done?' enquired the Woodman.

The Scarecrow decided to think, and he thought so hard that the pins and needles began to stick out of his brains.

Finally he said: 'Why not call the Winged Monkeys, and ask them to carry you over the desert?'

'I never thought of that!" said Dorothy, joyfully. 'It's just the thing. I'll go at once for the Golden Cap.'

When she brought it into the Throne Room she spoke the magic words, and soon the band of Winged Monkeys flew in through the open window and stood beside her.

'This is the second time you have called us,' said the Monkey King, bowing before the little girl. 'What do you wish?'

'I want you to fly with me to Kansas,' said Dorothy.

But the Monkey King shook his head.

'That cannot be done,' he said. 'We belong to this country alone, and cannot leave it. There has never been a Winged Monkey in Kansas yet, and I suppose there never will be, for they don't belong there. We shall be glad to serve you in any way in our power, but we cannot cross the desert. Goodbye.'

And with another bow the Monkey King spread his wings and flew away through the window, followed by all his band.

Dorothy was almost ready to cry with disappointment.

'I have wasted the charm of the Golden Cap to no purpose,' she said, 'for the Winged Monkey cannot help me.'

'It is certainly too bad!' said the tender-hearted Woodman.

The Scarecrow was thinking again, and his head bulged out so horribly that Dorothy feared it would burst.

'Let us call in the soldier with the green whiskers,' he said, 'and ask his advice.'

So the soldier was summoned and entered the Throne Room timidly, for while Oz was alive he never was allowed to come farther than the door.

'This little girl,' said the Scarecrow to the soldier, 'wishes to cross the desert. How can she do so?'

'I cannot tell,' answered the soldier; 'for nobody has ever crossed the desert, unless it is Oz himself.'

'Is there no one who can help me?' asked Dorothy earnestly.

'Glinda might,' he suggested.

'Who is Glinda?' enquired the Scarecrow.

'The Witch of the South. She is the most powerful of all the Witches, and rules over the Quadlings. Besides, her castle stands on the edge of the desert, so she may know a way to cross it.'

'Glinda is a good Witch, isn't she?' asked the child.

'The Quadlings think she is good,' said the soldier, 'and she is kind to everyone. I have heard that Glinda is a beautiful woman, who knows how to keep young in spite of the many years she has lived.'

'How can I get to her castle?' asked Dorothy.

'The road is straight to the South,' he answered, 'but it is said to be full of dangers to travellers. There are wild beasts in the woods, and a race of queer men who do not like strangers to cross their country. For this reason none of the Quadlings ever come to the Emerald City.'

The soldier then left them and the Scarecrow said, 'It seems, in spite of dangers, that the best thing Dorothy can do is to travel to the Land of the South and ask Glinda to help her. For, of course, if Dorothy stays here she will never get back to Kansas.'

'You must have been thinking again,' remarked the Tin Woodman.

'I have,' said the Scarecrow.

'I shall go with Dorothy,' declared the Lion, 'for I am tired of your city and long for the woods and the country again. I am really a wild beast, you know. Besides, Dorothy will need someone to protect her.'

'That is true,' agreed the Woodman. 'My axe may be of service to her; so I, also, will go with her to the Land of the South.'

'When shall we start?' asked the Scarecrow.

'Are you going?' they asked, in surprise.

'Certainly. If it wasn't for Dorothy I should never have had brains. She lifted me from the pole in the cornfield and brought me to the Emerald City. So my good luck is all due to her, and I shall never leave her until she starts back to Kansas for good and all.'

'Thank you,' said Dorothy, gratefully. 'You are all very kind to me. But I should like to start as soon as possible.'

'We shall go tomorrow morning,' returned the Scarecrow. 'So now let us all get ready, for it will be a long journey.'

CHAPTER NINETEEN

Attacked by the Fighting Trees

The next morning Dorothy kissed the pretty green girl goodbye, and they all shook hands with the soldier with the green whiskers, who had walked with them as far as the gate. When the Guardian of the Gates saw them again he wondered greatly that they could leave the beautiful City to get into new trouble. But he at once unlocked their spectacles, which he put back into the green box, and gave them many good wishes to carry with them.

'You are now our ruler,' he said to the Scarecrow; 'so you must come back to us as soon as possible.'

'I certainly shall if I am able,' the Scarecrow replied; 'but I must help Dorothy to get home first.'

As Dorothy bade the good-natured Guardian a last farewell she said, 'I have been very kindly treated in your lovely

City, and everyone has been good to me. I cannot tell you how grateful I am.'

'Don't try my dear,' he answered. 'We should like to keep you with us, but if it is your wish to return to Kansas I hope you will find a way.' He then opened the gate of the outer wall and they walked forth and started upon their journey.

The sun shone brightly as our friends turned their faces towards the Land of the South. They were all in the best of spirits, and laughed and chatted together. Dorothy was once more filled with the hope of getting home, and the Scarecrow and the Tin Woodman were glad to be of use to her. As for the Lion, he sniffed the fresh air with delight and whisked his tail from side to side in pure joy at being in the country again, while Toto ran around them and chased the moths and butterflies, barking merrily all the time.

'City life does not agree with me at all,' remarked the Lion, as they walked along at a brisk pace. 'I have lost much flesh since I lived there, and now I am anxious for a chance to show the other beasts how courageous I have grown.'

They now turned and took a last look at the Emerald City. All they could see was a mass of towers and steeples behind the green walls, and high up above everything the spires and dome of the Palace of Oz.

'Oz was not such a bad Wizard, after all,' said the Tin Woodman, as he felt his heart rattling around in his breast.

'He knew how to give me brains, and very good brains, too,' said the Scarecrow.

'If Oz had taken a dose of the same courage he gave me,' added the Lion, 'he would have been a brave man.'

Dorothy said nothing. Oz had not kept the promise he made her but he had done his best, so she forgave him. As he said, he was a good man, even if he was a bad Wizard.

The first day's journey was through the green fields and bright flowers that stretched about the Emerald City on every side. They slept that night on the grass, with nothing but the stars over them; and they rested very well indeed.

In the morning they travelled on until they came to a thick wood. There was no way of going around it, for it seemed to extend to the right and left as far as they could see; and, besides, they did not dare change the direction of their journey for fear of getting lost. So they looked for the place where it would be easiest to get into the forest.

The Scarecrow, who was in the lead, finally discovered a big tree with such wide spreading branches that there was room for the party to pass underneath. So he walked forward to the tree, but just as he came under the first branches they bent down and twined around him, and the next minute he was raised from the ground and flung headlong among his fellow travellers.

This did not hurt the Scarecrow, but it surprised him, and he looked rather dizzy when Dorothy picked him up.

'Here is another space between the trees,' called the Lion.

'Let me try it first,' said the Scarecrow, 'for it doesn't hurt me to get thrown about.' He walked up to another tree, as he spoke, but its branches immediately seized him and tossed him back again.

'This is strange,' exclaimed Dorothy; 'what shall we do?'

'The trees seem to have made up their minds to fight us, and stop our journey,' remarked the Lion.

'I believe I will try it myself,' said the Woodman, and shouldering his axe he marched up to the first tree that had handled the Scarecrow so roughly. When a big branch bent down to seize him the Woodman chipped at it so fiercely that he cut it in two. At once the tree began shaking all its branches as if in pain, and the Tin Woodman passed safely under it.

'Come on!' he shouted to the others; 'be quick!'

They all ran forward and passed under the tree without injury, except Toto, who was caught by a small branch and shaken until he howled. But the Woodman promptly chopped off the branch and set the little dog free.

The other trees of the forest did nothing to keep them back, so they made up their minds that only the first row of trees could bend down their branches, and that probably these were the policemen of the forest, and given this wonderful power in order to keep strangers out of it.

The four travellers walked with ease through the trees until they came to the farther edge of the wood. Then, to their surprise, they found before them a high wall which seemed to be made of white china. It was smooth, like the surface of a dish, and higher than their heads.

'What shall we do now?' asked Dorothy.

'I will make a ladder,' said the Tin Woodman, 'for we certainly must climb over the wall.'

CHAPTER TWENTY

The Dainty China Country

W**hile** the Woodman was making a ladder from wood which he found in the forest Dorothy lay down and slept, for she was tired by the long walk. The Lion also curled himself up to sleep and Toto lay beside him.

The Scarecrow watched the Woodman while he worked, and said to him: 'I cannot think why this wall is here, nor what it is made of.'

'Rest your brains and do not worry about the wall,' replied the Woodman; 'when we have climbed over it we shall know what is on the other side.'

After a time the ladder was finished. It looked clumsy, but the Tin Woodman was sure it was strong and would answer their purpose. The Scarecrow waked Dorothy and the Lion and Toto, and told them that the ladder was ready. The Scarecrow climbed up the ladder first, but he was so awkward that Dorothy had to follow close behind and keep him from falling off.

When he got his head over the top of the wall the Scarecrow said, 'Oh, my!'

'Go on,' exclaimed Dorothy.

So the Scarecrow climbed farther up and sat down on the top of the wall, and Dorothy put her head over and cried, 'Oh, my!' just as the Scarecrow had done.

Then Toto came up, and immediately began to bark but Dorothy made him be still.

The Lion climbed the ladder next, and the Tin Woodman came last; but both of them cried, 'Oh, my!' as soon as they looked over the wall. When they were all sitting in a row on the top of the wall they looked down and saw a strange sight.

Before them was a great stretch of country having a floor as smooth and shining and white as the bottom of a big platter. Scattered around were many houses made entirely of china and painted in the brightest colours. These houses were quite small, the biggest of them reaching only as high as Dorothy's waist. There were also pretty little farms, with china fences round them; and many cows and sheep and horses and pigs and chickens, all made of china, were standing about in groups.

But the strangest of all were the people who lived in this queer country. There were milkmaids and shepherdesses, with bright-coloured bodices and golden spots all over their gowns; and princesses with most gorgeous frocks of silver and gold and purple; and shepherds dressed in knee-breeches with pink and yellow and blue stripes down them, and golden buckles on their shoes; and princes with jewelled crowns upon their heads, wearing ermine robes and satin doublets, and funny clowns in ruffled gowns, with round red spots upon their cheeks and tall, pointed caps. And, strangest of

They were all made of china

all, these people were all made of china, even to their clothes, and were so small that the tallest of them was no higher than Dorothy's knee.

No one did so much as look at the travellers at first, except one little china dog with an extra-large head, which came to the wall and barked at them in a tiny voice, afterward running away again.

'How shall we get down?' asked Dorothy.

They found the ladder so heavy they could not pull it up, so the Scarecrow fell off the wall and the others jumped down upon him so that the hard floor would not hurt their feet. Of course they took pains not to light on his head and get the pins in their feet. When all were safely down they picked up the Scarecrow, whose body was quite flattened out, and patted his straw into shape again.

'We must cross this strange place in order to get to the other side,' said Dorothy; 'for it would be unwise for us to go any other way except due South.'

They began walking through the country of the china people, and the first thing they came to was a china milk-maid milking a china cow. As they drew near the cow suddenly gave a kick and kicked over the stool, the pail, and even the milkmaid herself, all falling on the china ground with a great clatter.

Dorothy was shocked to see that the cow had broken her leg short off, and that the pail was lying in several small pieces, while the poor milkmaid had a nick in her left elbow.

'There!' cried the milkmaid, angrily; 'see what you have done! My cow has broken her leg, and I must take her to the mender's shop and have it glued on again. What do you mean by coming here and frightening my cow?'

'I'm very sorry,' returned Dorothy; 'please forgive us.'

But the pretty milkmaid was much too vexed to make any answer. She picked up the leg sulkily and led her cow away, the poor animal limping on three legs. As she left them the milkmaid cast many reproachful glance over her shoulder at the clumsy strangers, holding her nicked elbow close to her side.

Dorothy was quite grieved at this mishap.

'We must be very careful here,' said the kind-hearted Woodman, 'or we may hurt these pretty little people so they will never get over it.'

A little farther on Dorothy met a most beautifully dressed young princess, who stopped short as she saw the strangers and started to run away.

Dorothy wanted to see more of the Princess, so she ran after her; but the china girl cried out, 'Don't chase me! don't chase me!'

She had such a frightened little voice that Dorothy stopped and said, 'Why not?'

'Because,' answered the Princess, also stopping a safe distance away, 'if I run I may fall down and break myself.'

'But could you not be mended?' asked the girl.

'Oh, yes; but one is never so pretty after being mended, you know,' replied the Princess.

'I suppose not,' said Dorothy.

'Now there is Mr Joker, one of our clowns,' continued the china lady, 'who is always trying to stand upon his head. He has broken himself so often that he is mended in a hundred places, and doesn't look at all pretty. Here he comes now, so you can see for yourself.'

Indeed, a jolly little clown now came walking towards them, and Dorothy could see that in spite of his pretty clothes of red and yellow and green he was completely covered with cracks, running every way and showing plainly that he had been mended in many places.

The Clown put his hands in his pockets, and after puffing out his cheeks and nodding his head at them saucily he said,

'My lady fair,
Why do you stare
At poor old Mr Joker?
You're quite as stiff
And prim as if
You'd eaten up a poker!'

'Be quiet, sir!' said the Princess; 'can't you see these are strangers, and should be treated with respect?'

'Well, that's respect, I expect,' declared the Clown, and immediately stood upon his head.

'Don't mind Mr Joker,' said the Princess to Dorothy; 'he is considerably cracked in his head, and that makes him foolish.'

'Oh, I don't mind him a bit,' said Dorothy. 'But you are so beautiful,' she continued, 'that I am sure I could love you dearly. Won't you let me carry you back to Kansas, and stand you on Aunt Em's mantelshelf? I could carry you in my basket.'

'That would make me very unhappy,' answered the china Princess. 'You see, here in our country we live contentedly, and can talk and move around as we please. But whenever any of us are taken away our joints at once stiffen, and we can only stand straight and look pretty. Of course that is all that is expected of us when we are on mantelshelves and cabinets and drawing-room tables, but our lives are much pleasanter here in our own country.'

'I would not make you unhappy for all the world!' exclaimed Dorothy; 'so I'll just say goodbye.'

'Goodbye,' replied the Princess.

They walked carefully through the china country. The little animals and all the people scampered out of their way, fearing the strangers would break them, and after an hour or so the travellers reached the other side of the country and came to another china wall.

It was not so high as the first, however, and by standing upon the Lion's back they all managed to scramble to the top. Then the Lion gathered his legs under him and jumped on the wall; but just as he jumped he upset a china church with his tail and smashed it all to pieces.

'That was too bad,' said Dorothy, 'but really I think we were lucky in not doing these little people more harm than breaking a cow's leg and a church. They are all so brittle!'

'They are, indeed,' said the Scarecrow, 'and I am thankful I am made of straw and cannot be easily damaged. There are worse things in the world than being a Scarecrow.'

CHAPTER TWENTY-ONE

The Lion Becomes the   King of Beasts

After climbing down from the china wall the travellers found themselves in a disagreeable country, full of bogs and marshes and covered with tall, rank grass. It was difficult to walk without falling into muddy holes, for the grass was so thick that it hid them from sight. However, by carefully picking their way, they got safely along until they reached solid ground. But here the country seemed wilder than ever, and after a long and tiresome walk through the underbush they entered another forest, where the trees were bigger and older than any they had ever seen.

'This forest is perfectly delightful,' declared the Lion, looking around him with joy; 'never have I seen a more beautiful place.'

'It seems gloomy,' said the Scarecrow.

'Not a bit of it,' answered the Lion; 'I should like to live here all my life. See how soft the dried leaves are under your feet and how rich and green the moss is that clings to these old trees. Surely no wild beast could wish a pleasanter home.'

'Perhaps there are wild beasts in the forest now,' said Dorothy.

'I suppose there are,' returned the Lion; 'but I do not see any of them about.'

They walked through the forest until it became too dark to go any farther. Dorothy and Toto and the Lion lay down to sleep, while the Woodman and the Scarecrow kept watch over them as usual.

When morning came they started again. Before they had gone far they heard a low rumble, as of the growling of many wild animals. Toto whimpered a little but none of the others was frightened and they kept along the well-trodden path until they came to an opening in the wood, in which were gathered hundreds of beasts of every variety. There were tigers and elephants and bears and wolves and foxes and all the others in the natural history, and for a moment Dorothy was afraid. But the Lion explained that the animals were holding a meeting, and he judged by their snarling and growling that they were in great trouble.

As he spoke several of the beasts caught sight of him, and at once the great assemblage hushed as if by magic. The biggest of the tigers came up to the Lion and bowed, saying, 'Welcome, O King of Beasts! You have come in good time to fight our enemy and bring peace to all the animals of the forest once more.'

'What is your trouble?' asked the Lion, quietly.

'We are all threatened,' answered the tiger, 'by a fierce enemy which has lately come into this forest. It is a most tremendous monster, like a great spider, with a body as big as an elephant and legs as long as a tree trunk. It has eight of these long legs, and as the monster crawls through the forest he seizes an animal with a leg and drags it to his mouth, where he eats it as a spider does a fly. Not one of us is safe while this fierce creature is alive, and we had called a meeting to decide how to take care of ourselves when you came among us.'

The Lion thought for a moment.

'Are there any other lions in this forest?' he asked.

'No; there were some, but the monster has eaten them all. And, besides, they were none of them nearly so large and brave as you.'

'If I put an end to your enemy will you bow down to me and obey me as King of the Forest?' enquired the Lion.

'We will do that gladly,' returned the tiger; and all the other beasts roared with a mighty roar: 'We will!'

'Where is this great spider of yours now?' asked the Lion.

'Yonder, among the oak trees,' said the tiger, pointing with his forefoot.

'Take good care of these friends of mine,' said the Lion, 'and I will go at once to fight the monster.'

He bade his comrades goodbye and marched proudly away to do battle with the enemy.

The great spider was lying asleep when the Lion found him, and it looked so ugly that its foe turned up his nose in disgust. Its legs were quite as long as the tiger had said, and its body covered with coarse black hair. It had a great mouth, with a row of sharp teeth a foot long; but its head was joined to the pudgy body by a neck as slender as a wasp's waist. This gave the Lion a hint of the best way to attack the creature, and as he knew it was easier to fight it asleep than awake, he gave a great spring and landed directly upon the monster's back. Then, with one blow of his heavy paw, all armed with sharp claws, he knocked the spider's head from its body. Jumping down, he watched it until the long legs stopped wriggling, when he knew it was quite dead.

The Lion went back to the opening where the beasts of the forest were waiting for him and said, proudly, 'You need fear your enemy no longer.'

Then the beasts bowed down to the Lion as their King, and he promised to come back and rule over them as soon as Dorothy was safely on her way to Kansas.

CHAPTER TWENTY-TWO

The Country of the Quadlings

The four travellers passed through the rest of the forest in safety, and when they came out from its gloom saw before them a steep hill, covered from top to bottom with great pieces of rock.

'That will be a hard climb,' said the Scarecrow, 'but we must get over the hill, nevertheless.'

So he led the way and the others followed. They had nearly reached the first rock when they heard a rough voice cry out, 'Keep back!'

'Who are you?' asked the Scarecrow.

Then a head showed itself over the rock and the same voice said, 'This hill belongs to us, and we don't allow anyone to cross it.'

'But we must cross it,' said the Scarecrow. 'We're going to the country of the Quadlings.'

'But you shall not!' replied the voice, and there stepped from behind the rock the strangest man the travellers had ever seen.

He was quite short and stout and had a big head, which was flat at the top and supported by a thick neck full of wrinkles. But he had no arms at all, and, seeing this, the Scarecrow did not fear that so helpless a creature could prevent them from climbing the hill.

So he said, 'I'm sorry not to do as you wish, but we must pass over your hill whether you like it or not,' and he walked boldly forward.

As quick as lightning the man's head shot forward and his neck stretched out until the top of the head, where it was flat, struck the Scarecrow in the middle and sent him tumbling, over and over, down the hill. Almost as quickly as it came the head went back to the body, and the man laughed harshly as he said, 'It isn't as easy as you think!'

A chorus of boisterous laughter came from the other rocks, and Dorothy saw hundreds of the armless Hammer-Heads upon the hillside, one behind every rock.

The Lion became quite angry at the laughter caused by the Scarecrow's mishap, and giving a loud roar that echoed like thunder he dashed up the hill.

Again a head shot swiftly out, and the great Lion went rolling down the hill as if he had been struck by a cannon ball.

Dorothy ran down and helped the Scarecrow to his feet, and the Lion came up to her, feeling rather bruised and sore, and said, 'It is useless to fight people with shooting heads; no one can withstand them.'

'What can we do, then?' she asked.

'Call the Winged Monkeys,' suggested the Tin Woodman; 'you have still the right to command them once more.'

'Very well,' she answered, and putting on the Golden Cap she uttered the magic words. The Monkeys were as prompt as ever, and in a few moments the entire band stood before her.

'What are your commands?' enquired the King of the Monkeys, bowing low.

'Carry us over the hill to the country of the Quadlings,' answered the girl.

'It shall be done,' said the King, and at once the Winged Monkeys caught the four travellers and Toto up in their arms and flew away with them. As they passed over the hill the Hammer-Heads yelled with vexation, and shot their heads high in the air but they could not reach the Winged Monkeys, which carried Dorothy and her comrades safely over the hill and set them down in the beautiful country of the Quadlings.

'This is the last time you can summon us,' said the leader to Dorothy; 'so goodbye and good luck to you.'

'Goodbye, and thank you very much,' returned the girl; and the Monkeys rose into the air and were out of sight in a twinkling.

The country of the Quadlings seemed rich and happy. There was field upon field of ripening grain, with well-paved roads running between, and pretty rippling brooks with strong bridges across them. The fences and houses and bridges were all painted bright red, just as they had been painted yellow in the country of the Winkies and blue in the country of the Munchkins. The Quadlings themselves, who were short and fat and looked chubby and good natured, were dressed all in red, which showed bright against the green grass and the yellowing grain.

The Monkeys had set them down near a farmhouse, and the four travellers walked up to it and knocked at the door. It was opened by the farmer's wife, and when Dorothy asked for something to eat the woman gave them all a good dinner, with three kinds of cake and four kinds of cookies, and a bowl of milk for Toto.

'How far is it to the Castle of Glinda?' asked the child.

'It is not a great way,' answered the farmer's wife. 'Take the road to the South and you will soon reach it.'

Thanking the good woman, they started afresh and walked by the fields and across the pretty bridges until they saw before them a very beautiful Castle. Before the gates were three young girls, dressed in handsome red uniforms trimmed with gold braid; and as Dorothy approached one of them said to her, 'Why have you come to the South Country?'

'To see the Good Witch who rules here,' she answered. 'Will you take me to her?'

'Let me have your name and I will ask Glinda if she will receive you.' They told who they were, and the girl soldier went into the Castle. After a few moments she came back to say that Dorothy and the others were to be admitted at once.

CHAPTER TWENTY-THREE

The Good Witch Grants Dorothy's Wish

Before they went to see Glinda, however, they were taken to a room of the Castle, where Dorothy washed her face and combed her hair, and the Lion shook the dust out of his mane, and the Scarecrow patted himself into his best shape, and the Woodman polished his tin and oiled his joints.

When they were all quite presentable they followed the soldier girl into a big room where the Witch Glinda sat upon a throne of rubies.

She was both beautiful and young to their eyes. Her hair was a rich red in colour and fell in flowing ringlets over her shoulders. Her dress was pure white but her eyes were blue, and they looked kindly upon the little girl.

'What can I do for you, my child?' she asked.

Dorothy told the Witch all her story: how the cyclone had brought her to the Land of Oz, how she had found her companions, and of the wonderful adventures they had met with.

'My greatest wish now,' she added, 'is to get back to Kansas, for Aunt Em will surely think something dreadful has happened to me, and that will make her put on mourning; and unless the crops are better this year than they were last I am sure Uncle Henry cannot afford it.'

Glinda leaned forward and kissed the sweet, upturned face of the loving little girl.

'Bless your dear heart,' she said, 'I am sure I can tell you of a way to get back to Kansas.' Then she added: 'But, if I do, you must give me the Golden Cap.'

'Willingly!' exclaimed Dorothy; 'indeed, it is of no use to me now, and when you have it you can command the Winged Monkeys three times.'

'And I think I shall need their service just those three times,' answered Glinda, smiling.

Dorothy then gave her the Golden Cap, and the Witch said to the Scarecrow, 'What will you do when Dorothy has left us?'

'I will return to the Emerald City,' he replied, 'for Oz has made me its ruler and the people like me. The only thing that worries me is how to cross the hill of the Hammer-Heads.'

'By means of the Golden Cap I shall command the Winged Monkeys to carry you to the gates of the Emerald City,' said Glinda, 'for it would be a shame to deprive the people of so wonderful a ruler.'

'Am I really wonderful?' asked the Scarecrow.

'You are unusual,' replied Glinda.

Turning to the Tin Woodman, she asked: 'What will become of you when Dorothy leaves this country?'

He leaned on his axe and thought a moment. Then he said, 'The Winkies were very kind to me, and wanted me to rule over them after the Wicked Witch died. I am fond of the Winkies, and if I could get back again to the country of the West I should like nothing better than to rule over them for ever.'

'My second command to the Winged Monkeys,' said Glinda, 'will be that they carry you safely to the land of the Winkies. Your brain may not be so large to look at as that of the Scarecrow, but you are really brighter than he is – when you are well polished – and I am sure you will rule the Winkies wisely and well.'

Then the Witch looked at the big, shaggy Lion and asked, 'When Dorothy has returned to her own home, what will become of you?'

'Over the hill of the Hammer-Heads,' he answered, 'lies a grand old forest, and all the beasts that live there have made me their King. If I could only get back to this forest I would pass my life very happily there.'

'My third command to the Winged Monkeys,' said Glinda, 'shall be to carry you to your forest. Then, having used up the powers of the Golden Cap, I shall give it to the King of the Monkeys, that he and his band may thereafter be free for evermore.'

The Scarecrow and the Tin Woodman and the Lion now thanked the Good Witch earnestly for her kindness, and Dorothy exclaimed, 'You are certainly as good as you are beautiful! But you have not yet told me how to get back to Kansas.'

'Your Silver Shoes will carry you over the desert,' replied Glinda. 'If you had known their power you could have gone back to your Aunt Em the very first day you came to this country.'

'But then I should not have had my wonderful brains!' cried the Scarecrow. 'I might have passed my whole life in the farmer's cornfield.'

'And I should not have had my lovely heart,' said the Tin Woodman. 'I might have stood and rusted in the forest till the end of the world.'

'And I should have lived a coward for ever,' declared the Lion, 'and no beast in all the forest would have had a good word to say to me.'

'This is all true,' said Dorothy, 'and I am glad I was of use to these good friends. But now that each of them has had what he most desired, and each is happy in having a kingdom to rule beside, I think I should like to go back to Kansas.'

'The Silver Shoes,' said the Good Witch, 'have wonderful powers. And one of the most curious things about them is that they can carry you to any place in the world in three steps, and each step will be made in the wink of an eye.

All you have to do is to knock the heels together three times and command the shoes to carry you wherever you wish to go.'

'If that is so,' said the child, joyfully, 'I will ask them to carry me back to Kansas at once.'

She threw her arms around the Lion's neck and kissed him, patting his big head tenderly. Then she kissed the Tin Woodman, who was weeping in a way most dangerous to his joints. But she hugged the soft, stuffed body of the Scarecrow in her arms instead of kissing his painted face and found she was crying herself at the sorrowful parting from her loving comrades.

Glinda the Good stepped down from her ruby throne to give the little girl a goodbye kiss, and Dorothy thanked her for all the kindness she had shown to her friends and herself.

Dorothy now took Toto up solemnly in her arms, and having said one last goodbye she clapped the heels of her shoes together three times, saying, 'Take me home to Aunt Em!'

*   *   *

Instantly she was whirling through the air, so swiftly that all she could see or feel was the wind whistling past her ears.

The Silver Shoes took but three steps, and then she stopped so suddenly that she rolled over upon the grass several times before she knew where she was.

At length, however, she sat up and looked about her.

'Good gracious!' she cried

For she was sitting on the broad Kansas prairie, and just before her was the new farmhouse Uncle Henry built after the cyclone had carried away the old one. Uncle Henry was milking the cows in the barnyard, and Toto had jumped out of her arms and was running towards the barn, barking joyously.

Dorothy stood up and found she was in her stocking-feet. For the Silver Shoes had fallen off in her flight through the air, and were lost for ever in the desert.

CHAPTER TWENTY-FOUR

Home Again

AUNT EM had just come out of the house to water the cabbages when she looked up and saw Dorothy running towards her.

'My darling child!' she cried, folding the little girl in her arms and covering her face with kisses; 'where in the world did you come from?'

'From the land of Oz,' said Dorothy, gravely. 'And here is Toto, too. And oh, Aunt Em, I'm so glad to be at home again!'

Glinda of Oz

In which are related the Exciting Experiences of Princess
Ozma of Oz and Dorothy in their hazardous journey
to the home of the Flatheads and to the Magic Isle
of the Skeezers, and how they were rescued
from dire peril by the sorcery of
Glinda the Good

This book is dedicated to my son
ROBERT STANTON BAUM

CONTENTS

CHAPTER ONE

The Call to Duty

GLINDA, THE GOOD SORCERESS OF OZ,

sat in the grand court of her palace, surrounded by her maids of honour – a hundred of the most beautiful girls of the Fairyland of Oz. The palace court was built of rare marbles, exquisitely polished. Fountains tinkled musically here and there; the vast colonnade, open to the south, allowed the maidens, as they raised their heads from their embroideries, to gaze upon a vista of rose-hued fields and groves of trees bearing fruits or laden with sweet-scented flowers. At times one of the girls would start a song, the others joining in the chorus, or one would rise and dance, gracefully swaying to the music of a harp played by a companion. And then Glinda smiled, glad to see her maids mixing play with work.

Presently among the fields an object was seen moving, threading the broad path that led to the castle gate. Some of the girls looked upon this object enviously; the Sorceress merely gave it a glance and nodded her stately head as if pleased, for it meant the coming of her friend and mistress – the only one in all the land that Glinda bowed to.

Then up the path trotted a wooden animal attached to a red wagon, and as the quaint steed halted at the gate there descended from the wagon two young girls, Ozma, Ruler of Oz, and her companion, Princess Dorothy. Both were dressed in simple white muslin gowns, and as they ran up the marble steps of the palace they laughed and chatted as gaily as if they were not the most important persons in the world's loveliest fairyland.

The maids of honour had risen and stood with bowed heads to greet the royal Ozma, while Glinda came forward with outstretched arms to greet her guests.

'We've just come on a visit, you know,' said Ozma. 'Both Dorothy and I were wondering how we should pass the day when we happened to think we'd not been to your Quadling Country for weeks, so we took the Sawhorse and rode straight here.'

'And we came so fast,' added Dorothy, 'that our hair is blown all fuzzy, for the Sawhorse makes a wind of his own. Usually it's a day's journey from the Em'rald City, but I don't s'pose we were two hours on the way.'

'You are most welcome,' said Glinda the Sorceress, and led them through the court to her magnificent reception hall. Ozma took the arm of her hostess, but Dorothy lagged behind, kissing some of the maids she knew best, talking with others, and making them all feel that she was their friend. When at last she joined Glinda and Ozma in the reception hall, she found them talking earnestly about the condition of the people, and how to make them more happy and contented – although they were already the happiest and most contented folks in all the world.

This interested Ozma, of course, but it didn't interest Dorothy very much, so the little girl ran over to a big table on which was lying open Glinda's *Great Book of Records*.

This book is one of the greatest treasures in Oz, and the Sorceress prizes it more highly than any of her magical possessions. That is the reason it is firmly attached to the big marble table by means of golden chains, and whenever Glinda leaves home she locks the *Great Book* together with five jewelled padlocks, and carries the keys safely hidden in her bosom.

I do not suppose there is any magical thing in any fairyland to compare with the *Great Book of Records*, on the pages of which are constantly being printed a record of every event that happens in any part of the world, at exactly the moment it happens. And the records are always truthful, although sometimes they do not give as many details as one could wish. But then, lots of things happen, and so the records have to be brief or even Glinda's *Great Book* could not hold them all.

Glinda looked at the records several times each day, and Dorothy, whenever she visited the Sorceress, loved to look in the book and see what was happening everywhere. Not much was recorded about the Land of Oz, which is usually peaceful and uneventful, but today Dorothy found something which interested her. Indeed, the printed letters were appearing on the page even while she looked.

'This is funny!' she exclaimed. 'Did you know, Ozma, that there were people in your Land of Oz called Skeezers?'

'Yes,' replied Ozma, coming to her side, 'I know that on Professor Wogglebug's map of the Land of Oz there is a place marked "Skeezer", but what the Skeezers are like I do not know. No one I know has ever seen them or heard of them. The Skeezer Country is 'way at the upper edge of the Gillikin Country, with the sandy, impassable desert on one side and the mountains of Oogaboo on another side. That is a part of the Land of Oz of which I know very little.'

'I guess no one else knows much about it either, unless it's the Skeezers themselves,' remarked Dorothy. 'But the book says: "The Skeezers of Oz have declared war on the Flatheads of Oz, and there is likely to be fighting and much trouble as the result." '

'Is that all the book says?' asked Ozma.

'Every word,' said Dorothy, and Ozma and Glinda both looked at the record and seemed surprised and perplexed.

'Tell me, Glinda,' said Ozma, 'who are the Flatheads?'

'I cannot, your Majesty,' confessed the Sorceress. 'Until

now I never have heard of them, nor have I ever heard the Skeezers mentioned. In the faraway corners of Oz are hidden many curious tribes of people, and those who never leave their own countries and never are visited by those from our favoured part of Oz, naturally are unknown to me. However, if you so desire, I can learn through my arts of sorcery something of the Skeezers and the Flatheads.'

'I wish you would,' answered Ozma seriously. 'You see, Glinda, if these are Oz people they are my subjects and I cannot allow any wars or troubles in the land I rule, if I can possibly help it.'

'Very well, your Majesty,' said the Sorceress, 'I will try to get some information to guide you. Please excuse me for a time, while I retire to my Room of Magic and Sorcery.'

'May I go with you?' asked Dorothy, eagerly.

'No, Princess,' was the reply. 'It would spoil the charm to have anyone present.'

So Glinda locked herself in her own Room of Magic and Dorothy and Ozma waited patiently for her to come out again.

In about an hour Glinda appeared, looking grave and thoughtful.

'Your Majesty,' she said to Ozma, 'the Skeezers live on a Magic Isle in a great lake. For that reason – because the Skeezers deal in magic – I can learn little about them.'

'Why, I didn't know there was a lake in that part of Oz,' exclaimed Ozma. 'The map shows a river running through the Skeezer Country, but no lake.'

'That is because the person who made the map never had visited that part of the country,' explained the Sorceress. 'The lake surely is there, and in the lake is an island – a Magic Isle – and on that island live the people called the Skeezers.'

'What are they like?' enquired the Ruler of Oz.

'My magic cannot tell me that,' confessed Glinda, 'for the

magic of the Skeezers prevents anyone outside their domain knowing anything about them.'

'The Flatheads must know, if they're going to fight the Skeezers,' suggested Dorothy.

'Perhaps so,' Glinda replied, 'but I can get little information concerning the Flatheads, either. They are people who inhabit a mountain just south of the Lake of the Skeezers. The mountain has steep sides and a broad, hollow top, like a basin, and in this basin the Flatheads have their dwellings. They also are magic-workers and usually keep to themselves and allow no one from outside to visit them. I have learned that the Flatheads number about one hundred people – men, women and children – while the Skeezers number just one hundred and one.'

'What did they quarrel about, and why do they wish to fight one another?' was Ozma's next question.

'I cannot tell your Majesty that,' said Glinda.

'But see here!' cried Dorothy, 'it's against the law for anyone but Glinda and the Wizard to work magic in the Land of Oz, so if these two strange people are magic-makers they are breaking the law and ought to be punished!' Ozma smiled upon her little friend.

'Those who do not know me or my laws,' she said, 'cannot be expected to obey my laws. If we know nothing of the Skeezers or the Flatheads, it is likely that they know nothing of us.'

'But they *ought* to know, Ozma, and we ought to know. Who's going to tell them, and how are we going to make them behave?'

'That,' returned Ozma, 'is what I am now considering. What would you advise, Glinda?'

The Sorceress took a little time to consider this question, before she made reply. Then she said: 'Had you not learned of the existence of the Flatheads and the Skeezers, through my *Book of Records*, you would never have worried about them or their quarrels. So, if you pay no attention to these peoples, you may never hear of them again.'

'But that wouldn't be right,' declared Ozma. 'I am Ruler of all the Land of Oz, which includes the Gillikin Country, the Quadling Country, the Winkie Country and the Munchkin Country, as well as the Emerald City, and being the Princess of this fairyland it is my duty to make all my people – wherever they may be – happy and content and to settle their disputes and keep them from quarrelling. So, while the Skeezers and Flatheads may not know me or that I am their lawful Ruler, I now know that they inhabit my kingdom and are my subjects, so I would not be doing my duty if I kept away from them and allowed them to fight.'

'That's a fact, Ozma,' commented Dorothy. 'You've got to go up to the Gillikin Country and make these people behave themselves and make up their quarrels. But how are you going to do it?'

'That is what is puzzling me also, your Majesty,' said the Sorceress. 'It may be dangerous for you to go into those strange countries, where the people are possibly fierce and warlike.'

'I am not afraid,' said Ozma, with a smile.

' 'Tisn't a question of being 'fraid,' argued Dorothy. 'Of course we know you're a fairy, and can't be killed or hurt, and we know you've a lot of magic of your own to help you. But, Ozma dear, in spite of all this you've been in trouble before, on account of wicked enemies, and it isn't right for the Ruler of all Oz to put herself in danger.'

'Perhaps I shall be in no danger at all,' returned Ozma, with a little laugh. 'You mustn't *imagine* danger, Dorothy, for one should only imagine nice things, and we do not know that the Skeezers and Flatheads are wicked people or my enemies. Perhaps they would be good and listen to reason.'

'Dorothy is right, your Majesty,' asserted the Sorceress.

'It is true we know nothing of these faraway subjects, except that they intend to fight one another, and have a certain amount of magic power at their command. Such folks do not like to submit to interference and they are more likely to resent your coming among them than to receive you kindly and graciously, as is your due.'

'If you had an army to take with you,' added Dorothy, 'it wouldn't be so bad; but there isn't such a thing as an army in all Oz.'

'I have one soldier,' said Ozma.

'Yes, the soldier with the green whiskers; but he's dreadful 'fraid of his gun and never loads it. I'm sure he'd run rather than fight. And one soldier, even if he were brave, couldn't do much against two hundred and one Flatheads and Skeezers.'

'What then, my friends, would you suggest?' enquired Ozma.

'I advise you to send the Wizard of Oz to them, and let him inform them that it is against the laws of Oz to fight, and that you command them to settle their differences and become friends,' proposed Glinda. 'Let the Wizard tell them they will be punished if they refuse to obey the commands of the Princess of all the Land of Oz.'

Ozma shook her head, to indicate that the advice was not to her satisfaction.

'If they refuse, what then?' she asked. 'I should be obliged to carry out my threat and punish them, and that would be an unpleasant and difficult thing to do. I am sure it would be better for me to go peacefully, without an army and armed only with my authority as Ruler, and plead with them to obey me. Then, if they prove obstinate I could resort to other means to win their obedience.'

'It's a ticklish thing, anyhow you look at it,' sighed Dorothy. 'I'm sorry now that I noticed the record in the *Great Book*.'

'But can't you realise, my dear, that I must do my duty, now that I am aware of this trouble?' asked Ozma. 'I am fully determined to go at once to the Magic Isle of the Skeezers and to the enchanted mountain of the Flatheads, and prevent war and strife between their inhabitants. The only question to decide is whether it is better for me to go alone or to assemble a party of my friends and loyal supporters to accompany me.'

'If you go I want to go, too,' declared Dorothy. 'Whatever happens it's going to be fun – 'cause all excitement is fun – and I wouldn't miss it for the world!'

Neither Ozma nor Glinda paid any attention to this statement, for they were gravely considering the serious aspect of this proposed adventure.

'There are plenty of friends who would like to go with you,' said the Sorceress, 'but none of them would afford your Majesty any protection in case you were in danger. You are yourself the most powerful fairy in Oz, although both I and the Wizard have more varied arts of magic at our command. However, you have one art that no other in all the world can equal – the art of winning hearts and making people love to bow to your gracious presence. For that reason I believe you can accomplish more good alone than with a large number of subjects in your train.'

'I believe that also,' agreed the Princess. 'I shall be quite able to take care of myself, you know, but might not be able to protect others so well. I do not look for opposition, however. I shall speak to these people in kindly words and settle their dispute – whatever it may be – in a just manner.'

'Aren't you going to take *me*?' pleaded Dorothy. 'You'll need *some* companion, Ozma.'

The Princess smiled upon her little friend.

'I see no reason why you should not accompany me,' was her reply. 'Two girls are not very warlike and they will not suspect us of being on any errand but a kindly and peaceful one. But, in order to prevent war and strife between these angry peoples, we must go to them at once. Let us return immediately to the Emerald City and prepare to start on our journey early tomorrow morning.'

Glinda was not quite satisfied with this plan, but could not think of any better way to meet the problem. She knew that Ozma, with all her gentleness and sweet disposition, was accustomed to abide by any decision she had made and could not easily be turned from her purpose. Moreover she could see no great danger to the fairy Ruler of Oz in the undertaking, even though the unknown people she was to visit proved obstinate. But Dorothy was not a fairy; she was a little girl who had come from Kansas to live in the Land of Oz. Dorothy might encounter dangers that to Ozma would be as nothing but to an 'Earth child' would be very serious.

The very fact that Dorothy lived in Oz, and had been made a Princess by her friend Ozma, prevented her from being killed or suffering any great bodily pain as long as she lived in that fairyland. She could not grow big, either, and would always remain the same little girl who had come to Oz, unless in some way she left that fairyland or was spirited away from it. But Dorothy was a mortal, nevertheless, and might possibly be destroyed, or hidden where none of her friends could ever find her. She could, for instance be cut into pieces, and the pieces, while still alive and free from pain, could be widely scattered; or she might be buried deep underground or 'destroyed' in other ways by evil magicians, were she not properly protected. These facts Glinda was considering while she paced with stately tread her marble hall.

Finally the good Sorceress paused and drew a ring from her finger, handing it to Dorothy.

'Wear this ring constantly until your return,' she said to the girl. 'If serious danger threatens you, turn the ring around on your finger once to the right and another turn to the left. That will ring the alarm bell in my palace and I will at once come to your rescue. But do not use the ring unless you are actually in danger of destruction. While you remain with Princess Ozma I believe she will be able to protect you from all lesser ills.'

'Thank you, Glinda,' responded Dorothy gratefully, as she placed the ring on her finger. 'I'm going to wear my Magic Belt which I took from the Nome King, too, so I guess I'll be safe from anything the Skeezers and Flatheads try to do to me.'

Ozma had many arrangements to make before she could leave her throne and her palace in the Emerald City, even for a trip of a few days, so she bade goodbye to Glinda and with Dorothy climbed into the Red Wagon. A word to the wooden Sawhorse started that astonishing creature on the return journey, and so swiftly did he run that Dorothy was unable to talk or do anything but hold tight to her seat all the way back to the Emerald City.

CHAPTER TWO

Ozma and Dorothy

RESIDING IN OZMA'S PALACE AT THIS time was a live Scarecrow, a most remarkable and intelligent creature who had once ruled the Land of Oz for a brief period and was much loved and respected by all the people. Once a Munchkin farmer had stuffed an old suit of clothes with straw and put stuffed boots on the feet and used a pair of stuffed cotton gloves for hands. The head of the Scarecrow was a stuffed sack fastened to the body, with eyes, nose, mouth and ears painted on the sack. When a hat had been put on the head, the thing was a good imitation of a man. The farmer placed the Scarecrow on a pole in his cornfield and it came to life in a curious manner. Dorothy, who was passing by the field, was hailed by the live Scarecrow and lifted him off his pole. He then went with her to the Emerald City, where the Wizard of Oz gave him some excellent brains, and the Scarecrow soon became an important personage.

Ozma considered the Scarecrow one of her best friends and most loyal subjects, so the morning after her visit to Glinda she asked him to take her place as Ruler of the Land of Oz while she was absent on a journey, and the Scarecrow at once consented without asking any questions.

Ozma had warned Dorothy to keep their journey a secret and say nothing to anyone about the Skeezers and Flatheads until their return, and Dorothy promised to obey. She longed to tell her girl friends, Tiny Trot and Betsy Bobbin, of the adventure they were undertaking, but refrained from saying a word on the subject although both these girls lived with her in Ozma's palace.

Indeed, only Glinda the Sorceress knew they were going, and even she didn't know what their errand might be.

Princess Ozma took the Sawhorse and the Red Wagon, although she was not sure there was a wagon road all the way to the Lake of the Skeezers. The Land of Oz is a pretty big place, surrounded on all sides by a Deadly Desert which it is impossible to cross, and the Skeezer Country, according to the map, was in the farthest northwestern part of Oz, bordering on the north desert. As the Emerald City was exactly in the centre of Oz, it was no small journey from there to the Skeezers.

Around the Emerald City the country is thickly settled in every direction, but the farther away you get from the city the fewer people there are, until those parts that border on the desert have small populations. Also those faraway sections are little known to the Oz people, except in the south, where Glinda lives and where Dorothy has often wandered on trips of exploration.

The least known of all is the Gillikin Country, which harbours many strange bands of people among its mountains and valleys and forests and streams, and Ozma was now bound for the most distant part of the Gillikin Country.

'I am really sorry,' said Ozma to Dorothy, as they rode away in the Red Wagon, 'not to know more about the wonderful land I rule. It is my duty to be acquainted with every tribe of people and every strange and hidden country in all Oz, but I am kept so busy at my palace making laws and planning for the comforts of those who live near the Emerald City, that I do not often find time to make long journeys.'

'Well,' replied Dorothy, 'we'll prob'bly find out a lot on this trip, and we'll learn all about the Skeezers and Flat-heads, anyhow. Time doesn't make much diff'rence in the Land of Oz, 'cause we don't grow up, or get old, or become sick and die, as they do in other places; so, if we explore one

place at a time, we'll by an' by know all about every nook
and corner in Oz.'

Dorothy wore around her waist the Nome King's Magic
Belt, which protected her from harm, and the Magic Ring
which Glinda had given her was on her finger. Ozma had
merely slipped a small silver wand into the bosom of her
gown, for fairies do not use chemicals and herbs and the
tools of wizards and sorcerers to perform their magic. The
Silver Wand was Ozma's one weapon of offence and defence
and by its use she could accomplish many things.

They had left the Emerald City just at sunrise and the
Sawhorse travelled very swiftly over the roads towards the
north, but in a few hours the wooden animal had to slacken
his pace because the farmhouses had become few and far
between and often there were no paths at all in the direction
they wished to follow. At such times they crossed the fields,
avoiding groups of trees and fording the streams and rivulets
whenever they came to them. But finally they reached a
broad hillside closely covered with scrubby brush, through
which the wagon could not pass.

'It will be difficult even for you and me to get through
without tearing our dresses,' said Ozma, 'so we must leave
the Sawhorse and the Wagon here until our return.'

'That's all right,' Dorothy replied, 'I'm tired of riding,
anyhow. Do you s'pose, Ozma, we're anywhere near the
Skeezer Country?'

'I cannot tell, Dorothy dear, but I know we've been going
in the right direction, so we are sure to find it in time.'

The scrubby brush was almost like a grove of small trees,
for it reached as high as the heads of the two girls, neither
of whom was very tall. They were obliged to thread their
way in and out, until Dorothy was afraid they would get
lost, and finally they were halted by a curious thing that
barred their further progress. It was a huge web – as if
woven by gigantic spiders – and the delicate, lacy film was

fastened stoutly to the branches of the bushes and continued to the right and left in the form of a half circle. The threads of this web were of a brilliant purple colour and woven into numerous artistic patterns, but it reached from the ground to branches above the heads of the girls and formed a sort of fence that hedged them in.

'It doesn't look very strong, though,' said Dorothy. 'I wonder if we couldn't break through.' She tried but found the web stronger than it seemed. All her efforts could not break a single thread.

'We must go back, I think, and try to get around this peculiar web,' Ozma decided.

So they turned to the right and, following the web found that it seemed to spread in a regular circle. On and on they went until finally Ozma said they had returned to the exact spot from which they had started. 'Here is a handkerchief you dropped when we were here before,' she said to Dorothy.

'In that case, they must have built the web behind us, after we walked into the trap,' exclaimed the little girl.

'True,' agreed Ozma, 'an enemy has tried to imprison us.'

'And they have, too,' said Dorothy. 'I wonder who it is.'

'It's a spider-web, I'm quite sure,' returned Ozma, 'but it must be the work of enormous spiders.'

'Quite right!' cried a voice behind them. Turning quickly around they beheld a huge purple spider sitting not two yards away and regarding them with its small bright eyes.

Then there crawled from the bushes a dozen more great purple spiders, which saluted the first one and said: 'The web is finished, O King, and the strangers are our prisoners.'

Dorothy did not like the look of these spiders at all. They had big heads, sharp claws, small eyes and fuzzy hair all over their purple bodies.

'They look wicked,' she whispered to Ozma. 'What shall we do?'

Ozma gazed upon the spiders with a serious face.

'What is your object in making us prisoners?' she enquired.

'We need someone to keep house for us,' answered the Spider King. 'There is sweeping and dusting to be done, and polishing and washing of dishes, and that is work my people dislike to do. So we decided that if any strangers came our way we would capture them and make them our servants.'

'I am Princess Ozma, Ruler of all Oz,' said the girl with dignity.

'Well, I am King of all Spiders,' was the reply, 'and that makes me your master. Come with me to my palace and I will instruct you in your work.'

'I won't,' said Dorothy indignantly. 'We won't have anything to do with you.'

'We'll see about that,' returned the spider in a severe tone, and the next instant he made a dive straight at Dorothy, opening the claws in his legs as if to grab and pinch her with the sharp points. But the girl was wearing her Magic Belt and was not harmed. The Spider King could not even touch her. He turned swiftly and made a dash at Ozma, but she held her Magic Wand over his head and the monster recoiled as if it had been struck.

'You'd better let us go,' Dorothy advised him, 'for you see you can't hurt us.'

'So I see,' returned the Spider King angrily. 'Your magic is greater than mine. But I'll not help you to escape. If you can break the magic web my people have woven you may go; if not you must stay here and starve.' With that the Spider King uttered a peculiar whistle and all the spiders disappeared.

'There is more magic in my fairyland than I dreamed of,' remarked the beautiful Ozma, with a sigh of regret. 'It seems that my laws have not been obeyed, for even these monstrous spiders defy me by means of magic.'

'Never mind that now,' said Dorothy; 'let's see what we can do to get out of this trap.'

They now examined the web with great care and were amazed at its strength. Although finer than the finest silken hairs, it resisted all their efforts to break through, even though both girls threw all their weight against it.

'We must find some instrument which will cut the threads of the web,' said Ozma, finally. 'Let us look about for such a tool.'

So they wandered among the bushes and finally came to a shallow pool of water, formed by a small bubbling spring. Dorothy stooped to get a drink and discovered in the water a green crab, about as big as her hand. The crab had two big, sharp claws, and as soon as Dorothy saw them she had an idea that those claws could save them.

'Come out of the water,' she called to the crab; 'I want to talk to you.'

Rather lazily the crab rose to the surface and caught hold of a bit of rock. With his head above the water he said in a cross voice: 'What do you want?'

'We want you to cut the web of the purple spiders with your claws, so we can get through it,' answered Dorothy. 'You can do that, can't you?'

'I suppose so,' replied the crab. 'But if I do what will you give me?'

'What do you wish?' Ozma enquired.

'I wish to be white, instead of green,' said the crab. 'Green crabs are very common, and white ones are rare; besides the purple spiders, which infest this hillside, are afraid of white crabs. Could you make me white if I should agree to cut the web for you?'

'Yes,' said Ozma, 'I can do that easily. And, so you may know I am speaking the truth, I will change your colour now.'

She waved her silver wand over the pool and the crab

instantly became snow-white – all except his eyes, which remained black. The creature saw his reflection in the water and was so delighted that he at once climbed out of the pool and began moving slowly towards the web, by backing away from the pool. He moved so very slowly that Dorothy cried out impatiently: 'Dear me, this will never do!' Catching the crab in her hands, she ran with him to the web.

She had to hold him up even then, so he could reach with his claws strand after strand of the filmy purple web, which he was able to sever with one nip.

When enough of the web had been cut to allow them to pass, Dorothy ran back to the pool and placed the white crab in the water, after which she rejoined Ozma. They were just in time to escape through the web, for several of the purple spiders now appeared, having discovered that their web had been cut, and had the girls not rushed through the opening the spiders would have quickly repaired the cuts and again imprisoned them.

Ozma and Dorothy ran as fast as they could and although the angry spiders threw a number of strands of web after them, hoping to lasso them or entangle them in the coils, they managed to escape and clamber to the top of the hill.

CHAPTER THREE

The Mist Maidens

FROM THE TOP OF THE HILL OZMA AND

Dorothy looked down into the valley beyond and were surprised to find it filled with a floating mist that was as dense as smoke. Nothing in the valley was visible except these rolling waves of mist, but beyond, on the other side, rose a grassy hill that appeared quite beautiful.

'Well,' said Dorothy, 'what are we to do, Ozma? Walk down into that thick fog, an' prob'bly get lost in it, or wait till it clears away?'

'I'm not sure it will clear away, however long we wait,' replied Ozma, doubtfully. 'If we wish to get on, I think we must venture into the mist.'

'But we can't see where we're going, or what we're stepping on,' protested Dorothy. 'There may be dreadful things mixed up in that fog, an' I'm scared just to think of wading into it.'

Even Ozma seemed to hesitate. She was silent and thoughtful for a little while, looking at the rolling drifts that were so grey and forbidding. Finally she said: 'I believe this is a Mist Valley, where these moist clouds always remain, for even the sunshine above does not drive them away. Therefore the Mist Maids must live here, and they are fairies and should answer my call.'

She placed her two hands before her mouth, forming a hollow with them, and uttered a clear, trilling, bird-like cry. It floated far out over the mist waves and presently was answered by a similar sound, as of a far-off echo.

Dorothy was much impressed. She had seen many strange

things since coming to this fairy country, but here was a new experience. At ordinary times Ozma was just like any little girl one might chance to meet – simple, merry, lovable as could be – yet with a certain reserve that lent her dignity in her most joyous moods. There were times, however, when seated on her throne and commanding her subjects, or when her fairy powers were called into use, when Dorothy and all others about her stood in awe of their lovely girl Ruler and realised her superiority.

Ozma waited. Presently out from the billows rose beautiful forms, clothed in fleecy, trailing garments of grey that could scarcely be distinguished from the mist. Their hair was mist-colour, too; only their gleaming arms and sweet, pallid faces proved they were living, intelligent creatures answering the call of a sister fairy.

Like sea nymphs they rested on the bosom of the clouds, their eyes turned questioningly upon the two girls who stood upon the bank. One came quite near and to her Ozma said: 'Will you please take us to the opposite hillside? We are afraid to venture into the mist. I am Princess Ozma of Oz, and this is my friend Dorothy, a Princess of Oz.'

The Mist Maids came nearer, holding out their arms. Without hesitation Ozma advanced and allowed them to embrace her and Dorothy plucked up courage to follow. Very gently the Mist Maids held them. Dorothy thought the arms were cold and misty – they didn't seem real at all – yet they supported the two girls above the surface of the billows and floated with them so swiftly to the green hillside opposite that the girls were astonished to find themselves set upon the grass before they realised they had fairly started.

'Thank you!' said Ozma gratefully, and Dorothy also added her thanks for the service.

The Mist Maids made no answer, but they smiled and waved their hands in goodbye as again they floated out into the mist and disappeared from view.

CHAPTER FOUR

The Magic Tent

'WELL,' SAID DOROTHY WITH A LAUGH, 'that was easier than I expected. It's worth while, sometimes, to be a real fairy. But I wouldn't like to be that kind, and live in a dreadful fog all the time.'

They now climbed the bank and found before them a delightful plain that spread for miles in all directions. Fragrant wild flowers were scattered throughout the grass; there were bushes bearing lovely blossoms and luscious fruits; now and then a group of stately trees added to the beauty of the landscape. But there were no dwellings or signs of life.

The farther side of the plain was bordered by a row of palms, and just in front of the palms rose a queerly shaped hill that towered above the plain like a mountain. The sides of this hill were straight up and down; it was round in shape and the top seemed flat and level.

'Oh, ho!' cried Dorothy; 'I'll bet that's the mountain Glinda told us of, where the Flatheads live.'

'If it is,' replied Ozma, 'the Lake of the Skeezers must be just beyond the line of palm trees. Can you walk that far, Dorothy?'

'Of course, in time,' was the prompt answer. 'I'm sorry we had to leave the Sawhorse and the Red Wagon behind us, for they'd come in handy just now; but with the end of our journey in sight a tramp across these pretty green fields won't tire us a bit.'

It was a longer tramp than they suspected, however, and night overtook them before they could reach the flat mountain. So Ozma proposed they camp for the night and Dorothy was quite ready to approve. She didn't like to admit to her friend she was tired, but she told herself that her legs 'had prickers in 'em', meaning they had begun to ache.

Usually when Dorothy started on a journey of exploration or adventure, she carried with her a basket of food, and other things that a traveller in a strange country might require, but to go away with Ozma was quite a different thing, as experience had taught her. The fairy Ruler of Oz only needed her silver wand – tipped at one end with a great sparkling emerald – to provide through its magic all that they might need. Therefore Ozma, having halted with her companion and selected a smooth, grassy spot on the plain, waved her wand in graceful curves and chanted some mystic words in her sweet voice, and in an instant a handsome tent appeared before them. The canvas was striped purple and white, and from the centre pole fluttered the royal banner of Oz.

'Come, dear,' said Ozma, taking Dorothy's hand, 'I am hungry and I'm sure you must be also; so let us go in and have our feast.'

On entering the tent they found a table set for two, with snowy linen, bright silver and sparkling glassware, a vase of roses in the centre and many dishes of delicious food, some smoking hot, waiting to satisfy their hunger. Also, on either side of the tent were beds, with satin sheets, warm blankets and pillows filled with swansdown. There were chairs, too, and tall lamps that lighted the interior of the tent with a soft, rosy glow.

Dorothy, resting herself at her fairy friend's command, and eating her dinner with unusual enjoyment, thought of the wonders of magic. If one were a fairy and knew the secret laws of nature and the mystic words and ceremonies that commanded those laws, then a simple wave of a silver wand would produce instantly all that men work hard and anxiously for through weary years. And Dorothy wished in her kindly, innocent heart, that all men and women could be fairies with silver wands, and satisfy all their needs without so much work and worry, for then, she imagined, they would have all their working hours to be happy in. But Ozma, looking into her friend's face and reading those thoughts, gave a laugh and said: 'No, no, Dorothy, that wouldn't do at all. Instead of happiness your plan would bring weariness to the world. If everyone could wave a wand and have his wants fulfilled there would be little to wish for. There would be no eager striving to obtain the difficult, for nothing would then be difficult, and the pleasure of earning something longed for, and only to be secured by hard work and careful thought, would be utterly lost. There would be nothing to do you see, and no interest in life and in our fellow creatures. That is all that makes life worth our while – to do good deeds and to help those less fortunate than ourselves.'

'Well, you're a fairy, Ozma. Aren't you happy?' asked Dorothy.

'Yes, dear, because I can use my fairy powers to make others happy. Had I no kingdom to rule, and no subjects to look after, I would be miserable. Also, you must realise that while I am a more powerful fairy than any other inhabitant of Oz, I am not as powerful as Glinda the Sorceress, who has studied many arts of magic that I know nothing of. Even the little Wizard of Oz can do some things I am unable to accomplish, while I can accomplish things unknown to the Wizard. This is to explain that I'm not all-powerful, by any means. My magic is simply fairy magic, and not sorcery or wizardry.'

'All the same,' said Dorothy, 'I'm mighty glad you could make this tent appear, with our dinners and beds all ready for us.'

Ozma smiled.

'Yes, it is indeed wonderful,' she agreed. 'Not all fairies know that sort of magic, but some fairies can do magic that fills me with astonishment. I think that is what makes us modest and unassuming – the fact that our magic arts are divided, some being given each of us. I'm glad I don't know everything, Dorothy, and that there still are things in both nature and in wit for me to marvel at.'

Dorothy couldn't quite understand this, so she said nothing more on the subject and presently had a new reason to marvel. For when they had quite finished their meal table and contents disappeared in a flash.

'No dishes to wash, Ozma!' she said with a laugh. 'I guess you'd make a lot of folks happy if you could teach 'em just that one trick.'

For an hour Ozma told stories, and talked with Dorothy about various people in whom they were interested. And then it was bedtime, and they undressed and crept into their soft beds and fell asleep almost as soon as their heads touched their pillows.

CHAPTER FIVE

The Magic Stairway

THE FLAT MOUNTAIN LOOKED MUCH
nearer in the clear light of the morning sun, but Dorothy
and Ozma knew there was a long tramp before them, even
yet. They finished dressing only to find a warm, delicious
breakfast awaiting them, and having eaten they left the tent
and started towards the mountain which was their first goal.
After going a little way Dorothy looked back and found
that the fairy tent had entirely disappeared. She was not
surprised, for she knew this would happen.

'Can't your magic give us a horse an' wagon, or an auto-
mobile?' enquired Dorothy.

'No, dear; I'm sorry that such magic is beyond my power,'
confessed her fairy friend.

'Perhaps Glinda could,' said Dorothy thoughtfully.

'Glinda has a stork chariot that carries her through the
air,' said Ozma, 'but even our great Sorceress cannot conjure
up other modes of travel. Don't forget what I told you last
night, that no one is powerful enough to do everything.'

'Well, I s'pose I ought to know that, having lived so long
in the Land of Oz,' replied Dorothy; 'but I can't do any
magic at all, an' so I can't figure out e'zactly how you an'
Glinda an' the Wizard do it.'

'Don't try,' laughed Ozma. 'But you have at least one
magical art, Dorothy: you know the trick of winning all
hearts.'

'No, I don't,' said Dorothy earnestly. 'If I really can do it,
Ozma, I am sure I don't know how I do it.'

It took them a good two hours to reach the foot of the

round, flat mountain, and then they found the sides so steep that they were like the wall of a house.

'Even my purple kitten couldn't climb 'em,' remarked Dorothy, gazing upwards.

'But there is some way for the Flatheads to get down and up again,' declared Ozma; 'otherwise they couldn't make war with the Skeezers, or even meet them and quarrel with them.'

'That's so, Ozma. Let's walk around the base; perhaps we'll find a ladder or something.'

They walked quite a distance, for it was a big mountain, and as they circled around it and came to the side that faced the palm trees, they suddenly discovered an entrance way cut out of the rock wall. This entrance was arched overhead and not very deep because it merely led to a short flight of stone stairs.

'Oh, we've found a way to the top at last,' announced Ozma, and the two girls hurried towards the entrance. Suddenly they bumped against something and stood still, unable to proceed farther.

'Dear me!' exclaimed Dorothy, rubbing her nose, which had struck something hard, although she could not see what it was; 'this isn't as easy as it looks. What has stopped us, Ozma? Is it magic of some sort?'

Ozma was feeling around, her bands outstretched before her.

'Yes, dear, it is magic,' she replied. 'The Flatheads had to have a way from their mountain top from the plain below, but to prevent enemies from rushing up the stairs to conquer them, they have built at a small distance before the entrance a wall of solid stone, the stones being held in place by cement, and then they have made the wall invisible.'

'I wonder why they did that?' mused Dorothy. 'A wall would keep folks out anyhow, whether it could be seen or not, so there wasn't any use making it invisible. Seems to me it would have been better to have left it solid, for then no one would have seen the entrance behind it. Now anybody can see the entrance, as we did. And prob'bly anybody that tries to go up the stairs gets bumped, as we did.'

Ozma made no reply at once. Her face was grave and thoughtful.

'I think I know the reason for making the wall invisible,' she said after a while. 'The Flatheads use the stairs for coming down and going up. If there was a solid stone wall to keep them from reaching the plain they would themselves be imprisoned by the wall. So they had to leave some place to get around the wall, and, if the wall was visible, all strangers or enemies would find the place to go around it and then the wall would be useless. So the Flatheads cunningly made their wall invisible, believing that everyone who saw the entrance to the mountain would walk straight towards it, as we did, and find it impossible to go any farther. I suppose the wall is really high and thick, and can't be broken through, so those who find it in their way are obliged to go away again.'

'Well,' said Dorothy, 'if there's a way around the wall, where is it?'

'We must find it,' returned Ozma, and began feeling her way along the wall. Dorothy followed and began to get discouraged when Ozma had walked nearly a quarter of a mile away from the entrance. But now the invisible wall curved in towards the side of the mountain and suddenly ended, leaving just space enough between the wall and the mountain for an ordinary person to pass through.

The girls went in, single file, and Ozma explained that they were now behind the barrier and could go back to the entrance. They met no further obstructions.

'Most people, Ozma, wouldn't have figured this thing out the way you did,' remarked Dorothy. 'If I'd been alone, the invisible wall surely would have stumped me.'

Reaching the entrance they began to mount the stone stairs. They went up ten stairs and then down five stairs, following a passage cut from the rock. The stairs were just wide enough for the two girls to walk abreast, arm in arm. At the bottom of the five stairs the passage turned to the right, and they ascended ten more stairs, only to find at the top of the flight five stairs leading straight down again. Again the passage turned abruptly, this time to the left, and ten more stairs led upwards.

The passage was now quite dark, for they were in the heart of the mountain and all daylight had been shut out by the turns of the passage. However, Ozma drew her silver wand from her bosom and the great jewel at its end gave out a lustrous, green-tinted light which lighted the place well enough for them to see their way plainly.

Ten steps up, five steps down, and a turn, this way or that. That was the programme, and Dorothy figured that they were only gaining five stairs upwards each advance they made.

'Those Flatheads must be funny people,' she said to Ozma. 'They don't seem to do anything in a bold straightforward manner. The design of this passage forces everyone to walk three times as far as is necessary. And of course this is just as tiresome to the Flatheads as it is to other folks.'

'That is true,' answered Ozma; 'yet it is a clever arrangement to prevent their being surprised by intruders. Every time we reach the tenth step of a flight, the pressure of our feet on the stone makes a bell ring on top of the mountain, to warn the Flatheads of our coming.'

'How do you know that?' demanded Dorothy, astonished.

'I've heard the bell ever since we started,' Ozma told her. 'You could not hear it, I know, but when I am holding my wand in my hand I can hear sounds a great distance off.'

'Do you hear anything on top of the mountain 'cept the bell?' enquired Dorothy.

'Yes. The people are calling to one another in alarm and

many footsteps are approaching the place where we will emerge on top of the mountain.'

This made Dorothy feel somewhat anxious. 'I'd thought we were going to visit just common, ordinary people,' she remarked, 'but they're pretty clever, it seems, and they know some kinds of magic, too. They may be dangerous, Ozma. P'raps we should have stayed at home.'

Finally the upstairs-and-downstairs passage seemed to be coming to an end, for daylight appeared ahead of the two girls and Ozma replaced her wand in the bosom of her gown. The last ten steps brought them to the surface, where they found themselves surrounded by such a throng of queer people that for a time they halted, speechless, and stared into the faces that confronted them.

Dorothy knew at once why these mountain people were called Flatheads. Their heads were really flat on top, as if they had been cut off just above the eyes and ears. Also the heads were bald, with no hair on top at all, and the ears were big and stuck straight out, and the noses were small and stubby, while the mouths of the Flatheads were well shaped and not unusual. Their eyes were perhaps their best feature, being large and bright and a deep violet in colour.

The costumes of the Flatheads were all made of metals dug from their mountain. Small gold, silver, tin and iron discs, about the size of pennies, and very thin, were cleverly wired together and made to form knee trousers and jackets for the men and skirts and bodices for the women. The coloured metals were skilfully mixed to form stripes and checks of various sorts, so that the costumes were quite gorgeous and reminded Dorothy of pictures she had seen of knights of old clothed in armour.

Aside from their flat heads, these people were not really bad looking. The men were armed with bows and arrows and had small axes of steel stuck in their metal belts. They wore no hats nor ornaments.

CHAPTER SIX

Flathead Mountain

WHEN THEY SAW THAT THE INTRUDERS on their mountain were only two little girls, the Flatheads grunted with satisfaction and drew back, permitting them to see what the mountain top looked like. It was shaped like a saucer, so that the houses and other buildings – all made of rocks – could not be seen over the edge by anyone standing on the plain below.

But now a big fat Flathead stood before the girls and in a gruff voice demanded: 'What are you doing here? Have the Skeezers sent you to spy upon us?'

'I am Princess Ozma, Ruler of all the Land of Oz.'

'Well, I've never heard of the Land of Oz, so you may be what you claim,' returned the Flathead.

'This is the Land of Oz – part of it, anyway,' exclaimed Dorothy. 'So Princess Ozma rules you Flathead people, as well as all the other people in Oz.'

The man laughed, and all the others who stood around laughed, too. Someone in the crowd called: 'She'd better not tell the Supreme Dictator about ruling the Flatheads. Eh, friends?'

'No, indeed!' they all answered in positive tones.

'Who is your Supreme Dictator?' answered Ozma.

'I think I'll let him tell you that himself,' answered the man who had first spoken. 'You have broken our laws by coming here; and whoever you are the Supreme Dictator must fix your punishment. Come along with me.'

He started down a path and Ozma and Dorothy followed him without protest, as they wanted to see the most important person in this queer country. The houses they passed seemed pleasant enough and each had a little yard in which were flowers and vegetables. Walls of rock separated the dwellings, and all the paths were paved with smooth slabs of rock. This seemed their only building material and they utilised it cleverly for every purpose.

Directly in the centre of the great saucer stood a larger building which the Flathead informed the girls was the palace of the Supreme Dictator. He led them through an entrance hall into a big reception room, where they sat upon stone benches and awaited the coming of the Dictator. Pretty soon he entered from another room – a rather lean and rather old Flathead, dressed much like the others of this strange race, and only distinguished from them by the sly and cunning expression of his face. He kept his eyes half closed and looked through the slits of them at Ozma and Dorothy, who rose to receive him.

'Are you the Supreme Dictator of the Flatheads?' enquired Ozma.

'Yes, that's me,' he said, rubbing his hands slowly together. 'My word is law. I'm the head of the Flatheads on this flat headland.'

'I am Princess Ozma of Oz, and I have come from the Emerald City to – '

'Stop a minute,' interrupted the Dictator, and turned to the man who had brought the girls there. 'Go away, Dictator Felo Flathead!' he commanded. 'Return to your duty and guard the stairway. I will look after these strangers.' The man bowed and departed, and Dorothy asked wonderingly: 'Is *he* a dictator, too?'

'Of course,' was the answer. 'Everybody here is a dictator of something or other. They're all office holders. That's what keeps them contented. But I'm the Supreme Dictator of all, and I'm elected once a year. This is a democracy, you know, where the people are allowed to vote for their rulers.

A good many others would like to be Supreme Dictator, but as I made a law that I am always to count the votes myself, I am always elected.'

'What is your name?' asked Ozma.

'I am called the Su-Dic, which is short for Supreme Dictator. I sent that man away because the moment you mentioned Ozma of Oz, and the Emerald City, I knew who you are. I suppose I'm the only Flathead that ever heard of you, but that's because I have more brains than the rest.'

Dorothy was staring hard at the Su-Dic.

'I don't see how you can have any brains at all,' she remarked, 'because the part of your head is gone where brains are kept.'

'I don't blame you for thinking that,' he said. 'Once the Flatheads had no brains because, as you say, there is no upper part to their heads, to hold brains. But long, long ago a band of fairies flew over this country and made it all a fairyland, and when they came to the Flatheads the fairies were sorry to find them all very stupid and quite unable to think. So, as there was no good place in their bodies in which to put brains the Fairy Queen gave each one of us a nice can of brains to carry in his pocket and that made us just as intelligent as other people. See,' he continued, 'here is one of the cans of brains the fairies gave us.' He took from a pocket a bright tin can having a pretty red label on it which said: 'Concentrated Brains, Extra Quality'.

'And does every Flathead have the same kind of brains?' asked Dorothy.

'Yes, they're all alike. Here's another can.' From another pocket he produced a second can of brains.

'Did the fairies give you a double supply?' enquired Dorothy.

'No, but one of the Flatheads thought he wanted to be the Su-Dic and tried to get my people to rebel against me, so I punished him by taking away his brains. One day my

wife scolded me severely, so I took away her can of brains.
She didn't like that and went out and robbed several women
of *their* brains. Then I made a law that if anyone stole
another's brains, or even tried to borrow them, he would
forfeit his own brains to the Su-Dic. So each one is content
with his own canned brains and my wife and I are the only
ones on the mountain with more than one can. I have three
cans and that makes me very clever – so clever that I'm a
good Sorcerer, if I do say it myself. My poor wife had four
cans of brains and became a remarkable witch, but alas! that
was before those terrible enemies, the Skeezers, transformed
her into a Golden Pig.'

'Good gracious!' cried Dorothy; 'is your wife really a
Golden Pig?'

'She is. The Skeezers did it and so I have declared war on
them. In revenge for making my wife a pig I intend to ruin
their Magic Island and make the Skeezers the slaves of the
Flatheads!'

The Su-Dic was very angry now; his eyes flashed and his
face took on a wicked and fierce expression. But Ozma said
to him, very sweetly and in a friendly voice: 'I am sorry to
hear this. Will you please tell me more about your troubles
with the Skeezers? Then perhaps I can help you.'

She was only a girl, but there was dignity in her pose and
speech which impressed the Su-Dic.

'If you are really Princess Ozma of Oz,' the Flathead said,
'you are one of that band of fairies who, under Queen
Lurline, made all Oz a Fairyland. I have heard that Lurline
left one of her own fairies to rule Oz, and gave the fairy the
name of Ozma.'

'If you knew this why did you not come to me at the
Emerald City and tender me your loyalty and obedience?'
asked the Ruler of Oz.

'Well, I only learned the fact lately, and I've been too busy
to leave home,' he explained, looking at the floor instead of

into Ozma's eyes. She knew he had spoken a falsehood, but only said: 'Why did you quarrel with the Skeezers?'

'It was this way,' began the Su-Dic, glad to change the subject. 'We Flatheads love fish, and as we have no fish on this mountain we would sometimes go to the Lake of the Skeezers to catch fish. This made the Skeezers angry, for they declared the fish in their lake belonged to them and were under their protection and they forbade us to catch them. That was very mean and unfriendly in the Skeezers, you must admit, and when we paid no attention to their orders they set a guard on the shore of the lake to prevent our fishing.

'Now, my wife, Rora Flathead, having four cans of brains, had become a wonderful witch, and fish being brain food, she loved to eat fish better than any one of us. So she vowed she would destroy every fish in the lake, unless the Skeezers let us catch what we wanted. They defied us, so Rora prepared a kettle full of magic poison and went down to the lake one night to dump it all in the water and poison the fish. It was a clever idea, quite worthy of my dear wife, but the Skeezer Queen – a young lady named Coo-ee-oh – hid on the bank of the lake and taking Rora unawares transformed her into a Golden Pig. The poison was spilled on the ground and wicked Queen Coo-ee-oh, not content with her cruel transformation, even took away my wife's four cans of brains, so she is now a common grunting pig without even brains enough to know her own name.'

'Then,' said Ozma thoughtfully, 'the Queen of the Skeezers must be a Sorceress.'

'Yes,' said the Su-Dic, 'but she doesn't know much magic, after all. She is not as powerful as Rora Flathead was, nor half as powerful as I am now, as Queen Coo-ee-oh will discover when we fight our great battle and destroy her.'

'The Golden Pig can't be a witch any more, of course,' observed Dorothy.

'No; even had Queen Coo-ee-oh left her the four cans of brains, poor Rora, in a pig's shape, couldn't do any witch-craft. A witch has to use her fingers, and a pig has only cloven hoofs.'

'It seems a sad story,' was Ozma's comment, 'and all the trouble arose because the Flatheads wanted fish that did not belong to them.'

'As for that,' said the Su-Dic, again angry, 'I made a law that any of my people could catch fish in the Lake of the Skeezers, whenever they wanted to. So the trouble was through the Skeezers defying my law.'

'You can only make laws to govern your own people,' asserted Ozma sternly. 'I, alone, am empowered to make laws that must be obeyed by all the peoples of Oz.'

'Pooh!' cried the Su-Dic scornfully. 'You can't make *me* obey your laws, I assure you. I know the extent of your powers, Princess Ozma of Oz, and I know that I am more powerful than you are. To prove it I shall keep you and your companion prisoners on this mountain until after we have fought and conquered the Skeezers. Then, if you promise to be good, I may let you go home again.'

Dorothy was amazed by this effrontery and defiance of the beautiful girl Ruler of Oz, whom all until now had obeyed without question. But Ozma, still unruffled and dignified, looked at the Su-Dic and said: 'You did not mean that. You are angry and speak unwisely, without reflection. I came here from my palace in the Emerald City to prevent war and to make peace between you and the Skeezers. I do not approve of Queen Coo-ee-oh's action in transforming your wife Rora into a pig, nor do I approve of Rora's cruel attempt to poison the fishes in the lake. No one has the right to work magic in my dominions without my consent, so the Flatheads and the Skeezers have both broken my laws – which must be obeyed.'

'If you want to make peace,' said the Su-Dic, 'make the Skeezers restore my wife to her proper form and give back her four cans of brains. Also make them agree to allow us to catch fish in their lake.'

'No,' returned Ozma, 'I will not do that, for it would be unjust. I will have the Golden Pig again transformed into your wife Rora, and give her one can of brains, but the other three cans must be restored to those she robbed. Neither may you catch fish in the Lake of the Skeezers, for it is their lake and the fish belong to them. This arrangement is just and honourable, and you must agree to it.'

'Never!' cried the Su-Dic. Just then a pig came running into the room, uttering dismal grunts. It was made of solid gold, with joints at the bends of the legs and in the neck and jaws. The Golden Pig's eyes were rubies, and its teeth were polished ivory.

'There!' said the Su-Dic, 'gaze on the evil work of Queen Coo-ee-oh, and then say if you can prevent my making war on the Skeezers. That grunting beast was once my wife – the most beautiful Flathead on our mountain and a skilful witch. Now look at her!'

'Fight the Skeezers, fight the Skeezers, fight the Skeezers!' grunted the Golden Pig.

'I *will* fight the Skeezers,' exclaimed the Flathead chief, 'and if a dozen Ozmas of Oz forbade me I would fight just the same.'

'Not if I can prevent it!' asserted Ozma.

'You can't prevent it. But since you threaten me, I'll have you confined in the bronze prison until the war is over,' said the Su-Dic. He whistled and four stout Flatheads, armed with axes and spears, entered the room and saluted him. Turning to the men he said: 'Take these two girls, bind them with wire ropes and cast them into the bronze prison.'

The four men bowed low and one of them asked: 'Where are the two girls, most noble Su-Dic?'

The Su-Dic turned to where Ozma and Dorothy had stood but they had vanished!

CHAPTER SEVEN

The Magic Isle

OZMA, SEEING IT WAS USELESS TO

argue with the Supreme Dictator of the Flatheads, had been considering how best to escape from his power. She realised that his sorcery might be difficult to overcome, and when he threatened to cast Dorothy and her into a bronze prison she slipped her hand into her bosom and grasped her silver wand. With the other hand she grasped the hand of Dorothy, but these motions were so natural that the Su-Dic did not notice them. Then when he turned to meet his four soldiers, Ozma instantly rendered both herself and Dorothy invisible and swiftly led her companion around the group of Flatheads and out of the room. As they reached the entry and descended the stone steps, Ozma whispered: 'Let us run, dear! We are invisible, so no one will see us.'

Dorothy understood and she was a good runner. Ozma had marked the place where the grand stairway that led to the plain was located, so they made directly for it. Some people were on the paths but these they dodged around. One or two Flatheads heard the pattering of footsteps of the girls on the stone pavement and stopped with bewildered looks to gaze around them, but no one interfered with the invisible fugitives.

The Su-Dic had lost no time in starting the chase. He and his men ran so fast that they might have overtaken the girls before they reached the stairway had not the Golden Pig suddenly run across their path. The Su-Dic tripped over the pig and fell flat, and his four men tripped over him and tumbled in a heap. Before they could scramble up and reach the mouth of the passage it was too late to stop the two girls.

There was a guard on each side of the stairway, but of course they did not see Ozma and Dorothy as they sped past and descended the steps. Then they had to go up five steps and down another ten, and so on, in the same manner in which they had climbed to the top of the mountain. Ozma lighted their way with her wand and they kept on without relaxing their speed until they reached the bottom. Then they ran to the right and turned the corner of the invisible wall just as the Su-Dic and his followers rushed out of the arched entrance and looked around in an attempt to discover the fugitives.

Ozma now knew they were safe, so she told Dorothy to stop and both of them sat down on the grass until they could breathe freely and become rested from their mad flight.

As for the Su-Dic, he realised he was foiled and soon turned and climbed his stairs again. He was very angry – angry with Ozma and angry with himself – because, now that he took time to think, he remembered that he knew very well the art of making people invisible, and visible again, and if he had only thought of it in time he could have used his magic knowledge to make the girls visible and so have captured them easily. However, it was now too late for regrets and he determined to make preparations at once to march all his forces against the Skeezers.

'What shall we do next?' asked Dorothy, when they were rested.

'Let us find the Lake of the Skeezers,' replied Ozma. 'From what that dreadful Su-Dic said I imagine the Skeezers are good people and worthy of our friendship, and if we go to them we may help them to defeat the Flatheads.'

'I s'pose we can't stop the war now,' remarked Dorothy reflectively, as they walked towards the row of palm trees.

'No; the Su-Dic is determined to fight the Skeezers, so all we can do is to warn them of their danger and help them as much as possible.'

'Of course you'll punish the Flatheads,' said Dorothy.

'Well, I do not think the Flathead people are as much to blame as their Supreme Dictator,' was the answer. 'If he is removed from power and his unlawful magic taken from him, the people will probably be good and respect the laws of the Land of Oz, and live at peace with all their neighbours in the future.'

'I hope so,' said Dorothy with a sigh of doubt

The palms were not far from the mountain and the girls reached them after a brisk walk. The huge trees were set close together, in three rows, and had been planted so as to keep people from passing them, but the Flatheads had cut a passage through this barrier and Ozma found the path and led Dorothy to the other side.

Beyond the palms they discovered a very beautiful scene. Bordered by a green lawn was a great lake fully a mile from shore to shore, the waters of which were exquisitely blue and sparkling, with little wavelets breaking its smooth surface where the breezes touched it. In the centre of this lake appeared a lovely island, not of great extent but almost entirely covered by a huge round building with glass walls and a high glass dome which glittered brilliantly in the sunshine. Between the glass building and the edge of the island there were no lawns, flowers or shrubbery, but only an expanse of highly polished white marble. There were no boats on either shore and no signs of life could be seen anywhere on the island.

'Well,' said Dorothy, gazing wistfully at the island, 'we've found the Lake of the Skeezers and their Magic Isle. I guess the Skeezers are in that big glass palace, but we can't get at 'em.'

CHAPTER EIGHT

Queen Coo-ee-oh

PRINCESS OZMA CONSIDERED THE
situation gravely. Then she tied her handkerchief to her
wand and, standing at the water's edge, waved the handkerchief like a flag, as a signal. For a time they could observe
no response.

'I don't see what good that will do,' said Dorothy. 'Even
if the Skeezers are on that island and see us, and know we're
friends, they haven't any boats to come and get us.'

But the Skeezers didn't need boats, as the girls soon
discovered. For on a sudden an opening appeared at the
base of the palace and from the opening came a slender
shaft of steel, reaching out slowly but steadily across the
water in the direction of the place where they stood. To the
girls this steel arrangement looked like a triangle, with the
base nearest the water. It came towards them in the form of
an arch, stretching out from the palace wall until its end
reached the bank and rested there, while the other end still
remained on the island.

Then they saw that it was a bridge, consisting of a steel
footway just broad enough to walk on, and two slender guide
rails, one on either side, which were connected with the
footway by steel bars. The bridge looked rather frail and
Dorothy feared it would not bear their weight, but Ozma at
once called, 'Come on!' and started to walk across, holding
fast to the rail on either side. So Dorothy summoned her
courage and followed after. Before Ozma had taken three
steps she halted and so forced Dorothy to halt, for the bridge
was again moving and returning to the island.

'We need not walk after all,' said Ozma. So they stood still in their places and let the steel bridge draw them onward. Indeed, the bridge drew them well into the glass-domed building which covered the island, and soon they found themselves standing in a marble room where two handsomely dressed young men stood on a platform to receive them.

Ozma at once stepped from the end of the bridge to the marble platform, followed by Dorothy, and then the bridge disappeared with a slight clang of steel and a marble slab covered the opening from which it had emerged.

The two young men bowed profoundly to Ozma, and one of them said: 'Queen Coo-ee-oh bids you welcome, O Strangers. Her Majesty is waiting to receive you in her palace.'

'Lead on,' replied Ozma with dignity.

But instead of 'leading on', the platform of marble began to rise, carrying them upward through a square hole above which just fitted it. A moment later they found themselves within the great glass dome that covered almost all of the island.

Within this dome was a little village, with houses, streets, gardens and parks. The houses were of coloured marbles, prettily designed, with many stained-glass windows, and the streets and gardens seemed well cared for. Exactly under the centre of the lofty dome was a small park filled with brilliant flowers and with an elaborate fountain, and facing this park stood a building larger and more imposing than the others. Towards this building the young men escorted Ozma and Dorothy.

On the streets and in the doorways or open windows of the houses were men, women and children, all richly dressed. These were much like other people in different parts of the Land of Oz, except that instead of seeming merry and contented they all wore expressions of much solemnity or of nervous irritation. They had beautiful homes, splendid clothes and ample food, but Dorothy at once decided something was wrong with their lives and that they were not happy. She said nothing, however, but looked curiously at the Skeezers.

At the entrance of the palace Ozma and Dorothy were met by two more young men, in uniform and armed with queer weapons that seemed about halfway between pistols and rifles, but were like neither. Their conductors bowed and left them, and the two in uniforms led the girls into the palace.

In a beautiful throne room, surrounded by a dozen or more young men and women, sat the Queen of the Skeezers, Coo-ee-oh. She was a girl who looked older than Ozma or Dorothy – fifteen or sixteen, at least – and although she was elaborately dressed as if she were going to a ball she was too thin and plain of feature to be pretty. But evidently Queen Coo-ee-oh did not realise this fact, for her air and manner betrayed her as proud and haughty and with a high regard for her own importance. Dorothy at once decided she was 'snippy' and that she would not like Queen Coo-ee-oh as a companion.

The Queen's hair was as black as her skin was white and her eyes were black, too. The eyes, as she calmly examined Ozma and Dorothy, had a suspicious and unfriendly look in them, but she said quietly: 'I know who you are, for I have consulted my Magic Oracle, which told me that one calls herself Princess Ozma, the Ruler of all the Land of Oz, and the other is Princess Dorothy of Oz, who came from a country called Kansas. I know nothing of the Land of Oz, and I know nothing of Kansas.'

'Why, *this* is the Land of Oz!' cried Dorothy. 'It's a *part* of the Land of Oz, anyhow, whether you know it or not.'

'Oh, in-deed!' answered Queen Coo-ee-oh, scornfully. 'I suppose you will claim next that this Princess Ozma, ruling the Land of Oz, rules me!'

'Of course,' returned Dorothy. 'There's no doubt of it.'

The Queen turned to Ozma.

'Do you dare make such a claim?' she asked.

By this time Ozma had made up her mind as to the character of this haughty and disdainful creature, whose self-pride evidently led her to believe herself superior to all others.

'I did not come here to quarrel with your Majesty,' said the girl Ruler of Oz, quietly. 'What and who I am is well established, and my authority comes from the Fairy Queen Lurline, of whose band I was a member when Lurline made all Oz a Fairyland. There are several countries and several different peoples in this broad land, each of which has its separate rulers, kings, emperors and queens. But all these render obedience to my laws and acknowledge me as the supreme Ruler.'

'If other kings and queens are fools that does not interest me in the least,' replied Coo-ee-oh, disdainfully. 'In the Land of the Skeezers I alone am supreme. You are impudent to think I would defer to you – or to anyone else.'

'Let us not speak of this now, please,' answered Ozma. 'Your island is in danger, for a powerful foe is preparing to destroy it.'

'Pah! The Flatheads. I do not fear them.'

'Their Supreme Dictator is a sorcerer.'

'My magic is greater than his. Let the Flatheads come! They will never return to their barren mountain-top. I will see to that.'

Ozma did not like this attitude, for it meant that the Skeezers were eager to fight the Flatheads, and Ozma's object in coming here was to prevent fighting and induce the two quarrelsome neighbours to make peace. She was also greatly disappointed in Coo-ee-oh, for the reports of the Su-Dic had led her to imagine the Queen more just and honourable than were the Flatheads. Indeed, Ozma reflected that the girl might be better at heart than her self-pride and overbearing manner indicated, and in any event it would be wise not to antagonise her but to try to win her friendship.

'I do not like wars, your Majesty,' said Ozma. 'In the Emerald City, where I rule thousands of people, and in the countries near to the Emerald City, where thousands more acknowledge my rule, there is no army at all, because there is no quarrelling and no need to fight. If differences arise between my people, they come to me and I judge the cases and award justice to all. So, when I learned there might be war between two faraway people of Oz, I came here to settle the dispute and adjust the quarrel.'

'No one asked you to come,' declared Queen Coo-ee-oh. 'It is *my* business to settle this dispute, not yours. You say my island is a part of the Land of Oz, which you rule, but that is all nonsense, for I've never heard of the Land of Oz, nor of you. You say you are a fairy, and that fairies gave you command over me. I don't believe it! What I *do* believe is that you are an impostor and have come here to stir up trouble among my people, who are already becoming difficult to manage. You two girls may even be spies of the vile Flatheads, for all I know, and may be trying to trick me. But understand this,' she added, proudly rising from her jewelled throne to confront them, 'I have magic powers greater than any fairy possesses, and greater than any Flathead possesses. I am a Krumbic Witch – the only Krumbic Witch in the world – and I fear the magic of no other creature that exists! You say you rule thousands. I rule one hundred and one Skeezers. But every one of them trembles at my word. Now that Ozma of Oz and Princess Dorothy are here, I shall rule one hundred and three subjects, for you also shall bow before my power. More than that, in ruling you I also rule the thousands you say you rule.'

Dorothy was very indignant at this speech.

'I've got a pink kitten that sometimes talks like that,' she said, 'but after I give her a good whipping she doesn't think she's so high and mighty after all. If you only knew who Ozma is you'd be scared to death to talk to her like that!'

Queen Coo-ee-oh gave the girl a supercilious look. Then she turned again to Ozma.

'I happen to know,' said she, 'that the Flatheads intend to attack us tomorrow, but we are ready for them. Until the battle is over, I shall keep you two strangers prisoners on my island, from which there is no chance for you to escape.'

She turned and looked around the band of courtiers who stood silently around her throne.

'Lady Aurex,' she continued, singling out one of the young women, 'take these children to your house and care for them, giving them food and lodging. You may allow them to wander anywhere under the Great Dome, for they are harmless. After I have attended to the Flatheads I will consider what next to do with these foolish girls.'

She resumed her seat and the Lady Aurex bowed low and said in a humble manner: 'I obey your Majesty's commands.' Then to Ozma and Dorothy she added, 'Follow me,' and turned to leave the throne room.

Dorothy looked to see what Ozma would do. To her surprise and a little to her disappointment Ozma turned and followed Lady Aurex. So Dorothy trailed after them, but not without giving a parting, haughty look towards Queen Coo-ee-oh, who had her face turned the other way and did not see the disapproving look.

CHAPTER NINE

Lady Aurex

LADY AUREX LED OZMA AND DOROTHY

along a street to a pretty marble house near to one edge of the great glass dome that covered the village. She did not speak to the girls until she had ushered them into a pleasant room, comfortably furnished, nor did any of the solemn people they met on the street venture to speak.

When they were seated Lady Aurex asked if they were hungry, and finding they were summoned a maid and ordered food to be brought.

This Lady Aurex looked to be about twenty years old, although in the Land of Oz where people have never changed in appearance since the fairies made it a fairyland – where no one grows old or dies – it is always difficult to say how many years anyone has lived. She had a pleasant, attractive face, even though it was solemn and sad as the faces of all Skeezers seemed to be, and her costume was rich and elaborate, as became a lady in waiting upon the Queen.

Ozma had observed Lady Aurex closely and now asked her in a gentle tone: 'Do you, also, believe me to be an impostor?'

'I dare not say,' replied Lady Aurex in a low tone.

'Why are you afraid to speak freely?' enquired Ozma.

'The Queen punishes us if we make remarks that she does not like.'

'Are we not alone then, in this house?'

'The Queen can hear everything that is spoken on this island – even the slightest whisper,' declared Lady Aurex.

'She is a wonderful witch, as she has told you, and it is folly to criticise her or disobey her commands.'

Ozma looked into her eyes and saw that she would like to say more if she dared. So she drew from her bosom her silver wand, and having muttered a magic phrase in a strange tongue, she left the room and walked slowly around the outside of the house, making a complete circle and waving her wand in mystic curves as she walked. Lady Aurex watched her curiously and, when Ozma had again entered the room and seated herself, she asked: 'What have you done?'

'I've enchanted this house in such a manner that Queen Coo-ee-oh, with all her witchcraft, cannot hear one word we speak within the magic circle I have made,' replied Ozma. 'We may now speak freely and as loudly as we wish, without fear of the Queen's anger.'

Lady Aurex brightened at this.

'Can I trust you?' she asked.

'Ev'rybody trusts Ozma,' exclaimed Dorothy. 'She is true and honest, and your wicked Queen will be sorry she insulted the powerful Ruler of all the Land of Oz.'

'The Queen does not know me yet,' said Ozma, 'but I want you to know me, Lady Aurex, and I want you to tell me why you, and all the Skeezers, are unhappy. Do not fear Coo-ee-oh's anger, for she cannot hear a word we say, I assure you.'

Lady Aurex was thoughtful a moment; then she said: 'I shall trust you, Princess Ozma, for I believe you are what you say you are – our supreme Ruler. If you knew the dreadful punishments our Queen inflicts upon us, you would not wonder we are so unhappy. The Skeezers are not bad people; they do not care to quarrel and fight, even with their enemies the Flatheads; but they are so cowed and fearful of Coo-ee-oh that they obey her slightest word, rather than suffer her anger.'

'Hasn't she any heart, then?' asked Dorothy.

'She never displays mercy. She loves no one but herself,' asserted Lady Aurex, but she trembled as she said it, as if afraid even yet of her terrible Queen.

'That's pretty bad,' said Dorothy, shaking her head gravely. 'I see you've a lot to do here, Ozma, in this forsaken corner of the Land of Oz. First place, you've got to take the magic away from Queen Coo-ee-oh, and from that awful Su-Dic, too. *My* idea is that neither of them is fit to rule anybody, 'cause they're cruel and hateful. So you'll have to give the Skeezers and Flatheads new rulers and teach all their people that they're part of the Land of Oz and must obey, above all, the lawful Ruler, Ozma of Oz. Then, when you've done that, we can go back home again.'

Ozma smiled at her little friend's earnest counsel, but Lady Aurex said in an anxious tone: 'I am surprised that you suggest these reforms while you are yet prisoners on this island and in Coo-ee-oh's power. That these things should be done, there is no doubt, but just now a dreadful war is likely to break out, and frightful things may happen to us all. Our Queen has such conceit that she thinks she can overcome the Su-Dic and his people, but it is said Su-Dic's magic is very powerful, although not as great as that possessed by his wife Rora, before Coo-ee-oh transformed her into a Golden Pig.'

'I don't blame her very much for doing that,' remarked Dorothy, 'for the Flatheads were wicked to try to catch your beautiful fish and the Witch Rora wanted to poison all the fishes in the lake.'

'Do you know the reason?' asked the Lady Aurex.

'I don't s'pose there *was* any reason, 'cept just wickedness,' replied Dorothy.

'Tell us the reason,' said Ozma earnestly.

'Well, your Majesty, once – a long time ago – the Flat-heads and the Skeezers were friendly. They visited our island and we visited their mountain, and everything was pleasant between the two peoples. At that time the Flat-heads were ruled by three Adepts in Sorcery, beautiful girls who were not Flatheads, but had wandered to the Flat Mountain and made their home there. These three Adepts used their magic only for good, and the mountain people gladly made them their rulers. They taught the Flatheads how to use their canned brains and how to work metals into clothing that would never wear out, and many other things that added to their happiness and content.

'Coo-ee-oh was our Queen then, as now, but she knew no magic and so had nothing to be proud of. But the three Adepts were very kind to Coo-ee-oh. They built for us this wonderful dome of glass and our houses of marble and taught us to make beautiful clothing and many other things. Coo-ee-oh pretended to be very grateful for these favours, but it seems that all the time she was jealous of the three Adepts and secretly tried to discover the secret of their magic arts. In this she was more clever than anyone suspected. She invited the three Adepts to a banquet one day, and while they were feasting Coo-ee-oh stole their charms and magical instruments and transformed them into three fishes – a gold fish, a silver fish and a bronze fish. While the poor fishes were gasping and flopping helplessly on the floor of the banquet room one of them said reproachfully: "You will be punished for this, Coo-ee-oh, for if one of us dies or is destroyed, you will become shrivelled and helpless, and all your stolen magic will depart from you." Frightened by this threat, Coo-ee-oh at once caught up the three fishes and ran with them to the shore of the lake, where she cast them into the water. This revived the three Adepts and they swam away and disappeared.

'I, myself, witnessed this shocking scene,' continued Lady Aurex, 'and so did many other Skeezers. The news was carried to the Flatheads, who then turned from friends to enemies. The Su-Dic and his wife Rora were the only ones on the mountain who were glad the three Adepts had been lost to them, and they at once became Rulers of the Flatheads and stole their canned brains from others to make themselves the more powerful. Some of the Adepts' magic tools had been left on the mountain, and these Rora seized and by the use of them she became a witch.

'The result of Coo-ee-oh's treachery was to make both the Skeezers and the Flatheads miserable instead of happy. Not only were the Su-Dic and his wife cruel to their people, but our Queen at once became proud and arrogant and treated us very unkindly. All the Skeezers knew she had stolen her magic powers and so she hated us and made us humble ourselves before her and obey her slightest word. If we disobeyed, or did not please her, or if we talked about her when we were in our own homes she would have us dragged to the whipping post in her palace and lashed with knotted cords. That is why we fear her so greatly.'

This story filled Ozma's heart with sorrow and Dorothy's heart with indignation.

'I now understand,' said Ozma, 'why the fishes in the lake have brought about war between the Skeezers and the Flatheads.'

'Yes,' Lady Aurex answered, 'now that you know the story it is easy to understand. The Su-Dic and his wife came to our lake hoping to catch the silver fish, or gold fish, or bronze fish – any one of them would do – and by destroying it deprive Coo-ee-oh of her magic. Then they could easily conquer her. Also they had another reason for wanting to catch the fish – they feared that in some way the three Adepts might regain their proper forms and then they would be sure to return to the mountain and punish Rora and the Su-Dic. That was why Rora finally tried to poison all the fishes in the lake, at the time Coo-ee-oh transformed her into a Golden Pig. Of course this attempt

to destroy the fishes frightened the Queen, for her safety
lies in keeping the three fishes alive.'

'I s'pose Coo-ee-oh will fight the Flatheads with all her
might,' observed Dorothy.

'And with all her magic,' added Ozma, thoughtfully.

'I do not see how the Flatheads can get to this island to
hurt us,' said Lady Aurex.

'They have bows and arrows, and I guess they mean to
shoot the arrows at your big dome, and break all the glass
in it,' suggested Dorothy.

But Lady Aurex shook her head with a smile.

'They cannot do that,' she replied.

'Why not?'

'I dare not tell you why, but if the Flatheads come
tomorrow morning you will yourselves see the reason.'

'I do not think they will attempt to harm the island,'
Ozma declared. 'I believe they will first attempt to destroy
the fishes, by poison or some other means. If they succeed
in that, the conquest of the island will not be difficult.'

'They have no boats,' said Lady Aurex, 'and Coo-ee-oh,
who has long expected this war, has been preparing for it in
many astonishing ways. I almost wish the Flatheads would
conquer us, for then we would be free from our dreadful
Queen; but I do not wish to see the three transformed
fishes destroyed, for in them lies our only hope of future
happiness.'

'Ozma will take care of you, whatever happens,' Dorothy
assured her. But the Lady Aurex, not knowing the extent of
Ozma's power – which was, in fact, not so great as Dorothy
imagined – could not take much comfort in this promise.

It was evident there would be exciting times on the
morrow, if the Flatheads really attacked the Skeezers of
the Magic Isle.

CHAPTER TEN

Underwater

WHEN NIGHT FELL ALL THE INTERIOR OF

the Great Dome, streets and houses, became lighted with brilliant incandescent lamps, which rendered it bright as day. Dorothy thought the island must look beautiful by night from the outer shore of the lake. There was revelry and feasting in the Queen's palace, and the music of the royal band could be plainly heard in Lady Aurex's house, where Ozma and Dorothy remained with their hostess and keeper. They were prisoners, but treated with much consideration.

Lady Aurex gave them a nice supper and when they wished to retire showed them to a pretty room with comfortable beds and wished them a good night and pleasant dreams.

'What do you think of all this, Ozma?' Dorothy anxiously enquired when they were alone.

'I am glad we came,' was the reply, 'for although there may be mischief done tomorrow, it was necessary I should know about these people, whose leaders are wild and lawless and oppress their subjects with injustice and cruelties. My task, therefore, is to liberate the Skeezers and the Flatheads and secure for them freedom and happiness. I have no doubt I can accomplish this in time.'

'Just now, though, we're in a bad fix,' asserted Dorothy. 'If Queen Coo-ee-oh conquers tomorrow, she won't be nice to us, and if the Su-Dic conquers, he'll be worse.'

'Do not worry, dear,' said Ozma, 'I do not think we are in danger, whatever happens, and the result of our adventure is sure to be good.'

Dorothy was not worrying, especially. She had confidence

in her friend, the fairy Princess of Oz, and she enjoyed the excitement of the events in which she was taking part. So she crept into bed and fell asleep as easily as if she had been in her own cosy room in Ozma's palace.

A sort of grating, grinding sound awakened her. The whole island seemed to tremble and sway, as it might do in an earthquake. Dorothy sat up in bed, rubbing her eyes to get the sleep out of them, and then found it was daybreak.

Ozma was hurriedly dressing herself.

'What is it?' asked Dorothy, jumping out of bed.

'I'm not sure,' answered Ozma 'but it feels as if the island is sinking.'

As soon as possible they finished dressing, while the creaking and swaying continued. Then they rushed into the living-room of the house and found Lady Aurex, fully dressed, awaiting them.

'Do not be alarmed,' said their hostess. 'Coo-ee-oh has decided to submerge the island, that is all. But it proves the Flatheads are coming to attack us.'

'What do you mean by sub-submerging the island?' asked Dorothy.

'Come here and see,' was the reply.

Lady Aurex led them to a window which faced the side of the great dome which covered all the village, and they could see that the island was indeed sinking, for the water of the lake was already half way up the side of the dome. Through the glass could be seen swimming fishes, and tall stalks of swaying seaweeds, for the water was clear as crystal and through it they could distinguish even the farther shore of the lake.

'The Flatheads are not here yet,' said Lady Aurex. 'They will come soon, but not until all of this dome is under the surface of the water.'

'Won't the dome leak?' Dorothy enquired anxiously.

'No, indeed.'

'Was the island ever sunk before?'

'Oh, yes; on several occasions. But Coo-ee-oh doesn't care to do that often, for it requires a lot of hard work to operate the machinery. The dome was built so that the island could disappear. I think,' she continued, 'that our Queen fears the Flatheads will attack the island and try to break the glass of the dome.'

'Well, if we're underwater, they can't fight us, and we can't fight them,' asserted Dorothy.

'They could kill the fishes, however,' said Ozma gravely.

'We have ways to fight, also, even though our island is underwater,' claimed Lady Aurex. 'I cannot tell you all our secrets, but this island is full of surprises. Also our Queen's magic is astonishing.'

'Did she steal it all from the three Adepts in Sorcery that are now fishes?'

'She stole the knowledge and the magic tools, but she has used them as the three Adepts never would have done.'

By this time the top of the dome was quite underwater and suddenly the island stopped sinking and became stationary.

'See!' cried Lady Aurex, pointing to the shore. 'The Flat-heads have come.'

On the bank, which was now far above their heads, a crowd of dark figures could be seen.

'Now let us see what Coo-ee-oh will do to oppose them,' continued Lady Aurex, in a voice that betrayed her excitement.

*   *   *

The Flatheads, pushing their way through the line of palm trees, had reached the shore of the lake just as the top of the island's dome disappeared beneath the surface. The water now flowed from shore to shore, but through the clear water the dome was still visible and the houses of the Skeezers could be dimly seen through the panes of glass.

'Good!' exclaimed the Su-Dic, who had armed all his followers and had brought with him two copper vessels, which he carefully set down upon the ground beside him. 'If Coo-ee-oh wants to hide instead of fighting our job will be easy, for in one of these copper vessels I have enough poison to kill every fish in the lake.'

'Kill them, then, while we have time, and then we can go home again,' advised one of the chief officers.

'Not yet,' objected the Su-Dic. 'The Queen of the Skeezers has defied me, and I want to get her into my power, as well as to destroy her magic. She transformed my poor wife into a Golden Pig, and I must have revenge for that, whatever else we do.'

'Look out!' suddenly exclaimed the officers, pointing into the lake; 'something's going to happen.'

From the submerged dome a door opened and something black shot swiftly out into the water. The door instantly closed behind it and the dark object cleaved its way through the water, without rising to the surface, directly towards the place where the Flatheads were standing.

'What is that?' Dorothy asked the Lady Aurex.

'That is one of the Queen's submarines,' was the reply. 'It is all enclosed, and can move underwater. Coo-ee-oh has several of these boats which are kept in little rooms in the basement under our village. When the island is submerged, the Queen uses these boats to reach the shore, and I believe she now intends to fight the Flatheads with them.'

The Su-Dic and his people knew nothing of Coo-ee-oh's submarines, so they watched with surprise as the underwater boat approached them. When it was quite near the shore it rose to the surface and the top parted and fell back, disclosing a boat full of armed Skeezers. At the head was the Queen, standing up in the bow and holding in one hand a coil of magic rope that gleamed like silver.

The boat halted and Coo-ee-oh drew back her arm to

throw the silver rope towards the Su-Dic, who was now but a few feet from her. But the wily Flathead leader quickly realised his danger and before the Queen could throw the rope he caught up one of the copper vessels and dashed its contents full in her face!

CHAPTER ELEVEN

The Conquest of the Skeezers

QUEEN COO-EE-OH DROPPED THE ROPE, tottered and fell headlong into the water, sinking beneath the surface, while the Skeezers in the submarine were too bewildered to assist her and only stared at the ripples in the water where she had disappeared. A moment later there arose to the surface a beautiful White Swan. This Swan was of large size, very gracefully formed, and scattered all over its white feathers were tiny diamonds, so thickly placed that as the rays of the morning sun fell upon them the entire body of the Swan glistened like one brilliant diamond. The head of the Diamond Swan had a bill of polished gold and its eyes were two sparkling amethysts.

'Hooray!' cried the Su-Dic, dancing up and down with wicked glee. 'My poor wife, Rora, is avenged at last. You made her a Golden Pig, Coo-ee-oh, and now I have made you a Diamond Swan. Float on your lake for ever, if you like, for your web feet can do no more magic and you are as powerless as the Pig you made of my wife!

'Villain! Scoundrel!' croaked the Diamond Swan. 'You will be punished for this. Oh, what a fool I was to let you enchant me!

'A fool you were, and a fool you are!' laughed the Su-Dic, dancing madly in his delight. And then he carelessly tipped over the other copper vessel with his heel and its contents spilled on the sands and were lost to the last drop.

The Su-Dic stopped short and looked at the overturned vessel with a rueful countenance.

'That's too bad – too bad!' he exclaimed sorrowfully. 'I've

lost all the poison I had to kill the fishes with, and I can't make any more because only my wife knew the secret of it, and she is now a foolish Pig and has forgotten all her magic.'

'Very well,' said the Diamond Swan scornfully, as she floated upon the water and swam gracefully here and there. 'I'm glad to see you are foiled. Your punishment is just beginning, for although you have enchanted me and taken away my powers of sorcery you have still the three magic fishes to deal with, and they'll destroy you in time, mark my words.'

The Su-Dic stared at the Swan a moment. Then he yelled to his men: 'Shoot her! Shoot the saucy bird!'

They let fly some arrows at the Diamond Swan, but she dived under the water and the missiles fell harmlessly. When Coo-ee-oh rose to the surface she was far from the shore and she swiftly swam across the lake to where no arrows or spears could reach her.

The Su-Dic rubbed his chin and thought what to do next. Near by floated the submarine in which the Queen had come, and now the Skeezers who were in it were puzzled what to do with themselves. Perhaps they were not sorry their cruel mistress had been transformed into a Diamond Swan, but the transformation had left them quite helpless. The underwater boat was not operated by machinery, but by certain mystic words uttered by Coo-ee-oh. They didn't know how to submerge it, or how to make the watertight shield cover them again, or how to make the boat go back to the castle, or make it enter the little basement room where it was usually kept. As a matter of fact, they were now shut out of their village under the Great Dome and could not get back again. So one of the men called to the Supreme Dictator of the Flatheads, saying: 'Please make us prisoners and take us to your mountain, and feed and keep us, for we have nowhere to go.'

Then the Su-Dic laughed and answered: 'Not so. I can't

be bothered to care for a lot of stupid Skeezers. Stay where you are, or go wherever you please, so long as you keep away from our mountain.' He turned to his men and added: 'We have conquered Queen Coo-ee-oh and made her a helpless swan. The Skeezers are underwater and may stay there. So, having won the war, let us go home again and make merry and feast, having after many years proved the Flatheads to be greater and more powerful than the Skeezers.'

So the Flatheads marched away and passed through the row of palms and went back to their mountain, where the Su-Dic and a few of his officers feasted and all the others were forced to wait on them.

'I'm sorry we couldn't have roast pig,' said the Su-Dic, 'but as the only pig we have is made of gold, we can't eat her. Also the Golden Pig happens to be my wife, and even were she not gold I am sure she would be too tough to eat.'

CHAPTER TWELVE

The Diamond Swan

WHEN THE FLATHEADS HAD GONE AWAY

the Diamond Swan swam back to the boat and one of the young Skeezers named Ervic said to her eagerly: 'How can we get back to the island, your Majesty?'

'Am I not beautiful?' asked Coo-ee-oh, arching her neck gracefully and spreading her diamond-sprinkled wings. 'I can see my reflection in the water, and I'm sure there is no bird nor beast, nor human as magnificent as I am!'

'How shall we get back to the island, your Majesty?' pleaded Ervic.

'When my fame spreads throughout the land, people will travel from all parts of this lake to look upon my loveliness,' said Coo-ee-oh, shaking her feathers to make the diamonds glitter more brilliantly.

'But, your Majesty, we must go home and we do not know how to get there,' Ervic persisted.

'My eyes,' remarked the Diamond Swan, 'are wonderfully blue and bright and will charm all beholders.'

'Tell us how to make the boat go – how to get back into the island,' begged Ervic and the others cried just as earnestly: 'Tell us, Coo-ee-oh; tell us!'

'I don't know,' replied the Queen in a careless tone.

'You are a magic-worker, a sorceress, a witch!'

'I was, of course, when I was a girl,' she said, bending her head over the clear water to catch her reflection in it; 'but now I've forgotten all such foolish things as magic. Swans are lovelier than girls, especially when they're sprinkled with diamonds. Don't you think so?' And she gracefully swam away, without seeming to care whether they answered or not.

Ervic and his companions were in despair. They saw plainly that Coo-ee-oh could not or would not help them. The former Queen had no further thought for her island, her people or her wonderful magic; she was only intent on admiring her own beauty.

'Truly,' said Ervic, in a gloomy voice, 'the Flatheads have conquered us!'

*   *   *

Some of these events had been witnessed by Ozma and Dorothy and Lady Aurex, who had left the house and gone close to the glass of the dome, in order to see what was going on. Many of the Skeezers had also crowded against the dome, wondering what would happen next. Although their vision was to an extent blurred by the water and the necessity of looking upward at an angle, they had observed the main points of the drama enacted above. They saw Queen Coo-ee-oh's submarine come to the surface and open; they saw the Queen standing erect to throw her magic rope; they saw her sudden transformation into a Diamond Swan, and a cry of amazement went up from the Skeezers inside the dome.

'Good!' exclaimed Dorothy. 'I hate that old Su-Dic, but I'm glad Coo-ee-oh is punished.'

'This is a dreadful misfortune!' cried Lady Aurex, pressing her hands upon her heart.

'Yes,' agreed Ozma, nodding her head thoughtfully; 'Coo-ee-oh's misfortune will prove a terrible blow to her people.'

'What do you mean by that?' asked Dorothy in surprise. 'Seems to me the Skeezers are in luck to lose their cruel Queen.'

'If that were all you would be right,' responded Lady Aurex; 'and if the island were above water it would not be so serious. But here we all are, at the bottom of the lake, and fast prisoners in this dome.'

'Can't you raise the island?' enquired Dorothy.

'No. Only Coo-ee-oh knew how to do that,' was the answer.

'We can try,' insisted Dorothy. 'If it can be made to go down, it can be made to come up. The machinery is still here, I suppose.

'Yes; but the machinery works by magic, and Coo-ee-oh would never share her secret power with any one of us.'

Dorothy's face grew grave; but she was thinking.

'Ozma knows a lot of magic,' she said.

'But not that kind of magic,' Ozma replied.

'Can't you learn how, by looking at the machinery?'

'I'm afraid not, my dear. It isn't fairy magic at all; it is witchcraft.'

'Well,' said Dorothy, turning to Lady Aurex, 'you say there are other sinking boats. We can get in one of those, and shoot out to the top of the water, like Coo-ee-oh did, and so escape. And then we can help to rescue all the Skeezers down here.'

'No one knows how to work the underwater boats but the Queen,' declared Lady Aurex.

'Isn't there any door or window in this dome that we could open?'

'No; and, if there were, the water would rush in to flood the dome, and we could not get out.'

'The Skeezers,' said Ozma, 'could not drown; they'd only get wet and soggy and in that condition they would be very uncomfortable and unhappy. But you are a mortal girl, Dorothy, and if your Magic Belt protected you from death you would have to lie for ever at the bottom of the lake.'

'No, I'd rather die quickly,' asserted the little girl. 'But there are doors in the basement that open – to let out the bridges and the boats – and that would not flood the dome, you know.'

'Those doors open by a magic word, and only Coo-ee-oh knows the word that must be uttered,' said Lady Aurex.

'Dear me!' exclaimed Dorothy, 'that dreadful Queen's witchcraft upsets all my plans to escape. I guess I'll give it up, Ozma, and let you save us.'

Ozma smiled, but her smile was not so cheerful as usual. The Princess of Oz found herself confronted with a serious problem, and although she had no thought of despairing she realised that the Skeezers and their island, as well as Dorothy and herself, were in grave trouble and that unless she could find a means to save them they would be lost to the Land of Oz for all future time.

'In such a dilemma,' said she, musingly, 'nothing is gained by haste. Careful thought may aid us, and so may the course of events. The unexpected is always likely to happen, and cheerful patience is better than reckless action.'

'All right,' returned Dorothy; 'take your time, Ozma; there's no hurry. How about some breakfast, Lady Aurex?'

Their hostess led them back to the house, where she ordered her trembling servants to prepare and serve breakfast. All the Skeezers were frightened and anxious over the transformation of their Queen into a swan. Coo-ee-oh was feared and hated, but they had depended on her magic to conquer the Flatheads and she was the only one who could raise their island to the surface of the lake again.

Before breakfast was over several of the leading Skeezers came to Aurex to ask her advice and to question Princess Ozma, of whom they knew nothing except that she claimed to be a fairy and the Ruler of all the land, including the Lake of the Skeezers.

'If what you told Queen Coo-ee-oh was the truth,' they said to her, 'you are our lawful mistress, and we may depend on you to get us out of our difficulties.'

'I will try to do that,' Ozma graciously assured them, 'but you must remember that the powers of fairies are granted them to bring comfort and happiness to all who appeal to them. On the contrary, such magic as Coo-ee-oh knew and practised is unlawful witchcraft and her arts are such as no fairy would condescend to use. However, it is sometimes necessary to consider evil in order to accomplish good, and perhaps by studying Coo-ee-oh's tools and charms of witchcraft I may be able to save us. Do you promise to accept me as your Ruler and to obey my commands?'

They promised willingly.

'Then,' continued Ozma, 'I will go to Coo-ee-oh's palace and take possession of it. Perhaps what I find there will be of use to me. In the meantime tell all the Skeezers to fear nothing, but have patience. Let them return to their homes and perform their daily tasks as usual. Coo-ee-oh's loss may not prove a misfortune, but rather a blessing.'

This speech cheered the Skeezers amazingly. Really, they had no one now to depend upon but Ozma, and in spite of their dangerous position their hearts were lightened by the transformation and absence of their cruel Queen.

They got out their brass band and a grand procession escorted Ozma and Dorothy to the palace, where all of Coo-ee-oh's former servants were eager to wait upon them. Ozma invited Lady Aurex to stay at the palace also, for she knew all about the Skeezers and their island and had also been a favourite of the former Queen, so her advice and information were sure to prove valuable.

Ozma was somewhat disappointed in what she found in the palace. One room of Coo-ee-oh's private suite was entirely devoted to the practice of witchcraft, and here were countless queer instruments and jars of ointments and bottles of potions labelled with queer names, and strange machines that Ozma could not guess the use of, and pickled toads and snails and lizards, and a shelf of books that were

written in blood, but in a language which the Ruler of Oz
did not know.

'I do not see,' said Ozma to Dorothy, who accompanied
her in her search, 'how Coo-ee-oh knew the use of the
magic tools she stole from the three Adept Witches. Moreover, from all reports these Adepts practised only good
witchcraft, such as would be helpful to their people, while
Coo-ee-oh performed only evil.'

'Perhaps she turned the good things to evil uses?' suggested
Dorothy.

'Yes, and with the knowledge she gained Coo-ee-oh
doubtless invented many evil things quite unknown to the
good Adepts, who are now fishes,' added Ozma. 'It is
unfortunate for us that the Queen kept her secrets so
closely guarded, for no one but herself could use any of
these strange things gathered in this room.'

'Couldn't we capture the Diamond Swan and make her
tell the secrets?' asked Dorothy.

'No; even were we able to capture her, Coo-ee-oh now
has forgotten all the magic she ever knew. But until we
ourselves escape from this dome we could not capture the
Swan, and were we to escape we would have no use for
Coo-ee-oh's magic.'

'That's a fact,' admitted Dorothy. 'But – say, Ozma,
here's a good idea! Couldn't we capture the three fishes –
the gold and silver and bronze ones, and couldn't you
transform 'em back to their own shapes, and then couldn't
the three Adepts get us out of here?'

'You are not very practical, Dorothy dear. It would be as
hard for us to capture the three fishes, from among all the
other fishes in the lake, as to capture the Swan.'

'But if we could, it would be of more help to us,' persisted
the little girl.

'That is true,' answered Ozma, smiling at her friend's
eagerness. 'You find a way to catch the fishes, and I'll

promise when they are caught to restore them to their proper forms.'

'I know you think I can't do it,' replied Dorothy, 'but I'm going to try.'

She left the palace and went to a place where she could look through a clear pane of the glass dome into the surrounding water. Immediately she became interested in the queer sights that met her view.

The Lake of the Skeezers was inhabited by fishes of many kinds and many sizes. The water was so transparent that the girl could see for a long distance and the fishes came so close to the glass of the dome that sometimes they actually touched it. On the white sands at the bottom of the lake were starfish, lobsters, crabs and many shellfish of strange shapes and with shells of gorgeous hues. The water foliage was of brilliant colours and to Dorothy it resembled a splendid garden.

But the fishes were the most interesting of all. Some were big and lazy, floating slowly along or lying at rest with just their fins waving. Many with big round eyes looked full at the girl as she watched them and Dorothy wondered if they could hear her through the glass if she spoke to them. In Oz, where all the animals and birds can talk, many fishes are able to talk also, but usually they are more stupid than birds and animals because they think slowly and haven't much to talk about.

In the Lake of the Skeezers the fish of smaller size were more active than the big ones and darted quickly in and out among the swaying weeds, as if they had important business and were in a hurry. It was among the smaller varieties that Dorothy hoped to spy the gold and silver and bronze fishes. She had an idea the three would keep together, being companions now as they were in their natural forms, but such a multitude of fishes constantly passed, the scene shifting every moment, that she was not sure she could pick them out even if they appeared in view. Her eyes couldn't look in all directions and the fishes she sought might be on the other side of the dome, or far away in the lake.

'P'raps, because they were afraid of Coo-ee-oh, they've hid themselves somewhere, and don't know their enemy has been transformed,' she reflected.

She watched the fishes for a long time, until she became hungry and went back to the palace for lunch. But she was not discouraged.

'Anything new, Ozma?' she asked.

'No, dear. Did you discover the three fishes?'

'Not yet. But there isn't anything better for me to do, Ozma, so I guess I'll go back and watch again.'

CHAPTER THIRTEEN

The Alarm Bell

GLINDA THE GOOD, IN HER PALACE IN THE Quadling Country, had many things to occupy her mind, for not only did she look after the weaving and embroidery of her bevy of maids, and assist all those who came to her to implore her help – beasts and birds as well as people – but she was a close student of the arts of sorcery and spent much time in her Magical Laboratory, where she strove to find a remedy for every evil and to perfect her skill in magic.

Nevertheless, she did not forget to look in the *Great Book of Records* each day to see if any mention was made of the visit of Ozma and Dorothy to the Enchanted Mountain of the Flatheads and the Magic Isle of the Skeezers. The *Records* told her that Ozma had arrived at the mountain, that she had escaped, with her companion, and gone to the island of the Skeezers, and that Queen Coo-ee-oh had submerged the island so that it was entirely underwater. Then came the statement that the Flatheads had come to the lake to poison the fishes and that their Supreme Dictator had transformed Queen Coo-ee-oh into a swan.

No other details were given in the *Great Book* and so Glinda did not know that since Coo-ee-oh had forgotten her magic none of the Skeezers knew how to raise the island to the surface again. So Glinda was not worried about Ozma and Dorothy until one morning, while she sat with her maids, there came a sudden clang of the great alarm bell. This was so unusual that every maid gave a start and even the Sorceress for a moment could not think what the alarm meant.

Then she remembered the ring she had given Dorothy when she left the palace to start on her venture. In giving the ring, Glinda had warned the little girl not to use its magic powers unless she and Ozma were in real danger, but then she was to turn it on her finger once to the right and once to the left and Glinda's alarm bell would ring.

So the Sorceress now knew that danger threatened her beloved Ruler and Princess Dorothy, and she hurried to her magic room to seek information as to what sort of danger it was. The answer to her question was not very satisfactory, for it was only: 'Ozma and Dorothy are prisoners in the great Dome of the Isle of the Skeezers, and the Dome is under the water of the lake.'

'Hasn't Ozma the power to raise the island to the surface?' enquired Glinda.

'No,' was the reply, and the *Records* refused to say more except that Queen Coo-ee-oh, who alone could command the island to rise, had been transformed by the Flathead Su-Dic into a Diamond Swan.

Then Glinda consulted the past *Records* of the Skeezers in the *Great Book*. After diligent search she discovered that Coo-ee-oh was a powerful sorceress who had gained most of her power by treacherously transforming the Adepts of Magic, who were visiting her, into three fishes – gold, silver and bronze – after which she had them cast into the lake.

Glinda reflected earnestly on this information and decided that someone must go to Ozma's assistance. While there was no great need of haste, because Ozma and Dorothy could live in a submerged dome a long time, it was evident they could not get out until someone was able to raise the island.

The Sorceress looked through all her recipes and books of sorcery, but could find no magic that would raise a sunken island. Such a thing had never before been required in sorcery. Then Glinda made a little island, covered by a glass dome, and sunk it in a pond near her castle, and experimented in magical ways to bring it to the surface. She made several such experiments, but all were failures. It seemed a simple thing to do, yet she could not do it.

Nevertheless, the wise Sorceress did not despair of finding a way to liberate her friends. Finally she concluded that the best thing to do was to go to the Skeezer country and examine the lake. While there she was more likely to discover a solution to the problem that bothered her, and to work out a plan for the rescue of Ozma and Dorothy.

So Glinda summoned her storks and her aerial chariot, and telling her maids she was going on a journey and might not soon return, she entered the chariot and was carried swiftly to the Emerald City.

In Princess Ozma's palace the Scarecrow was now acting as Ruler of the Land of Oz. There wasn't much for him to do, because all the affairs of state moved so smoothly, but he was there in case anything unforeseen should happen.

Glinda found the Scarecrow playing croquet with Trot and Betsy Bobbin, two little girls who lived at the palace under Ozma's protection and were great friends of Dorothy and much loved by all the Oz people.

'Something's happened!' cried Trot, as the chariot of the Sorceress descended near them. 'Glinda never comes here 'cept something's gone wrong.'

'I hope no harm has come to Ozma, or Dorothy,' said Betsy anxiously, as the lovely Sorceress stepped down from her chariot.

Glinda approached the Scarecrow and told him of the dilemma of Ozma and Dorothy and she added: 'We must save them, somehow, Scarecrow.'

'Of course,' replied the Scarecrow, stumbling over a wicket and falling flat on his painted face.

The girls picked him up and patted his straw stuffing into shape, and he continued, as if nothing had occurred: 'But you'll have to tell me what to do, for I never have raised a sunken island in all my life.'

'We must have a Council of State as soon as possible,' proposed the Sorceress. 'Please send messengers to summon all of Ozma's counsellors to this palace. Then we can decide what is best to be done.'

The Scarecrow lost no time in doing this. Fortunately most of the royal counsellors were in the Emerald City or near to it, so they all met in the throne room of the palace that same evening.

CHAPTER FOURTEEN

Ozma's Counsellors

NO RULER EVER HAD SUCH A QUEER assortment of advisers as the Princess Ozma had gathered about her throne. Indeed, in no other country could such amazing people exist. But Ozma loved them for their peculiarities and could trust every one of them.

First there was the Tin Woodman. Every bit of him was tin, brightly polished. All his joints were kept well oiled and moved smoothly. He carried a gleaming axe to prove he was a woodman, but seldom had cause to use it because he lived in a magnificent tin castle in the Winkie Country of Oz and was the Emperor of all the Winkies. The Tin Woodman's name was Nick Chopper. He had a very good mind, but his heart was not of much account, so he was very careful to do nothing unkind or to hurt anyone's feelings.

Another counsellor was Scraps, the Patchwork Girl of Oz, who was made of a gaudy patchwork quilt, cut into shape and stuffed with cotton. This Patchwork Girl was very intelligent, but so full of fun and mad pranks that a lot of more stupid folks thought she must be crazy. Scraps was jolly under all conditions, however grave they might be, but her laughter and good spirits were of value in cheering others and in her seemingly careless remarks much wisdom could often be found.

Then there was the Shaggy Man – shaggy from head to foot, hair and whiskers, clothes and shoes – but very kind and gentle and one of Ozma's most loyal supporters.

Tik-Tok was there, a copper man with machinery inside him, so cleverly constructed that he moved, spoke and thought by three separate clockworks. Tik-Tok was very reliable because he always did exactly what he was wound up to do, but his machinery was liable to run down at times and then he was quite helpless until wound up again.

A different sort of person was Jack Pumpkinhead, one of Ozma's oldest friends and her companion on many adventures. Jack's body was very crude and awkward, being formed of limbs of trees of different sizes, jointed with wooden pegs. But it was a substantial body and not likely to break or wear out, and when it was dressed the clothes covered much of its roughness. The head of Jack Pumpkinhead was, as you have guessed, a ripe pumpkin, with the eyes, nose and mouth carved upon one side. The pumpkin was stuck on Jack's wooden neck and was liable to get turned sidewise or backwards and then he would have to straighten it with his wooden hands.

The worst thing about this sort of a head was that it did not keep well and was sure to spoil sooner or later. So Jack's main business was to grow a field of fine pumpkins each year, and always before his old head spoiled he would select a fresh pumpkin from the field and carve the features on it very neatly, and have it ready to replace the old head whenever it became necessary. He didn't always carve it the same way, so his friends never knew exactly what sort of an expression they would find on his face. But there was no mistaking him, because he was the only pumpkin-headed man alive in the Land of Oz.

A one-legged sailor-man was a member of Ozma's council. His name was Cap'n Bill and he had come to the Land of Oz with Trot, and had been made welcome on account of his cleverness, honesty and good nature. He wore a wooden leg to replace the one he had lost and was a great friend of all the children in Oz because he could whittle all sorts of toys out of wood with his big jackknife.

Professor H. M. Wogglebug, T. E. was another member

of the council. The 'H. M.' meant Highly Magnified, for the professor was once a little bug, who became magnified to the size of a man and always remained so. The 'T. E.' meant that he was Thoroughly Educated. He was at the head of Princess Ozma's Royal Athletic College, and so that the students would not have to study and so lose much time that could be devoted to athletic sports, such as football, baseball and the like, Professor Wogglebug had invented the famous Educational Pills. If one of the college students took a Geography Pill after breakfast, he knew his geography lesson in an instant; if he took a Spelling Pill he at once knew his spelling lesson, and an Arithmetic Pill enabled the student to do any kind of sum without having to think about it.

These useful pills made the college very popular and taught the boys and girls of Oz their lessons in the easiest possible way. In spite of this, Professor Wogglebug was not a favourite outside his college, for he was very conceited and admired himself so much and displayed his cleverness and learning so constantly, that no one cared to associate with him. Ozma found him of value in her councils, nevertheless.

Perhaps the most splendidly dressed of all those present was a great frog as large as a man, called the Frogman, who was noted for his wise sayings. He had come to the Emerald City from the Yip Country of Oz and was a guest of honour. His long-tailed coat was of velvet, his waistcoat of satin and his trousers of finest silk. There were diamond buckles on his shoes and he carried a gold-headed cane and a high silk hat. All of the bright colours were represented in his rich attire, so it tired one's eyes to look at him for long, until one became used to his splendour.

The best farmer in all Oz was Uncle Henry, who was Dorothy's own uncle, and who now lived near the Emerald City with his wife Aunt Em. Uncle Henry taught the Oz people how to grow the finest vegetables and fruits and grains and was of much use to Ozma in keeping the Royal Storehouses well filled. He, too, was a counsellor.

The reason I mention the little Wizard of Oz last is because he was the most important man in the Land of Oz. He wasn't a big man in size but he was a big man in power and intelligence and second only to Glinda the Good in all the mystic arts of magic. Glinda had taught him, and the Wizard and the Sorceress were the only ones in Oz permitted by law to practise wizardry and sorcery, which they applied only to good uses and for the benefit of the people.

The Wizard wasn't exactly handsome but he was pleasant to look at. His bald head was as shiny as if it had been varnished; there was always a merry twinkle in his eyes and he was as spry as a schoolboy. Dorothy says the reason the Wizard is not as powerful as Glinda is because Glinda didn't teach him all she knows, but what the Wizard knows he knows very well and so he performs some very remarkable magic.

The ten I have mentioned assembled, with the Scarecrow and Glinda, in Ozma's throne room, right after dinner that evening, and the Sorceress told them all she knew of the plight of Ozma and Dorothy.

'Of course we must rescue them,' she continued, 'and the sooner they are rescued the better pleased they will be; but what we must now determine is how they can be saved. That is why I have called you together in council.'

'The easiest way,' remarked the Shaggy Man, 'is to raise the sunken island of the Skeezers to the top of the water again.'

'Tell me how,' said Glinda.

'I don't know how, your Highness, for I have never raised a sunken island.'

'We might all get under it and lift,' suggested Professor Wogglebug.

'How can we get under it when it rests on the bottom of the lake?' asked the Sorceress.

'Couldn't we throw a rope around it and pull it ashore?' enquired Jack Pumpkinhead.

'Why not pump the water out of the lake?' suggested the Patchwork Girl with a laugh.

'Do be sensible!' pleaded Glinda. 'This is a serious matter, and we must give it serious thought.'

'How big is the lake and how big is the island?' was the Frogman's question.

'None of us can tell, for we have not been there.'

'In that case,' said the Scarecrow, 'it appears to me we ought to go to the Skeezer country and examine it carefully.'

'Quite right,' agreed the Tin Woodman.

'We–will–have–to–go–there–anyhow,' remarked Tik-Tok in his jerky machine voice.

'The question is which of us shall go, and how many of us?' said the Wizard.

'I shall go of course,' declared the Scarecrow.

'And I,' said Scraps.

'It is my duty to Ozma to go,' asserted the Tin Woodman.

'I could not stay away, knowing our loved Princess is in danger,' said the Wizard.

'We all feel like that,' Uncle Henry said.

Finally one and all present decided to go to the Skeezer country, with Glinda and the little Wizard to lead them. Magic must meet magic in order to conquer it, so these two skilful magic-workers were necessary to ensure the success of the expedition.

They were all ready to start at a moment's notice, for none had any affairs of importance to attend to. Jack was wearing a newly made pumpkin head and the Scarecrow had recently been stuffed with fresh straw. Tik-Tok's machinery was in good running order and the Tin Woodman always was well oiled.

'It is quite a long journey,' said Glinda, 'and while I might travel quickly to the Skeezer country by means of my stork chariot the rest of you would be obliged to walk. So, as we must keep together, I will send my chariot back to my castle and we will plan to leave the Emerald City at sunrise tomorrow.'

CHAPTER FIFTEEN

The Great Sorceress

BETSY AND TROT, WHEN THEY HEARD OF
the rescue expedition, begged the Wizard to permit them
to join it and he consented. The Glass Cat, overhearing the
conversation, wanted to go also and to this the Wizard
made no objection.

This Glass Cat was one of the real curiosities of Oz. It
had been made and brought to life by a clever magician
named Dr Pipt, who was not now permitted to work magic
and was an ordinary citizen of the Emerald City. The cat
was of transparent glass, through which one could plainly
see its ruby heart beating and its pink brains whirling
around in the top of the head.

The Glass Cat's eyes were emeralds; its fluffy tail was of
spun glass and very beautiful. The ruby heart, while pretty
to look at, was hard and cold and the Glass Cat's disposition
was not pleasant at all times. It scorned to catch mice, did
not eat, and was extremely lazy. If you complimented the
remarkable cat on her beauty, she would be very friendly,
for she loved admiration above everything. The pink brains
were always working and their owner was indeed more
intelligent than most common cats.

Three other additions to the rescue party were made the
next morning, just as they were setting out upon their
journey. The first was a little boy called Button Bright,
because he had no other name that anyone could remember.
He was a fine, manly little fellow, well mannered and good
humoured, who had only one bad fault. He was continually
getting lost. To be sure, Button Bright got found as often

as he got lost, but when he was missing his friends could not help being anxious about him.

'Someday,' predicted the Patchwork Girl, 'he won't be found, and that will be the last of him.' But that didn't worry Button Bright, who was so careless that he did not seem to be able to break the habit of getting lost.

The second addition to the party was a Munchkin boy of about Button Bright's age, named Ojo. He was often called 'Ojo the Lucky', because good fortune followed him wherever he went. He and Button Bright were close friends, although of such different natures, and Trot and Betsy were fond of both.

The third and last to join the expedition was an enormous lion, one of Ozma's regular guardians and the most important and intelligent beast in all Oz. He called himself the Cowardly Lion, saying that every little danger scared him so badly that his heart thumped against his ribs, but all who knew him knew that the Cowardly Lion's fears were coupled with bravery and that however much he might be frightened he summoned courage to meet every danger he encountered. Often he had saved Dorothy and Ozma in times of peril, but afterwards he moaned and trembled and wept because he had been so scared.

'If Ozma needs help, I'm going to help her,' said the great beast. 'Also, I suspect the rest of you may need me on the journey – especially Trot and Betsy – for you may pass through a dangerous part of the country. I know that wild Gillikin country pretty well. Its forests harbour many ferocious beasts.'

They were glad the Cowardly Lion was to join them, and in good spirits the entire party formed a procession and marched out of the Emerald City amid the shouts of the people, who wished them success and a safe return with their beloved Ruler.

They followed a different route from that taken by Ozma

and Dorothy, for they went through the Winkie Country and up north towards Oogaboo. But before they got there they swerved to the left and entered the Great Gillikin Forest, the nearest thing to a wilderness in all Oz. Even the Cowardly Lion had to admit that certain parts of this forest were unknown to him, although he had often wandered among the trees, and the Scarecrow and Tin Woodman, who were great travellers, never had been there at all.

The forest was only reached after a tedious tramp, for some of the Rescue Expedition were quite awkward on their feet. The Patchwork Girl was as light as a feather and very spry; the Tin Woodman covered the ground as easily as Uncle Henry and the Wizard; but Tik-Tok moved slowly and the slightest obstruction in the road would halt him until the others cleared it away. Then, too, Tik-Tok's machinery kept running down, so Betsy and Trot took turns in winding it up.

The Scarecrow was more clumsy but less bother, for although he often stumbled and fell he could scramble up again and a little patting of his straw-stuffed body would put him in good shape again.

Another awkward one was Jack Pumpkinhead, for walking would jar his head around on his neck and then he would be likely to go in the wrong direction. But the Frogman took Jack's arm and then he followed the path more easily.

Cap'n Bill's wooden leg didn't prevent him from keeping up with the others for the old sailor could walk as far as any of them.

When they entered the forest the Cowardly Lion took the lead. There was no path here for men, but many beasts had made paths of their own which only the eyes of the Lion, practised in woodcraft, could discern. So he stalked ahead and wound his way in and out, the others following in single file, Glinda being next to the Lion.

There were dangers in the forest, of course, but as the

huge Lion headed the party he kept the wild denizens of the wilderness from bothering the travellers. Once, to be sure, an enormous leopard sprang upon the Glass Cat and caught her in his powerful jaws, but he broke several of his teeth and with howls of pain and dismay dropped his prey and vanished among the trees.

'Are you hurt?' Trot anxiously enquired of the Glass Cat.

'How silly!' exclaimed the creature in an irritated tone of voice; 'nothing can hurt glass, and I'm too solid to break easily. But I'm annoyed at that leopard's impudence. He has no respect for beauty or intelligence. If he had noticed my pink brains working, I'm sure he would have realised I'm too important to be grabbed in a wild beast's jaws.'

'Never mind,' said Trot consolingly; 'I'm sure he won't do it again.'

They were almost in the centre of the forest when Ojo, the Munchkin boy, suddenly said: 'Why, where's Button Bright?'

They halted and looked around them. Button Bright was not with the party.

'Dear me,' remarked Betsy, 'I expect he's lost again!'

'When did you see him last, Ojo?' enquired Glinda.

'It was some time ago,' replied Ojo. 'He was trailing along at the end and throwing twigs at the squirrels in the trees. Then I went to talk to Betsy and Trot, and just now I noticed he was gone.'

'This is too bad,' declared the Wizard, 'for it is sure to delay our journey. We must find Button Bright before we go any farther, for this forest is full of ferocious beasts that would not hesitate to tear the boy to pieces.'

'But what shall we do?' asked the Scarecrow. 'If any of us leaves the party to search for Button Bright he or she might fall a victim to the beasts, and if the Lion leaves us we will have no protector.'

'The Glass Cat could go,' suggested the Frogman. 'The beasts can do her no harm, as we have discovered.'

The Wizard turned to Glinda.

'Cannot your sorcery discover where Button Bright is?' he asked.

'I think so,' replied the Sorceress.

She called to Uncle Henry, who had been carrying her wicker box, to bring it to her, and when he obeyed she opened it and drew out a small round mirror. On the surface of the glass she dusted a white powder and then wiped it away with her handkerchief and looked in the mirror. It reflected a part of the forest, and there, beneath a wide-spreading tree, Button Bright was lying asleep. On one side of him crouched a tiger, ready to spring; on the other side was a big grey wolf, its bared fangs glistening in a wicked way.

'Goodness me!' cried Trot, looking over Glinda's shoulder. 'They'll catch and kill him sure.'

Everyone crowded around for a glimpse at the magic mirror.

'Pretty bad – pretty bad!' said the Scarecrow sorrowfully.

'Comes of getting lost!' said Cap'n Bill, sighing.

'Guess he's a goner!' said the Frogman, wiping his eyes on his purple silk handkerchief.

'But where is he? Can't we save him?' asked Ojo the Lucky.

'If we knew where he is we could probably save him,' replied the little Wizard, 'but that tree looks so much like all the other trees that we can't tell whether it's far away or near by.'

'Look at Glinda!' exclaimed Betsy

Glinda, having handed the mirror to the Wizard, had stepped aside and was making strange passes with her out-stretched arms and reciting in low, sweet tones a mystical incantation. Most of them watched the Sorceress with anxious eyes, despair giving way to the hope that she might be able to save their friend. The Wizard, however, watched

the scene in the mirror, while over his shoulders peered
Trot, the Scarecrow and the Shaggy Man.

What they saw was more strange than Glinda's actions.
The tiger started to spring on the sleeping boy, but suddenly
lost its power to move and lay flat upon the ground. The
grey wolf seemed unable to lift its feet from the ground.
It pulled first at one leg and then at another, and finding
itself strangely confined to the spot began to back and snarl
angrily. They couldn't hear the barkings and snarls, but they
could see the creature's mouth open and its thick lips move.
Button Bright, however, being but a few feet away from the
wolf, heard its cries of rage, which wakened him from his
untroubled sleep. The boy sat up and looked first at the tiger
and then at the wolf. His face showed that for a moment he
was quite frightened, but he soon saw that the beasts were
unable to approach him and so he got upon his feet and
examined them curiously, with a mischievous smile upon his
face. Then he deliberately kicked the tiger's head with his
foot and catching up a fallen branch of a tree he went to the
wolf and gave it a good whacking. Both the beasts were
furious at such treatment but could not prevent it.

Button Bright now threw down the stick and with his
hands in his pockets wandered carelessly away.

'Now,' said Glinda, 'let the Glass Cat run and find him.
He is in that direction,' pointing the way, 'but how far off I
do not know. Make haste and lead him back to us as quickly
as you can.'

The Glass Cat did not obey everyone's orders, but she
really feared the great Sorceress, so as soon as the words
were spoken the crystal animal darted away and was quickly
lost to sight.

The Wizard handed the mirror back to Glinda, for the
woodland scene had now faded from the glass. Then those
who cared to rest sat down to await Button Bright's coming.
It was not long before he appeared through the trees and as

he rejoined his friends he said in a peevish tone: 'Don't ever send that Glass Cat to find me again. She was very impolite and, if we didn't all know that she had no manners, I'd say she insulted me.'

Glinda turned upon the boy sternly.

'You have caused all of us much anxiety and annoyance,' said she. 'Only my magic saved you from destruction. I forbid you to get lost again.'

'Indeed,' he answered, 'it won't be *my* fault if I get lost again; and it wasn't my fault *this* time.'

CHAPTER SIXTEEN

The Enchanted Fishes

I MUST NOW TELL YOU WHAT HAPPENED

to Ervic and the three other Skeezers who were left floating in the iron boat after Queen Coo-ee-oh had been transformed into a Diamond Swan by the magic of the Flathead Su-Dic.

The four Skeezers were all young men and their leader was Ervic. Coo-ee-oh had taken them with her in the boat to assist her if she captured the Flathead chief, as she hoped to do by means of her silver rope. They knew nothing about the witchcraft that moved the submarine and so, when left floating upon the lake, were at a loss what to do. The submarine could not be submerged by them or made to return to the sunken island. There were neither oars nor sails in the boat, which was not anchored but drifted quietly upon the surface of the lake.

The Diamond Swan had no further thought or care for her people. She had glided over to the other side of the lake and all the calls and pleadings of Ervic and his companions were unheeded by the vain bird. As there was nothing else for them to do, they sat quietly in their boat and waited as patiently as they could for someone to come to their aid.

The Flatheads had refused to help them and had gone back to their mountain. All the Skeezers were imprisoned in the Great Dome and could not help even themselves. When evening came, they saw the Diamond Swan, still keeping to the opposite shore of the lake, walk out of the water on to the sands, shake her diamond-sprinkled feathers, and then disappear among the bushes to seek a resting place for the night.

'I'm hungry,' said Ervic.

'I'm cold,' said another Skeezer.

'I'm tired,' said a third.

'I'm afraid,' said the last one of them.

But it did them no good to complain. Night fell and the moon rose and cast a silvery sheen over the surface of the water.

'Go to sleep,' said Ervic to his companions. 'I'll stay awake and watch, for we may be rescued in some unexpected way.'

So the other three laid themselves down in the bottom of the boat and were soon fast asleep.

Ervic watched. He rested himself by leaning over the bow of the boat, his face near to the moonlit water, and thought dreamily of the day's surprising events and wondered what would happen to the prisoners in the Great Dome.

Suddenly a tiny gold fish popped its head above the surface of the lake, not more than a foot from his eyes. A silver fish then raised its head beside that of the gold fish, and a moment later a bronze fish lifted its head beside the others. The three fishes, all in a row, looked earnestly with their round, bright eyes into the astonished eyes of Ervic the Skeezer.

'We are the three Adepts whom Queen Coo-ee-oh betrayed and wickedly transformed,' said the gold fish, its voice low and soft but distinctly heard in the stillness of the night.

'I know of our Queen's treacherous deed,' replied Ervic, 'and I am sorry for your misfortune. Have you been in the lake ever since?'

'Yes,' was the reply.

'I – I hope you are well – and comfortable,' stammered Ervic, not knowing what else to say.

'We knew that someday Coo-ee-oh would meet with the

fate she so richly deserved,' declared the bronze fish. 'We have waited and watched all this time. Now if you will promise to help us and will be faithful and true, you can aid us in regaining our natural forms, and save yourself and all your people from the dangers that now threaten you.'

'Well,' said Ervic, 'you can depend on my doing the best I can. But I'm no witch, nor magician, you must know.'

'All we ask is that you obey our instructions,' returned the silver fish. 'We know that you are honest and that you served Coo-ee-oh only because you were obliged to in order to escape her anger. Do as we command and all will be well.'

'I promise!' exclaimed the young man. 'Tell me what I am to do first.'

'You will find in the bottom of your boat the silver cord which dropped from Coo-ee-oh's hand when she was transformed,' said the gold fish. 'Tie one end of that cord to the bow of your boat and drop the other end to us in the water. Together we will pull your boat to the shore.'

Ervic much doubted that the three small fishes could move so heavy a boat, but he did as he was told and the fishes all seized their end of the silver cord in their mouths and headed towards the nearest shore, which was the very place where the Flatheads had stood when they conquered Queen Coo-ee-oh.

At first the boat did not move at all, although the fishes pulled with all their strength. But presently the strain began to tell. Very slowly the boat crept towards the shore, gaining more speed at every moment. A couple of yards away from the sandy beach the fishes dropped the cord from their mouths and swam to one side, while the iron boat, being now underway, continued to move until its prow grated upon the sand.

Ervic leaned over the side and said to the fishes: 'What next?'

'You will find upon the sand,' said the silver fish, 'a copper kettle, which the Su-Dic forgot when he went away. Cleanse it thoroughly in the water of the lake, for it has had poison in it. When it is cleaned, fill it with fresh water and hold it over the side of the boat, so that we three may swim into the kettle. We will then instruct you further.'

'Do you wish me to catch you, then?' asked Ervic in surprise.

'Yes,' was the reply.

So Ervic jumped out of the boat and found the copper kettle. Carrying it a little way down the beach, he washed it well, scrubbing away every drop of the poison it had contained with sand from the shore.

Then he went back to the boat.

Ervic's comrades were still sound asleep and knew nothing of the three fishes or what strange happenings were taking place about them. Ervic dipped the kettle in the lake, holding fast to the handle until it was underwater. The gold and silver and bronze fishes promptly swam into the kettle. The young Skeezer then lifted it, poured out a little of the water so it would not spill over the edge, and said to the fishes: 'What next?'

'Carry the kettle along the shore. Take one hundred steps to the east, keeping to the edge of the lake, and then you will see a path leading through the meadows, up hill and down dale. Follow the path until you come to a cottage which is painted a purple colour with white trimmings. When you stop at the gate of this cottage we will tell you what to do next. Be careful, above all, not to stumble and spill the water from the kettle, or you will destroy us and all you have done will be in vain.'

The gold fish issued these commands and Ervic promised to be careful and started to obey. He left his sleeping comrades in the boat, stepping cautiously over their bodies, and once on the beach took exactly one hundred steps to the east. Then he looked for the path and the moonlight was so bright that he easily discovered it, although it was hidden from view by tall weeds until he was almost upon it. This path was very narrow and did not seem to be much used, but it was quite distinct and Ervic had no difficulty in following it. He walked through a broad meadow, covered with tall grass and weeds, up a hill and down into a valley and then up another hill and down again.

It seemed to Ervic that he had walked miles and miles. Indeed the moon sank low and day was beginning to dawn when finally he discovered by the roadside a pretty little cottage, painted purple with white trimmings. It was a lonely place – no other buildings were anywhere about and the ground was not tilled at all. No farmer lived here, that was certain. Who would care to dwell in such an isolated place?

But Ervic did not bother his head long with such questions. He went up to the gate that led to the cottage, set the copper kettle carefully down and bending over it asked: 'What next?'

CHAPTER SEVENTEEN

Under the Great Dome

WHEN GLINDA THE GOOD AND HER followers of the Rescue Expedition came in sight of the Enchanted Mountain of the Flatheads, it was away to the left of them, for the route they had taken through the Great Forest was some distance from that followed by Ozma and Dorothy.

They halted awhile to decide whether they should call upon the Supreme Dictator first, or go on to the Lake of the Skeezers.

'If we go to the mountain,' said the Wizard, 'we may get into trouble with that wicked Su-Dic, and then we would be delayed in rescuing Ozma and Dorothy. So I think our best plan will be to go to the Skeezer Country, raise the sunken island and save our friends and the imprisoned Skeezers. Afterwards we can visit the mountain and punish the cruel magician of the Flatheads.'

'That is sensible,' approved the Shaggy Man. 'I quite agree with you.'

The others, too, seemed to think the Wizard's plan the best, and Glinda herself commended it, so on they marched towards the line of palm trees that hid the Skeezers' lake from view.

Pretty soon they came to the palms. These were set so closely together at this point that the branches, which came quite to the ground, were so tightly interlaced that even the Glass Cat could scarcely find a place to squeeze through. The path which the Flatheads used was some distance away.

'Here's a job for the Tin Woodman,' said the Scarecrow.

So the Tin Woodman, who was always glad to be of use, set to work with his sharp, gleaming axe, which he always carried, and in a surprisingly short time had chopped away enough branches to permit them all to pass easily through the trees.

Now the clear waters of the beautiful lake were before them and by looking closely they could see the outline of the Great Dome of the sunken island, far from shore and directly in the centre of the lake.

Of course every eye was at first fixed upon this dome, where Ozma and Dorothy and the Skeezers were still fast prisoners. But soon their attention was caught by a more brilliant sight, for here was the Diamond Swan swimming just before them, its long neck arched proudly, the amethyst eyes gleaming and all the diamond-sprinkled feathers glistening splendidly under the rays of the sun.

'That,' said Glinda, 'is Queen Coo-ee-oh, the haughty and wicked witch who betrayed the three Adepts at Magic and treated her people like slaves.'

'She's wonderfully beautiful now,' remarked the Frogman.

'It doesn't seem like much of a punishment,' said Trot. 'The Flathead Su-Dic ought to have made her a toad.'

'I am sure Coo-ee-oh is punished,' said Glinda, 'for she has lost all her magic powers and her grand palace and can no longer misrule the poor Skeezers.'

'Let us call to her, and hear what she has to say,' proposed the Wizard.

So Glinda beckoned the Diamond Swan, which swam gracefully to a position near them. Before anyone could speak, Coo-ee-oh called to them in a rasping voice – for the voice of a swan is always harsh and unpleasant – and said with much pride: 'Admire me, strangers! Admire the lovely Coo-ee-oh, the handsomest creature in all Oz. Admire me!'

'Handsome is as handsome does,' replied the Scarecrow. 'Are your deeds lovely, Coo-ee-oh?'

'Deeds? What deeds can a swan do but swim around and give pleasure to all beholders?' said the sparkling bird.

'Have you forgotten your former life? Have you forgotten your magic and witchcraft?' enquired the Wizard.

'Magic – witchcraft? Pshaw, who cares for such silly things?' retorted Coo-ee-oh. 'As for my past life, it seems like an unpleasant dream. I wouldn't go back to it if I could. Don't you admire my beauty, strangers?'

'Tell us, Coo-ee-oh,' said Glinda earnestly, 'if you can recall enough of your witchcraft to enable us to raise the sunken island to the surface of the lake. Tell us that and I'll give you a string of pearls to wear around your neck and add to your beauty.'

'Nothing can add to my beauty, for I'm the most beautiful creature anywhere in the whole world.'

'But how can we raise the island?'

'I don't know and I don't care. If ever I knew I've forgotten, and I'm glad of it,' was the response. 'Just watch me circle around and see me glitter!

'It's no use,' said Button Bright; 'the old Swan is too much in love with herself to think of anything else.'

'That's a fact,' agreed Betsy with a sigh; 'but we've got to get Ozma and Dorothy out of that lake, somehow or other.'

'And we must do it in our own way,' added the Scarecrow.

'But how?' asked Uncle Henry in a grave voice, for he could not bear to think of his dear niece Dorothy being out there under the water; 'how shall we do it?'

'Leave that to Glinda,' advised the Wizard, realising he was unable to do it himself.

'If it were just an ordinary sunken island,' said the powerful sorceress, 'there would be several ways by which I might bring it to the surface again. But this is a Magic Isle, and by some curious art of witchcraft, unknown to any but Queen Coo-ee-oh, it obeys certain commands of magic and will not respond to any other. I do not despair in the least, but it will require some deep study to solve this difficult problem. If the Swan could only remember the witchcraft that she invented and knew as a woman, I could force her to tell me the secret, but all her former knowledge is now forgotten.'

'It seems to me,' said the Wizard after a brief silence had followed Glinda's speech, 'that there are three fishes in this lake that used to be Adepts at Magic and from whom Coo-ee-oh stole much of her knowledge. If we could find those fishes and return them to their former shapes, they could doubtless tell us what to do to bring the sunken island to the surface.'

'I have thought of those fishes,' replied Glinda, 'but among so many fishes as this lake contains how are we to single them out?'

You will understand, of course, that had Glinda been at home in her castle, where the *Great Book of Records* was, she would have known that Ervic the Skeezer already had taken the gold and silver and bronze fishes from the lake. But that act had been recorded in the *Book* after Glinda had set out on this journey, so it was all unknown to her.

'I think I see a boat yonder on the shore,' said Ojo the Munchkin boy, pointing to a place around the edge of the lake. 'If we could get that boat and row all over the lake, calling to the magic fishes, we might be able to find them.'

'Let us go to the boat,' said the Wizard.

They walked around the lake to where the boat was stranded upon the beach, but found it empty. It was a mere shell of blackened steel, with a collapsible roof that, when in position, made the submarine watertight, but at present the roof rested in slots on either side of the magic craft. There were no oars or sails, no machinery to make the boat go, and although Glinda promptly realised it was meant to be operated by witchcraft, she was not acquainted with that sort of magic.

'However,' said she, 'the boat is merely a boat, and I

believe I can make it obey a command of sorcery as well as a command of witchcraft. After I have given a little thought to the matter, the boat will take us wherever we desire to go.'

'Not all of us,' returned the Wizard, 'for it won't hold so many. But, most noble Sorceress, provided you can make the boat go, of what use will it be to us?'

'Can't we use it to catch the three fishes?' asked Button Bright.

'It will not be necessary to use the boat for that purpose,' replied Glinda. 'Wherever in the lake the enchanted fishes may be, they will answer to my call. What I am trying to discover is how the boat came to be on this shore, while the island on which it belongs is underwater yonder. Did Coo-ee-oh come here in the boat to meet the Flatheads before the island was sunk, or afterwards?'

No one could answer that question, of course; but while they pondered the matter three young men advanced from the line of trees, and rather timidly bowed to the strangers.

'Who are you, and where did you come from?' enquired the Wizard.

'We are Skeezers,' answered one of them, 'and our home is on the Magic Isle of the Lake. We ran away when we saw you coming, and hid behind the trees, but as you are strangers and seem to be friendly we decided to meet you, for we are in great trouble and need assistance.'

'If you belong on the island, why are you here?' demanded Glinda.

So they told her all the story: How the Queen had defied the Flatheads and submerged the whole island so that her enemies could not get to it or destroy it; how, when the Flatheads came to the shore, Coo-ee-oh had commanded them, together with their friend Ervic, to go with her in the submarine to conquer the Su-Dic, and how the boat had shot out from the basement of the sunken isle, obeying a magic word, and risen to the surface, where it opened and floated upon the water. Then followed the account of how the Su-Dic had transformed Coo-ee-oh into a swan, after which she had forgotten all the witchcraft she ever knew. The young men told how, in the night when they were asleep, their comrade Ervic had mysteriously disappeared, while the boat in some strange manner had floated to the shore and stranded upon the beach.

That was all they knew. They had searched in vain for three days for Ervic. As their island was underwater and they could not get back to it, the three Skeezers had no place to go, and so had waited patiently beside the boat for something to happen.

Being questioned by Glinda and the Wizard, they told all they knew about Ozma and Dorothy and declared the two girls were still in the village under the Great Dome. They were quite safe and would be well cared for by Lady Aurex, now that the Queen who opposed them was out of the way.

When they had gleaned all the information they could from these Skeezers, the Wizard said to Glinda: 'If you find you can make this boat obey your sorcery, you could have it return to the island, submerge itself, and enter the door in the basement from which it came. But I cannot see that our going to the sunken island would enable our friends to escape. We would only join them as prisoners.'

'Not so, friend Wizard,' replied Glinda. 'If the boat would obey my commands to enter the basement door, it would also obey my commands to come out again, and I could bring Ozma and Dorothy back with me.'

'And leave all of our people still imprisoned?' asked one of the Skeezers reproachfully.

'By making several trips in the boat, Glinda could fetch all your people to the shore,' replied the Wizard.

'But what could they do then?' enquired another Skeezer.

'They would have no homes and no place to go, and would be at the mercy of their enemies, the Flatheads.'

'That is true,' said Glinda the Good. 'And as these people are Ozma's subjects, I think she would refuse to escape with Dorothy and leave the others behind, or to abandon the island which is the lawful home of the Skeezers. I believe the best plan will be to summon the three fishes and learn from them how to raise the island.'

The little Wizard seemed to think that this was rather a forlorn hope.

'How will you summon them,' he asked the lovely Sorceress, 'and how can they hear you?'

'That is something we must consider carefully,' responded stately Glinda, with a serene smile. 'I think I can find a way.'

All of Ozma's counsellors applauded this sentiment, for they knew well the powers of the Sorceress.

'Very well,' agreed the Wizard. 'Summon them, most noble Glinda.'

CHAPTER EIGHTEEN

The Cleverness of Ervic

WE MUST NOW RETURN TO ERVIC THE

Skeezer, who, when he had set down the copper kettle containing the three fishes at the gate of the lonely cottage, had asked, 'What next?'

The gold fish stuck its head above the water in the kettle and said in its small but distinct voice: 'You are to lift the latch, open the door and walk boldly into the cottage. Do not be afraid of anything you see, for however you seem to be threatened with dangers, nothing can harm you. The cottage is the home of a powerful Yookoohoo, named Reera the Red, who assumes all sorts of forms, sometimes changing her form several times in a day, according to her fancy. What her real form may be we do not know. This strange creature cannot be bribed with treasure or coaxed through friendship or won by pity. She has never assisted anyone or done wrong to anyone, that we know of. All her wonderful powers are used for her own selfish amusement. She will order you out of the house but you must refuse to go. Remain and watch Reera closely and try to see what she uses to accomplish her transformations. If you can discover the secret whisper it to us and we will then tell you what to do next.'

'That sounds easy,' returned Ervic, who had listened carefully. 'But are you sure she will not hurt me, or try to transform me?'

'She may change your form,' replied the gold fish, 'but do not worry if that happens, for we can break that enchantment easily. You may be sure that nothing will harm you, so you must not be frightened at anything you see or hear.'

Now Ervic was as brave as any ordinary young man, and he knew the fishes who spoke to him were truthful and to be relied upon, nevertheless he experienced a strange sinking of the heart as he picked up the kettle and approached the door of the cottage. His hand trembled as he raised the latch, but he was resolved to obey his instructions. He pushed the door open, took three strides into the middle of the one room the cottage contained, and then stood still and looked around him.

The sights that met his gaze were enough to frighten anyone who had not been properly warned. On the floor just before Ervic lay a great crocodile, its red eyes gleaming wickedly and its wide open mouth displaying rows of sharp teeth. Horned toads hopped about; each of the four upper corners of the room was festooned with a thick cobweb in the centre of which sat a spider, as big around as a washbasin and armed with pincher-like claws; a red-and-green lizard was stretched at full length on the window-sill and black rats darted in and out of the holes they had gnawed in the floor of the cottage.

But the most startling thing was a huge grey ape which sat upon a bench and knitted. It wore a lace cap, such as old ladies wear, and a little apron of lace, but no other clothing. Its eyes were bright and looked as if coals were burning in them. The ape moved as naturally as an ordinary person might, and on Ervic's entrance stopped knitting and raised its head to look at him.

'Get out!' cried a sharp voice, seeming to come from the ape's mouth.

Ervic saw another bench, empty, just beyond him, so he stepped over the crocodile, sat down upon the bench and carefully placed the kettle beside him.

'Get out!' again cried the voice.

Ervic shook his head.

'No,' said he, 'I'm going to stay.'

The spiders left their four corners, dropped to the floor and made a rush towards the young Skeezer, circling around his legs with their pinchers extended. Ervic paid no attention to them. An enormous black rat ran up Ervic's body, passed around his shoulders and uttered piercing squeals in his ears, but he did not wince. The green-and-red lizard, coming from the window-sill, approached Ervic and began spitting a flaming fluid at him, but Ervic merely stared at the creature and its flame did not touch him.

The crocodile raised its tail and, swinging around, swept Ervic off the bench with a powerful blow. But the Skeezer managed to save the kettle from upsetting and he got up, shook off the horned toads that were crawling over him and resumed his seat on the bench.

All the creatures, after this first attack, remained motionless, as if awaiting orders. The old grey ape knitted on, not looking towards Ervic now, and the young Skeezer stolidly kept his seat. He expected something else to happen, but nothing did. A full hour passed and Ervic was growing nervous.

'What do you want?' the ape asked at last.

'Nothing,' said Ervic.

'You may have that!' retorted the ape, and at this all the strange creatures in the room broke into a chorus of cackling laughter.

Another long wait.

'Do you know who I am?' questioned the ape.

'You must be Reera the Red – the Yookoohoo,' Ervic answered.

'Knowing so much, you must also know that I do not like strangers. Your presence here in my home annoys me. Do you not fear my anger?'

'No,' said the young man.

'Do you intend to obey me, and leave this house?'

'No,' replied Ervic, speaking just as quietly as the Yookoohoo.

The ape knitted for a long time before resuming the conversation.

'Curiosity,' it said, 'has led to many a man's undoing. I suppose in some way you have learned that I do tricks of magic, and so through curiosity you have come here. You may have been told that I do not injure anyone, so you are bold enough to disobey my commands to go away. You imagine that you may witness some of the rites of witch-craft, and that they may amuse you. Have I spoken truly?'

'Well,' remarked Ervic, who had been pondering on the strange circumstances of his coming here, 'you are right in some ways, but not in others. I am told that you work magic only for your own amusement. That seems to me very selfish. Few people understand magic. I'm told that you are the only real Yookoohoo in all Oz. Why don't you amuse others as well as yourself?'

'What right have you to question my actions?'

'None at all.'

'And you say you are not here to demand any favours of me?'

'For myself I want nothing from you.'

'You are wise in that. I never grant favours.'

'That doesn't worry me,' declared Ervic.

'But you are curious? You hope to witness some of my magic transformations?'

'If you wish to perform any magic, go ahead,' said Ervic. 'It may interest me and it may not. If you'd rather go on with your knitting, it's all the same to me. I am in no hurry at all.'

This may have puzzled Red Reera, but the face beneath the lace cap could show no expression, being covered with hair. Perhaps in all her career the Yookoohoo had never been visited by anyone who, like this young man, asked for nothing, expected nothing, and had no reason for coming except curiosity. This attitude somewhat disarmed the witch and she began to regard the Skeezer in a more friendly way. She knitted for some time, seemingly in deep thought, and then she arose and walked to a big cupboard that stood against the wall of the room. When the cupboard door was opened Ervic could see a lot of drawers inside, and into one of these drawers – the second from the bottom – Reera thrust a hairy hand.

Until now Ervic could see over the bent form of the ape, but suddenly the form, with its back to him, seemed to straighten up and blot out the drawers. The ape had changed to the form of a woman, dressed in the pretty Gillikin costume, and when she turned around he saw that it was a young woman, whose face was quite attractive.

'Do you like me better this way?' Reera enquired with a smile.

'You *look* better,' he said calmly, 'but I'm not sure I *like* you any better.'

She laughed, saying: 'During the heat of the day I like to be an ape, for an ape doesn't wear any clothes to speak of. But if one has gentlemen callers it is proper to dress up.'

Ervic noticed her right hand was closed, as if she held something in it. She shut the cupboard door, bent over the crocodile and in a moment the creature had changed to a red wolf. It was not pretty even now, and the wolf crouched beside its mistress as a dog might have done. Its teeth looked as dangerous as had those of the crocodile.

Next the Yookoohoo went about touching all the lizards and toads, and at her touch they became kittens. The rats she changed into chipmunks. Now the only horrid creatures remaining were the four great spiders, which hid themselves behind their thick webs.

'There!' Reera cried, 'now my cottage presents a more comfortable appearance. I love the toads and lizards and rats, because most people hate them, but I would tire of them if they always remained the same. Sometimes I change their forms a dozen times a day.'

'You are clever,' said Ervic. 'I did not hear you utter any incantations or magic words. All you did was to touch the creatures.'

'Oh, do you think so?' she replied. 'Well, touch them yourself, if you like, and see if you can change their forms.'

'No,' said the Skeezer, 'I don't understand magic and if I did I would not try to imitate your skill. You are a wonderful Yookoohoo, while I am only a common Skeezer.'

This confession seemed to please Reera, who liked to have her witchcraft appreciated.

'Will you go away now?' she asked. 'I prefer to be alone.'

'I prefer to stay here,' said Ervic.

'In another person's home, where you are not wanted?'

'Yes.'

'Is not your curiosity yet satisfied?' demanded Reera, with a smile.

'I don't know. Is there anything else you can do?'

'Many things. But why should I exhibit my powers to a stranger?'

'I can think of no reason at all,' he replied.

She looked at him curiously.

'You want no power for yourself, you say, and you're too stupid to be able to steal my secrets. This isn't a pretty cottage, and outside are sunshine, broad prairies and beautiful wild flowers. Yet you insist on sitting on that bench and annoying me with your unwelcome presence. What have you in that kettle?'

'Three fishes,' he answered readily.

'Where did you get them?'

'I caught them in the Lake of the Skeezers.'

'What do you intend to do with the fishes?'

'I shall carry them to the home of a friend of mine who

has three children. The children will love to have the fishes for pets.'

She came over to the bench and looked into the kettle, where the three fishes were swimming quietly in the water.

'They're pretty,' said Reera. 'Let me transform them into something else.'

'No,' objected the Skeezer.

'I love to transform things; it's so interesting. And I've never transformed any fishes in all my life.'

'Let them alone,' said Ervic.

'What shapes would you prefer them to have? I can make them turtles, or cute little sea-horses; or I could make them piglets, or rabbits, or guinea-pigs; or, if you like, I can make chickens of them, or eagles, or bluejays.'

'Let them alone!' repeated Ervic.

'You're not a very pleasant visitor,' laughed Red Reera. 'People accuse *me* of being cross and crabbed and unsociable, and they are quite right. If you had come here pleading and begging for favours, and half afraid of my Yookoohoo magic, I'd have abused you until you ran away; but you're quite different from that. *You're* the unsociable and crabbed and disagreeable one, and so I like you, and bear with your grumpiness. It's time for my midday meal; are you hungry?'

'No,' said Ervic, although he really desired food.

'Well, I am,' Reera declared and clapped her hands together. Instantly a table appeared, spread with linen and bearing dishes of various foods, some smoking hot. There were two plates laid, one at each end of the table, and as soon as Reera seated herself all her creatures gathered around her, as if they were accustomed to be fed when she ate. The wolf squatted at her right hand and the kittens and chipmunks gathered at her left.

'Come, stranger, sit down and eat,' she called cheerfully, 'and while we're eating let us decide into what forms we shall change your fishes.'

'They're all right as they are,' asserted Ervic, drawing up his bench to the table. 'The fishes are beauties – one gold, one silver and one bronze. Nothing that has life is more lovely than a beautiful fish.'

'What! Am *I* not more lovely?' Reera asked, smiling at his serious face.

'I don't object to you – for a Yookoohoo, you know,' he said, helping himself to the food and eating with good appetite.

'And don't you consider a beautiful girl more lovely than a fish, however pretty the fish may be?'

'Well,' replied Ervic, after a period of thought, 'that might be. If you transformed my three fish into three girls – girls who would be Adepts at Magic, you know, they might please me as well as the fish do. You won't do that of course, because you can't, with all your skill. And, should you be able to do so, I fear my troubles would be more than I could bear. They would not consent to be my slaves – especially if they were Adepts at Magic – and so they would command *me* to obey *them*. No, Mistress Reera, let us not transform the fishes at all.'

The Skeezer had put his case with remarkable cleverness. He realised that if he appeared anxious for such a transformation the Yookoohoo would not perform it, yet he had skilfully suggested that they be made Adepts at Magic.

CHAPTER NINETEEN

Red Reera, the Yookoohoo

AFTER THE MEAL WAS OVER AND REERA
had fed her pets, including the four monster spiders which
had come down from their webs to secure their share, she
made the table disappear from the floor of the cottage.

'I wish you'd consent to my transforming your fishes,' she
said, as she took up her knitting again.

The Skeezer made no reply. He thought it unwise to
hurry matters. All during the afternoon they sat silent.
Once Reera went to her cupboard and after thrusting her
hand into the same drawer as before, touched the wolf and
transformed it into a bird with gorgeous coloured feathers.
This bird was larger than a parrot and of a somewhat
different form, and Ervic had never seen one like it before.

'Sing!' said Reera to the bird, which had perched itself on
a big wooden peg – as if it had been in the cottage before
and knew just what to do.

And the bird sang jolly, rollicking songs with words to
them – just as a person who had been carefully trained
might do. The songs were entertaining and Ervic enjoyed
listening to them. In an hour or so the bird stopped singing,
tucked its head under its wing and went to sleep. Reera
continued knitting but seemed thoughtful.

Now Ervic had marked this cupboard drawer well and
had concluded that Reera took something from it which
enabled her to perform her transformations. He thought
that if he managed to remain in the cottage, and Reera fell
asleep, he could slyly open the cupboard, take a portion of
whatever was in the drawer, and by dropping it into the

copper kettle transform the three fishes into their natural shapes. Indeed, he had firmly resolved to carry out this plan when the Yookoohoo put down her knitting and walked towards the door.

'I'm going out for a few minutes,' said she; 'do you wish to go with me, or will you remain here?'

Ervic did not answer but sat quietly on his bench. So Reera went out and closed the cottage door.

As soon as she was gone, Ervic rose and tiptoed to the cupboard.

'Take care! Take care!' cried several voices, coming from the kittens and chipmunks. 'If you touch anything we'll tell the Yookoohoo!'

Ervic hesitated a moment but, remembering that he need not consider Reera's anger if he succeeded in transforming the fishes, he was about to open the cupboard when he was arrested by the voices of the fishes, which stuck their heads above the water in the kettle and called out: 'Come here, Ervic!'

So he went back to the kettle and bent over it.

'Let the cupboard alone,' said the gold fish to him earnestly. 'You could not succeed by getting that magic powder, for only the Yookoohoo knows how to use it. The best way is to allow her to transform us into three girls, for then we will have our natural shapes and be able to perform all the Arts of Magic we have learned and well understand. You are acting wisely and in the most effective manner. We did not know you were so intelligent, or that Reera could be so easily deceived by you. Continue as you have begun and try to persuade her to transform us. But insist that we be given the forms of girls.'

The gold fish ducked its head down just as Reera re-entered the cottage. She saw Ervic bent over the kettle, so she came and joined him.

'Can your fishes talk?' she asked.

'Sometimes,' he replied, 'for all fishes in the Land of Oz know how to speak. Just now they were asking me for some bread. They are hungry.'

'Well, they can have some bread,' said Reera. 'But it is nearly supper-time, and if you would allow me to transform your fishes into girls they could join us at the table and have plenty of food much nicer than crumbs. Why not let me transform them?'

'Well,' said Ervic, as if hesitating, 'ask the fishes. If they consent, why – why, then, I'll think it over.'

Reera bent over the kettle and asked: 'Can you hear me, little fishes?'

All three popped their heads above water.

'We can hear you,' said the bronze fish.

'I want to give you other forms, such as rabbits, or turtles or girls, or something; but your master, the surly Skeezer, does not wish me to. However, he has agreed to the plan if you will consent.'

'We'd like to be girls,' said the silver fish.

'No, no!' exclaimed Ervic.

'If you promise to make us three beautiful girls, we will consent,' said the gold fish.

'No, no!' exclaimed Ervic again.

'Also make us Adepts at Magic,' added the bronze fish.

'I don't know exactly what that means,' replied Reera musingly, 'but as no Adept at Magic is as powerful as a Yookoohoo, I'll add that to the transformation.'

'We won't try to harm you, or to interfere with your magic in any way,' promised the gold fish. 'On the contrary, we will be your friends.'

'Will you agree to go away and leave me alone in my cottage, whenever I command you to do so?' asked Reera.

'We promise that,' cried the three fishes.

'Don't do it! Don't consent to the transformation,' urged Ervic.

'They have already consented,' said the Yookoohoo, laughing in his face, 'and you have promised me to abide by their decision. So, friend Skeezer, I shall perform the transformation whether you like it or not.'

Ervic seated himself on the bench again, a deep scowl on his face but joy in his heart. Reera moved over to the cupboard, took something from the drawer and returned to the copper kettle. She was clutching something tightly in her right hand, but with her left she reached within the kettle, took out the three fishes and laid them carefully on the floor, where they gasped in distress at being out of water.

Reera did not keep them in misery more than a few seconds, for she touched each one with her right hand and instantly the fishes were transformed into three tall and slender young women, with fine, intelligent faces and clothed in handsome, clinging gowns. The one who had been a gold fish had beautiful golden hair and blue eyes and was exceedingly fair of skin; the one who had been a bronze fish had dark brown hair and clear grey eyes and her complexion matched these lovely features. The one who had been a silver fish had snow-white hair of the finest texture and deep brown eyes. The hair contrasted exquisitely with her pink cheeks and ruby-red lips, nor did it make her look a day older than her two companions.

As soon as they secured these girlish shapes, all three bowed low to the Yookoohoo and said: 'We thank you, Reera.'

Then they bowed to the Skeezer and said: 'We thank you, Ervic.'

'Very good!' cried the Yookoohoo, examining her work with critical approval. 'You are much better and more interesting than fishes, and this ungracious Skeezer would scarcely allow me to do the transformations. You surely have nothing to thank *him* for. But now let us dine in honour of the occasion.'

She clapped her hands together and again a table loaded with food appeared in the cottage. It was a longer table, this time, and places were set for the three Adepts as well as for Reera and Ervic.

'Sit down, friends, and eat your fill,' said the Yookoohoo, but instead of seating herself at the head of the table she went to the cupboard, saying to the Adepts: 'Your beauty and grace, my fair friends, quite outshine my own. So that I may appear properly at the banquet table I intend, in honour of this occasion, to take upon myself my natural shape.'

Scarcely had she finished this speech before Reera transformed herself into a young woman fully as lovely as the three Adepts. She was not quite so tall as they, but her form was more rounded and more handsomely clothed, with a wonderful jewelled girdle and a necklace of shining pearls. Her hair was a bright auburn red, and her eyes large and dark.

'Do you claim this is your natural form?' asked Ervic of the Yookoohoo.

'Yes,' she replied. 'This is the only form I am really entitled to wear. But I seldom assume it because there is no one here to admire or appreciate it and I get tired of admiring it myself.'

'I see now why you are named Reera the Red,' remarked Ervic.

'It is on account of my red hair,' she explained smiling. 'I do not care for red hair myself, which is one reason I usually wear other forms.'

'It is beautiful,' asserted the young man; and then, remembering the other women present, he added: 'But, of course, all women should not have red hair, because that would make it too common. Gold and silver and brown hair are equally handsome.'

The smiles that he saw interchanged between the four

filled the poor Skeezer with embarrassment, so he fell silent and attended to eating his supper, leaving the others to do the talking. The three Adepts frankly told Reera who they were, how they became fishes and how they had planned secretly to induce the Yookoohoo to transform them. They admitted that they had feared, had they asked her to help, that she would have refused them.

'You were quite right,' returned the Yookoohoo. 'I make it my rule never to perform magic to assist others, for if I did there would always be a crowd at my cottage demanding help and I hate crowds and want to be left alone.

'However, now that you are restored to your proper shapes, I do not regret my action and I hope you will be of use in saving the Skeezer people by raising their island to the surface of the lake, where it really belongs. But you must promise me that after you go away you will never come here again, nor tell anyone what I have done for you.'

The three Adepts and Ervic thanked the Yookoohoo warmly. They promised to remember her wish that they should not come to her cottage again and so, with a good-bye, took their departure.

CHAPTER TWENTY

A Puzzling Problem

GLINDA THE GOOD, HAVING DECIDED TO

try her sorcery upon the abandoned submarine, so that it would obey her commands, asked all of her party, including the Skeezers, to withdraw from the shore of the lake to the line of palm trees. She kept with her only the little Wizard of Oz, who was her pupil and knew how to assist her in her magic rites. When they two were alone beside the stranded boat, Glinda said to the Wizard: 'I shall first try my magic recipe No. 1163, which is intended to make inanimate objects move at my command. Have you a skeropythrope with you?'

'Yes, I always carry one in my bag,' replied the Wizard. He opened his black bag of magic tools and took out a brightly polished skeropythrope, which he handed to the Sorceress. Glinda had also brought a small wicker bag, containing various requirements of sorcery, and from this she took a parcel of powder and a vial of liquid. She poured the liquid into the skeropythrope and added the powder. At once the skeropythrope began to sputter and emit sparks of a violet colour, which spread in all directions. The Sorceress instantly stepped into the middle of the boat and held the instrument so that the sparks fell all around her and covered every bit of the blackened steel craft. At the same time Glinda crooned a weird incantation in the language of sorcery, her voice sounding low and musical.

After a little the violet sparks ceased, and those that had fallen upon the boat had disappeared and left no mark upon its surface. The ceremony was ended and Glinda returned the skeropythrope to the Wizard, who put it away in his black bag.

'That ought to do the business all right,' he said confidently.

'Let us make a trial and see,' she replied.

So they both entered the boat and seated themselves.

Speaking in a tone of command the Sorceress said to the boat: 'Carry us across the lake, to the farther shore.'

At once the boat backed off the sandy beach, turned its prow and moved swiftly over the water.

'Very good – very good indeed!' cried the Wizard, when the boat slowed up at the shore opposite that whence they had departed. 'Even Coo-ee-oh, with all her witchcraft, could do no better.'

The Sorceress now said to the boat: 'Close up, submerge and carry us to the basement door of the sunken island – the door from which you emerged at the command of Queen Coo-ee-oh.'

The boat obeyed. As it sank into the water the top sections rose from the sides and joined together over the heads of Glinda and the Wizard, who were thus enclosed in a waterproof chamber. There were four glass windows in this covering, one on each side and one at either end, so that the passengers could see exactly where they were going. Moving under the water more slowly than on the surface, the submarine gradually dived down and halted with its bow pressed against the huge marble door in the basement under the Dome. This door was tightly closed and it was evident to both Glinda and the Wizard that it would not open to admit the underwater boat unless a magic word was spoken by them or someone from within the basement of the island. But what was this magic word? Neither of them knew.

'I'm afraid,' said the Wizard regretfully, 'that we can't get in, after all. Unless your sorcery can discover the word to open the marble door.'

'That is probably some word only known to Coo-ee-oh,' replied the Sorceress. 'I may be able to discover what it is, but that will require time. Let us go back again to our companions.'

'It seems a shame, after we have made the boat obey us, to be balked by just a marble door,' grumbled the Wizard.

At Glinda's command the boat rose until it was on a level with the Skeezer village, when the Sorceress made it slowly circle all around the Great Dome.

Many faces were pressed against the glass from the inside, eagerly watching the submarine, and in one place were Dorothy and Ozma, who quickly recognised Glinda and the Wizard through the glass windows of the boat. Glinda saw them, too, and held the boat close to the Dome while the friends exchanged greetings in pantomime. Their voices, unfortunately, could not be heard through the Dome and the water and the side of the boat. The Wizard tried to make the girls understand, through signs, that he and Glinda had come to their rescue, and Ozma and Dorothy understood this from the very fact that the Sorceress and the Wizard had appeared. The two girl prisoners were smiling and in safety, and knowing this Glinda felt she could take all the time necessary in order to effect their final rescue.

As nothing more could be done just then, Glinda ordered the boat to return to shore and it obeyed readily. First it ascended to the surface of the water, then the roof parted and fell into the slots at the sides of the boat, and then the magic craft quickly made the shore and beached itself on the sands at the very spot from which it had departed at Glinda's command. All the Oz people and the Skeezers at once ran to the boat to ask if they had reached the island, and whether they had seen Ozma and Dorothy. The Wizard told them of the obstacle they had met in the way of a marble door, and how Glinda would now undertake to find a magic way to conquer the door.

Realising that it would require several days to succeed in raising the island and liberating their friends and the Skeezer people, Glinda now prepared a camp halfway between the lake shore and the palm trees.

The Wizard's wizardry made a number of tents appear and the sorcery of the Sorceress furnished these tents all complete, with beds, chairs, tables, rugs, lamps and even books with which to pass idle hours. All the tents had the Royal Banner of Oz flying from the centre poles and one big tent, not now occupied, had Ozma's own banner moving in the breeze.

Betsy and Trot had a tent to themselves, and Button Bright and Ojo had another. The Scarecrow and the Tin Woodman paired together in one tent, as did Jack Pumpkinhead and the Shaggy Man, Cap'n Bill and Uncle Henry, Tik-Tok and Professor Wogglebug. Glinda had the most splendid tent of all, except that reserved for Ozma, while the Wizard had a little one of his own. Whenever it was mealtime, tables loaded with food magically appeared in the tents of those who were in the habit of eating, and these complete arrangements made the rescue party just as comfortable as they would have been in their own homes.

Far into the night Glinda sat in her tent studying a roll of mystic scrolls, in search of the word that would open the basement door of the island and admit her to the Great Dome. She also made many magical experiments, hoping to discover something that would aid her. Yet the morning found the powerful Sorceress still unsuccessful.

Glinda's art could have opened any ordinary door, you may be sure, but you must realise that this marble door of the island had been commanded not to open save in obedience to one magic word, and therefore all other magic words could have no effect upon it. The magic word that guarded the door had probably been invented by Coo-ee-oh, who had now forgotten it. The only way, then, to gain

entrance to the sunken island was to break the charm that
held the door fast shut. If this could be done no magic
would be required to open it.

The next day the Sorceress and the Wizard again entered
the boat and made it submerge and go to the marble door,
which they tried in various ways to open, but without success.

'We shall have to abandon this attempt, I think,' said
Glinda. 'The easiest way to raise the island would be for us
to gain admittance to the Dome and then descend to the
basement and see in what manner Coo-ee-oh made the
entire island sink or rise at her command. It naturally
occurred to me that the easiest way to gain admittance
would be by having the boat take us into the basement
through the marble door from which Coo-ee-oh launched
it. But there must be other ways to get inside the Dome
and join Ozma and Dorothy, and such ways we must find
by study and the proper use of our powers of magic.'

'It won't be easy,' declared the Wizard, 'for we must not
forget that Ozma herself understands considerable magic,
and has doubtless tried to raise the island or find other
means of escape from it and failed.'

'That is true,' returned Glinda, 'but Ozma's magic is fairy
magic, while you are a Wizard and I am a Sorceress. In this
way the three of us have a great variety of magic to work
with, and if we should all fail it will be because the island is
raised and lowered by a magic power none of us is acquainted
with. My idea therefore is to seek – by such magic as we
possess – to accomplish our object in another way.'

They made the circle of the Dome again in their boat, and
once more saw Ozma and Dorothy through their windows
and exchanged signals with the two imprisoned girls.

Ozma realised that her friends were doing all in their
power to rescue her and smiled encouragement to their
efforts. Dorothy seemed a little anxious but was trying to
be as brave as her companion.

After the boat had returned to the camp and Glinda was seated in her tent, working out various ways by which Ozma and Dorothy could be rescued, the Wizard stood on the shore dreamily eying the outline of the Great Dome which showed beneath the clear water; when he raised his eyes he saw a group of strange people approaching from around the lake. Three were young women of stately presence, very beautifully dressed, who moved with remarkable grace. They were followed at a little distance by a good-looking young Skeezer.

The Wizard saw at a glance that these people might be very important, so he advanced to meet them. The three maidens received him graciously and the one with the golden hair said: 'I believe you are the famous Wizard of Oz, of whom I have often heard. We are seeking Glinda, the Sorceress, and perhaps you can lead us to her.'

'I can, and will, right gladly,' answered the Wizard. 'Follow me, please.'

The little Wizard was puzzled as to the identity of the three lovely visitors but he gave no sign that might embarrass them.

He understood they did not wish to be questioned, and so he made no remarks as he led the way to Glinda's tent.

With a courtly bow the Wizard ushered the three visitors into the gracious presence of Glinda the Good.

CHAPTER TWENTY-ONE

The Three Adepts

THE SORCERESS LOOKED UP FROM HER work as the three maidens entered, and something in their appearance and manner led her to rise and bow to them in her most dignified manner. The three knelt an instant before the great Sorceress and then stood upright and waited for her to speak.

'Whoever you may be,' said Glinda, 'I bid you welcome.'

'My name is Audah,' said one.

'My name is Aurah,' said another.

'My name is Aujah,' said the third.

Glinda had never heard these names before, but looking closely at the three she asked: 'Are you witches or workers in magic?'

'Some of the secret arts we have gleaned from Nature,' replied the brown-haired maiden modestly, 'but we do not place our skill beside that of the Great Sorceress, Glinda the Good.'

'I suppose you are aware it is unlawful to practice magic in the Land of Oz, without the permission of our Ruler, Princess Ozma?'

'No, we were not aware of that,' was the reply. 'We have heard of Ozma, who is the appointed Ruler of all this great fairyland, but her laws have not reached us, as yet.'

Glinda studied the strange maidens thoughtfully; then she said to them: 'Princess Ozma is even now imprisoned in the Skeezer village, for the whole island with its Great Dome, was sunk to the bottom of the lake by the witchcraft of Coo-ee-oh, whom the Flathead Su-Dic transformed into a silly swan. I am seeking some way to overcome Coo-ee-oh's magic and raise the isle to the surface again. Can you help me do this?'

The maidens exchanged glances, and the white-haired one replied: 'We do not know; but we will try to assist you.'

'It seems,' continued Glinda musingly, 'that Coo-ee-oh derived most of her witchcraft from three Adepts at Magic, who at one time ruled the Flatheads. While the Adepts were being entertained by Coo-ee-oh at a banquet in her palace, she cruelly betrayed them and after transforming them into fishes cast them into the lake.

'If I could find these three fishes and return them to their natural shapes, they might know what magic Coo-ee-oh used to sink the island. I was about to go to the shore and call these fishes to me when you arrived. So, if you will join me, we will try to find them.'

The maidens exchanged smiles now, and the golden-haired one, Audah, said to Glinda: 'It will not be necessary to go to the lake. We are the three fishes.'

'Indeed!' cried Glinda. 'Then you are the three Adepts at Magic, restored to your proper forms?'

'We are the three Adepts,' admitted Aujah.

'Then,' said Glinda, 'my task is half accomplished. But who destroyed the transformation that made you fishes?'

'We have promised not to tell,' answered Aurah; 'but this young Skeezer was largely responsible for our release; he is brave and clever, and we owe him our gratitude.'

Glinda looked at Ervic, who stood modestly behind the Adepts, hat in hand. 'He shall be properly rewarded,' she declared, 'for in helping you he has helped us all, and perhaps saved his people from being imprisoned for ever in the sunken isle.'

The Sorceress now asked her guests to seat themselves and a long talk followed, in which the Wizard of Oz shared.

'We are quite certain,' said Aurah, 'that if we could get

inside the Dome we could discover Coo-ee-oh's secrets, for in all her work, after we became fishes, she used the formulas and incantations and arts that she stole from us. She may have added to these things, but they were the foundation of all her work.'

'What means do you suggest for our getting into the Dome?' enquired Glinda.

The three Adepts hesitated to reply, for they had not yet considered what could be done to reach the inside of the Great Dome. While they were in deep thought, and Glinda and the Wizard were quietly awaiting their suggestions, into the tent rushed Trot and Betsy, dragging between them the Patchwork Girl.

'Oh, Glinda,' cried Trot, 'Scraps has thought of a way to rescue Ozma and Dorothy and all of the Skeezers.'

The three Adepts could not avoid laughing merrily, for not only were they amused by the queer form of the Patchwork Girl, but Trot's enthusiastic speech struck them as really funny. If the Great Sorceress and the famous Wizard and the three talented Adepts at Magic were unable as yet to solve the important problem of the sunken isle, there was little chance for a patched girl stuffed with cotton to succeed.

But Glinda, smiling indulgently at the earnest faces turned towards her, patted the children's heads and said: 'Scraps is very clever. Tell us what she has thought of, my dear.'

'Well,' said Trot, 'Scraps says that if you could dry up all the water in the lake the island would be on dry land, an' everyone could come and go whenever they liked.'

Glinda smiled again, but the Wizard said to the girls: 'If we should dry up the lake, what would become of all the beautiful fishes that now live in the water?'

'Dear me! That's so,' admitted Betsy, crestfallen; 'we never thought of that, did we Trot?'

'Couldn't you transform 'em into polliwogs?' asked Scraps,

turning a somersault and then standing on one leg. 'You could give them a little teeny pond to swim in, and they'd be just as happy as they are as fishes.'

'No indeed!' replied the Wizard, severely. 'It is wicked to transform any living creatures without their consent, and the lake is the home of the fishes and belongs to them.'

'All right,' said Scraps, making a face at him; 'I don't care.'

'It's too bad,' sighed Trot, 'for I thought we'd struck a splendid idea.'

'So you did,' declared Glinda, her face now grave and thoughtful. 'There is something in the Patchwork Girl's idea that may be of real value to us.'

'I think so, too,' agreed the golden-haired Adept. 'The top of the Great Dome is only a few feet below the surface of the water. If we could reduce the level of the lake until the Dome sticks a little above the water, we could remove some of the glass and let ourselves down into the village by means of ropes.'

'And there would be plenty of water left for the fishes to swim in,' added the white-haired maiden.

'If we succeed in raising the island we could fill up the lake again,' suggested the brown-haired Adept.

'I believe,' said the Wizard, rubbing his hands together in delight, 'that the Patchwork Girl has shown us the way to success.'

The girls were looking curiously at the three beautiful Adepts, wondering who they were, so Glinda introduced them to Trot and Betsy and Scraps, and then sent the children away while she considered how to carry the new idea into effect.

Not much could be done that night, so the Wizard prepared another tent for the Adepts, and in the evening Glinda held a reception and invited all her followers to meet the new arrivals. The Adepts were greatly astonished at the extraordinary personages presented to them, and marvelled that Jack Pumpkinhead and the Scarecrow and the Tin Woodman and Tik-Tok could really live and think and talk just like other people. They were especially pleased with the lively Patchwork Girl and loved to watch her antics.

It was quite a pleasant party, for Glinda served some dainty refreshments to those who could eat, and the Scarecrow recited some poems, and the Cowardly Lion sang a song in his deep bass voice. The only thing that marred their joy was the thought that their beloved Ozma and dear little Dorothy were yet confined in the Great Dome of the Sunken island.

CHAPTER TWENTY-TWO

The Sunken Island

AS SOON AS THEY HAD BREAKFASTED

the next morning, Glinda and the Wizard and the three Adepts went down to the shore of the lake and formed a line with their faces towards the submerged island. All the others came to watch them, but stood at a respectful distance in the background.

At the right of the Sorceress stood Audah and Aurah, while at the left stood the Wizard and Aujah. Together they stretched their arms over the water's edge and in unison the five chanted a rhythmic incantation.

This chant they repeated again and again, swaying their arms gently from side to side, and in a few minutes the watchers behind them noticed that the lake had begun to recede from the shore. Before long the highest point of the dome appeared above the water. Gradually the water fell, making the dome appear to rise. When it was three or four feet above the surface Glinda gave the signal to stop, for their work had been accomplished.

The blackened submarine was now entirely out of the water, but Uncle Henry and Cap'n Bill managed to push it back into the lake. Glinda, the Wizard, Ervic and the Adepts got into the boat, taking with them a coil of strong rope, and at the command of the Sorceress the craft cleaved its way through the water towards the part of the Dome which was now visible.

'There's still plenty of water for the fish to swim in,' observed the Wizard as they rode along. 'They might like more but I'm sure they can get along until we have raised the island and can fill up the lake again.'

The boat touched gently on the sloping glass of the Dome, and the Wizard took some tools from his black bag and quickly removed one large pane of glass, thus making a hole large enough for their bodies to pass through. Stout frames of steel supported the glass of the Dome, and around one of these frames the Wizard tied the end of a rope.

'I'll go down first,' said he, 'for while I'm not as spry as Cap'n Bill I'm sure I can manage it easily. Are you sure the rope is long enough to reach the bottom?'

'Quite sure,' replied the Sorceress.

So the Wizard let down the rope and climbing through the opening lowered himself down, hand over hand, clinging to the rope with his legs and feet. Below in the streets of the village were gathered all the Skeezers, men, women and children, and you may be sure that Ozma and Dorothy, with Lady Aurex, were filled with joy that their friends were at last coming to their rescue.

The Queen's palace, now occupied by Ozma, was directly in the centre of the Dome, so that when the rope was let down the end of it came just in front of the palace entrance. Several Skeezers held fast to the rope's end to steady it and the Wizard reached the ground in safety. He hugged first Ozma and then Dorothy, while all the Skeezers cheered as loud as they could.

The Wizard now discovered that the rope was long enough to reach from the top of the Dome to the ground when doubled, so he tied a chair to one end of the rope and called to Glinda to sit in the chair while he and some of the Skeezers lowered her to the pavement. In this way the Sorceress reached the ground quite comfortably and the three Adepts and Ervic soon followed her.

The Skeezers quickly recognised the three Adepts at Magic, whom they had learned to respect before their wicked Queen betrayed them, and welcomed them as friends. All the inhabitants of the village had been greatly frightened by their imprisonment under the water, but now realised that an attempt was to be made to rescue them.

Glinda, the Wizard and the Adepts followed Ozma and Dorothy into the palace, and they asked Lady Aurex and Ervic to join them. After Ozma had told of her adventures in trying to prevent war between the Flatheads and the Skeezers, and Glinda had told all about the Rescue Expedition and the restoration of the three Adepts by the help of Ervic, a serious consultation was held as to how the island could be made to rise.

'I've tried every way in my power,' said Ozma, 'but Coo-ee-oh used a very unusual sort of magic which I do not understand. She seems to have prepared her witchcraft in such a way that a spoken word is necessary to accomplish her designs, and these spoken words are known only to herself.'

'That is a method we taught her,' declared Aurah the Adept.

'I can do no more, Glinda,' continued Ozma, 'so I wish you would try what your sorcery can accomplish.'

'First, then,' said Glinda, 'let us visit the basement of the island, which I am told is underneath the village.'

A flight of marble stairs led from one of Coo-ee-oh's private rooms down to the basement, but when the party arrived all were puzzled by what they saw. In the centre of a broad, low room, stood a mass of great cog-wheels, chains and pulleys, all interlocked and seeming to form a huge machine; but there was no engine or other motive power to make the wheels turn.

'This, I suppose, is the means by which the island is lowered or raised,' said Ozma, 'but the magic word which is needed to move the machinery is unknown to us.'

The three Adepts were carefully examining the mass of wheels, and soon the golden-haired one said: 'These wheels do not control the island at all. On the contrary, one set of them is used to open the doors of the little rooms where the submarines are kept, as may be seen from the chains and pulleys used. Each boat is kept in a little room with two doors, one to the basement room where we are now and the other opening on to the lake.

'When Coo-ee-oh used the boat in which she attacked the Flatheads, she first commanded the basement door to open and with her followers she got into the boat and made the top close over them. Then the basement door being closed, the outer door was slowly opened, letting the water fill the room to float the boat, which then left the island, keeping underwater.'

'But how could she expect to get back again?' asked the Wizard.

'Why the boat would enter the room filled with water and after the outer door was closed a word of command started a pump which pumped all the water from the room. Then the boat would open and Coo-ee-oh could enter the basement.'

'I see,' said the Wizard. 'It is a clever contrivance, but won't work unless one knows the magic words.'

'Another part of this machinery,' explained the white-haired Adept, 'is used to extend the bridge from the island to the mainland. The steel bridge is in a room much like that in which the boats are kept, and at Coo-ee-oh's command it would reach out, joint by joint, until its far end touched the shore of the lake. The same magic command would make the bridge return to its former position. Of course the bridge could not be used unless the island was on the surface of the water.'

'But how do you suppose Coo-ee-oh managed to sink the island, and make it rise again?' enquired Glinda.

This the Adepts could not yet explain. As nothing more could be learned from the basement they mounted the steps to the Queen's private suite again, and Ozma showed them to a special room where Coo-ee-oh kept her magical instruments and performed all her arts of witchcraft.

CHAPTER TWENTY-THREE

The Magic Words

MANY INTERESTING THINGS WERE TO BE

seen in the Room of Magic, including much that had been stolen from the Adepts when they were transformed into fishes, but they had to admit that Coo-ee-oh had a rare genius for mechanics, and had used her knowledge in inventing a lot of mechanical apparatus that ordinary witches, wizards and sorcerers could not understand.

They all carefully inspected this room, taking care to examine every article they came across.

'The island,' said Glinda thoughtfully, 'rests on a base of solid marble. When it is submerged, as it is now, the base of the island is upon the bottom of the lake. What puzzles me is how such a great weight can be lifted and suspended in the water, even by magic.'

'I now remember,' returned Aujah, 'that one of the arts we taught Coo-ee-oh was the way to expand steel, and I think that explains how the island is raised and lowered. I noticed in the basement a big steel pillar that passed through the floor and extended upwards to this palace. Perhaps the end of it is concealed in this very room. If the lower end of the steel pillar is firmly embedded in the bottom of the lake, Coo-ee-oh could utter a magic word that would make the pillar expand, and so lift the entire island to the level of the water.'

'I've found the end of the steel pillar. It's just here,' announced the Wizard, pointing to one side of the room where a great basin of polished steel seemed to have been set upon the floor.

They all gathered around, and Ozma said: 'Yes, I am

quite sure that is the upper end of the pillar that supports the island. I noticed it when I first came here. It has been hollowed out, you see, and something has been burned in the basin, for the fire has left its marks. I wondered what was under the great basin and got several of the Skeezers to come up here and try to lift it for me. They were strong men, but could not move it at all.'

'It seems to me,' said Audah the Adept, 'that we have discovered the manner in which Coo-ee-oh raised the island. She would burn some sort of magic powder in the basin, utter the magic word, and the pillar would lengthen out and lift the island with it.'

'What's this?' asked Dorothy, who had been searching around with the others, and now noticed a slight hollow in the wall, near to where the steel basin stood. As she spoke Dorothy pushed her thumb into the hollow and instantly a small drawer popped out from the wall.

The three Adepts, Glinda and the Wizard sprang forward and peered into the drawer. It was half filled with a greyish powder, the tiny grains of which constantly moved as if impelled by some living force.

'It may be some kind of radium,' said the Wizard.

'No,' replied Glinda, 'it is more wonderful than even radium, for I recognise it as a rare mineral powder called Gaulau by the sorcerers. I wonder how Coo-ee-oh discovered it and where she obtained it.'

'There is no doubt,' said Aujah the Adept, 'that this is the magic powder Coo-ee-oh burned in the basin. If only we knew the magic word, I am quite sure we could raise the island.'

'How can we discover the magic word?' asked Ozma, turning to Glinda as she spoke.

'That we must now seriously consider,' answered the Sorceress.

So all of them sat down in the Room of Magic and began to

think. It was so still that after a while Dorothy grew nervous. The little girl never could keep silent for long, and at the risk of displeasing her magic-working friends she suddenly said: 'Well, Coo-ee-oh used just three magic words, one to make the bridge work, and one to make the submarines go out of their holes, and one to raise and lower the island. Three words. And Coo-ee-oh's name is made up of just three words. One is "Coo", and one is "ee", and one is "oh".'

The Wizard frowned but Glinda looked wonderingly at the young girl and Ozma cried out: 'A good thought, Dorothy dear! You may have solved our problem.'

'I believe it is worth a trial,' agreed Glinda. 'It would be quite natural for Coo-ee-oh to divide her name into three magic syllables, and Dorothy's suggestion seems like an inspiration.'

The three Adepts also approved the trial but the brown-haired one said: 'We must be careful not to use the wrong word, and send the bridge out underwater. The main thing, if Dorothy's idea is correct, is to hit upon the one word that moves the island.'

'Let us experiment,' suggested the Wizard.

In the drawer with the moving grey powder was a tiny golden cup, which they thought was used for measuring. Glinda filled this cup with the powder and carefully poured it into the shallow basin, which was the top of the great steel pillar supporting the island. Then Aurah the Adept lighted a taper and touched it to the powder, which instantly glowed fiery red and tumbled about the basin with astonishing energy. While the grains of powder still glowed red the Sorceress bent over it and said in a voice of command: 'Coo!'

They waited motionless to see what would happen. There was a grating noise and a whirl of machinery, but the island did not move a particle.

Dorothy rushed to the window, which overlooked the glass side of the dome.

'The boats!' she exclaimed. 'The boats are all loose an' sailing underwater.'

'We've made a mistake,' said the Wizard gloomily.

'But it's one which shows we are on the right track,' declared Aujah the Adept. 'We know now that Coo-ee-oh used the syllables of her name for the magic words.'

'If "Coo" sends out the boats, it is probable that "ee" works the bridge,' suggested Ozma. 'So the last part of the name may raise the island.'

'Let us try that next then,' proposed the Wizard.

He scraped the embers of the burned powder out of the basin and Glinda again filled the golden cup from the drawer and poured the powder on top of the steel pillar. Aurah lighted it with her taper and Ozma bent over the basin and murmured the long drawn syllable: 'Oh–h–h!'

Instantly the island trembled and with a weird groaning noise it moved upwards – slowly, very slowly, but with a steady motion, while all the company stood by in awed silence. It was a wonderful thing, even to those skilled in the arts of magic, wizardry and sorcery, to realise that a single word could raise that great, heavy island, with its immense glass Dome.

'Why, we're way *above* the lake now!' exclaimed Dorothy from the window, when at last the island ceased to move.

'That is because we lowered the level of the water,' explained Glinda.

They could hear the Skeezers cheering lustily in the streets of the village as they realised that they were saved.

'Come,' said Ozma eagerly, 'let us go down and join the people.'

'Not just yet,' returned Glinda, a happy smile upon her lovely face, for she was overjoyed at their success. 'First let us extend the bridge to the mainland, where our friends from the Emerald City are waiting.'

It didn't take long to put more powder in the basin, light

it and utter the syllable 'ee!' The result was that a door in the basement opened and the steel bridge moved out, extended itself joint by joint, and finally rested its far end on the shore of the lake just in front of the encampment.

'Now,' said Glinda, 'we can go up and receive the congratulations of the Skeezers and of our friends of the Rescue Expedition.'

Across the water, on the shore of the lake, the Patchwork Girl was waving them a welcome.

CHAPTER TWENTY-FOUR

Glinda's Triumph

OF COURSE ALL THOSE WHO HAD JOINED
Glinda's expedition at once crossed the bridge to the island,
where they were warmly welcomed by the Skeezers. Before
all the concourse of people Princess Ozma made a speech
from a porch of the palace and demanded that they
recognise her as their lawful Ruler and promise to obey the
laws of the Land of Oz. In return she agreed to protect
them from all future harm and declared they would no
longer be subjected to cruelty and abuse.

This pleased the Skeezers greatly, and when Ozma told
them they might elect a Queen to rule over them, who in
turn would be subject to Ozma of Oz, they voted for Lady
Aurex, and that same day the ceremony of crowning the
new Queen was held and Aurex was installed as mistress of
the palace.

For her Prime Minister the Queen selected Ervic, for the
three Adepts had told of his good judgement, faithfulness
and cleverness, and all the Skeezers approved the appoint-
ment.

Glinda, the Wizard and the Adepts stood on the bridge
and recited an incantation that quite filled the lake with
water again, and the Scarecrow and the Patchwork Girl
climbed to the top of the Great Dome and replaced the
pane of glass that had been removed to allow Glinda and
her followers to enter.

When evening came Ozma ordered a great feast prepared,
to which every Skeezer was invited. The village was
beautifully decorated and brilliantly lighted and there was

music and dancing until a late hour to celebrate the liberation of the people. For the Skeezers had been freed, not only from the water of the lake but from the cruelty of their former Queen.

As the people from the Emerald City prepared the next morning to depart Queen Aurex said to Ozma: 'There is only one thing I now fear for my people, and that is the enmity of the terrible Su-Dic of the Flatheads. He is liable to come here at any time and try to annoy us, and my Skeezers are peaceful folk and unable to fight the wild and wilful Flatheads.'

'Do not worry,' returned Ozma, reassuringly. 'We intend to stop on our way at the Flatheads' Enchanted Mountain and punish the Su-Dic for his misdeeds.'

That satisfied Aurex and when Ozma and her followers trooped over the bridge to the shore, having taken leave of their friends, all the Skeezers cheered them and waved their hats and handkerchiefs, and the band played and the departure was indeed a ceremony long to be remembered.

The three Adepts at Magic, who had formerly ruled the Flatheads wisely and considerately, went with Princess Ozma and her people, for they had promised Ozma to stay on the mountain and again see that the laws were enforced.

Glinda had been told all about the curious Flatheads and she had consulted with the Wizard and formed a plan to render them more intelligent and agreeable.

When the party reached the mountain Ozma and Dorothy showed them how to pass around the invisible wall – which had been built by the Flatheads after the Adepts were transformed – and how to gain the up-and-down stairway that led to the mountain top.

The Su-Dic had watched the approach of the party from the edge of the mountain and was frightened when he saw that the three Adepts had recovered their natural forms and were coming back to their former home. He realised that his power would soon be gone and yet he determined to fight to the last. He called all the Flatheads together and armed them, and told them to arrest all who came up the stairway and hurl them over the edge of the mountain to the plain below. But although they feared the Supreme Dictator, who had threatened to punish them if they did not obey his commands, as soon as they saw the three Adepts they threw down their arms and begged their former rulers to protect them.

The three Adepts assured the excited Flatheads that they had nothing to fear.

Seeing that his people had rebelled the Su-Dic ran away and tried to hide, but the Adepts found him and had him cast into a prison, all his cans of brains being taken away from him.

After this easy conquest of the Su-Dic, Glinda told the Adepts of her plan, which had already been approved by Ozma of Oz, and they joyfully agreed to it. So, during the next few days, the great Sorceress transformed, in a way, every Flathead on the mountain.

Taking them one at a time, she had the can of brains that belonged to each one opened and the contents spread on the flat head, after which, by means of her arts of sorcery, she caused the head to grow over the brains – in the manner most people wear them – and they were thus rendered as intelligent and good looking as any of the other inhabitants of the Land of Oz.

When all had been treated in this manner there were no more Flatheads at all, and the Adepts decided to name their people Mountaineers. One good result of Glinda's sorcery was that no one could now be deprived of the brains that belonged to him and each person had exactly the share he was entitled to.

Even the Su-Dic was given his portion of brains and his flat head made round, like the others, but he was deprived of all power to work further mischief, and with the Adepts constantly watching him he would be forced to become obedient and humble.

The Golden Pig, which ran grunting about the streets, with no brains at all, was disenchanted by Glinda, and in her woman's form was given brains and a round head. This wife of the Su-Dic had once been even more wicked than her evil husband, but she had now forgotten all her wickedness and was likely to be a good woman thereafter.

These things being accomplished in a satisfactory manner, Princess Ozma and her people bade farewell to the three Adepts and departed for the Emerald City, well pleased with their interesting adventures.

They returned by the road over which Ozma and Dorothy had come, stopping to collect the Sawhorse and the Red Wagon from where they had left them.

'I'm very glad I went to see these peoples,' said Princess Ozma, 'for I not only prevented any further warfare between them, but they have been freed from the rule of the Su-Dic and Coo-ee-oh and are now happy and loyal subjects of the Land of Oz. Which proves that it is always wise to do one's duty, however unpleasant that duty may seem to be.'